CAROLE GIFT PAGE

THOMAS NELSON PUBLISHERS
Nashville • Atlanta • London • Vancouver
Printed in the United States of America

Published in Nashville, Tennessee, by Thomas Nelson, Inc., Publishers, and distributed in Canada by Word Communications, Ltd., Richmond, British Columbia.

The Bible version used in this publication is THE KING JAMES VERSION.

Library of Congress Cataloging-in-Publication Data

Page, Carole Gift.
The hope of Herrick House / Carole Gift Page.
p. cm.
ISBN 0-8407-6780-3
I. Title.
PS3566.A3326H67 1996
813'.54—dc20 96-17029
CIP

Printed in the United States of America.

1 2 3 4 5 6—01 00 99 98 97 96

To my husband, Bill, with all my love.

Thanks to my editor, Janet, and her in-house team, Emily and Esther, for all their help and support in "birthing" this book. It's been a labor of love.

1

Heat lightning.

The sky was filled with it that night.

Bethany Rose could almost smell the air sizzling.

It gave everything a nervous edge and sent a streak of foreboding along her spine that dazzled her senses.

Everything ended and began that night.

The night of the kiss.

The night of the fire.

The night her mama died.

For months afterward, memories of that fateful August night in 1949 would reel and collide in Bethany's head like dead leaves scattered in a dry wind. Images hazy as a mirage on a lonesome road at twilight would spring back vivid as sun glare. She would relive every moment, obsessed by the tricks memory plays on the mind—the strange way trivial incidents attach themselves to shattering events that alter one's life forever.

It started in the barn—the kind of gray, ramshackle barn that dotted the flat, bountiful Indiana landscape. Bethany remembered the barn's muggy closeness with an aching clarity. The air was pungent with the acrid smells of a spindly newborn calf wobbling in wet straw. Jake Witherspoon had come from down the road to see the calf, but Bethany knew he had really come to see her. He was older than she by two years—he had turned twenty-one the first day of summer and she had baked him a spice cake to celebrate.

Everything about Jake was bigger than life—the blunt, granite cut of his features, the way he swung his arms to match his loose-jointed swagger, and the enormous space he filled with his vigorous presence. He was tall as a lumberjack and as massive as a tree trunk, with a thick neck, broad shoulders, and a hard, muscled torso from years of backbreaking farm work. He was a mixture of startling contrasts—curly blond hair and brows bleached white by the sun and squinty eyes pale as rainwater against sun-baked skin that shone like mahogany.

Bethany Rose should have known better than to linger in the barn with the likes of Jake Witherspoon, knowing how taken he was with her. She blamed her foolishness on the sweltering heat. After all, how could a girl think straight in such wilting humidity? For days now she hadn't been able to concentrate on chores, eat a decent supper, or sleep through the night, so how was she to have the good sense to ward off the advances of an uninvited suitor?

Not that Jake was exactly uninvited. She teased him sometimes with a coquettish smile or an evocative glance; on some guileless, unconscious level she had practiced her wiles on him for as long as she could remember. Who better to practice on? Jake had been her brother Luke's best friend since childhood and was like a brother to her as well. Until recently, that is, when he stopped looking at her the way a brother does.

Lately his pale blue eyes glinted with a curious expression that made her want to flinch and turn away or cover up even though she was fully dressed. He was looking at her that way now as they stood together in the weathered barn, watching the teetering calf.

Her fingers moved through her tawny curls to the back of her neck, wet with perspiration. "I thought you came to see the calf," she said, her voice demure, yet mildly accusing.

"I seen lots of calves. I'd rather watch you."

She turned abruptly and headed for the door, but Jake stepped in front of her and pushed her up against the splintery pine wall, pinning her arms to her sides. The rough grain of the wood prickled through her thin cotton frock.

Jake's warm breath on her face was spicy and strong, but not unpleasant. "I just want a kiss," he whispered.

She craned her neck away. "Why should I kiss you, Jake Witherspoon?"

"Because you want to. I know you got hot blood in those veins, Beth."

She met his gaze with a sly little smile. "If I kiss you, are you going to marry me and take me away to some place grand?"

"Come on, Bethany Rose. You been reading too many of them movie magazines." He rubbed his nose teasingly against hers. "I'll marry you and take you home to my mama and daddy's farm. It's big enough for all of us. Big enough for all the children we'll have someday."

She wriggled against his grasp. "I told you a dozen times I don't want to be a farmer's wife. I've been doing chores—cleaning stalls and planting corn and harvesting crops—since I could walk. I want a man who can give me pretty things and a fine house and a happy life."

"It ain't gonna happen, Bethany Rose. You are what you are. A poor, ordinary farm girl."

She kicked at his shin, just missing. "I may be poor, but I'm not ordinary!"

"Okay, you're the prettiest farm girl I ever laid eyes on—small as a button, with big brown eyes like a baby deer's, and hair like cornsilk in a red sunset. But you're still a farm girl, born to work the land and take care of your man and raise his children."

"And end up old and exhausted before my time, like your mama and my mama?" she shot back, lifting her chin defiantly. "I won't! I was born for more than this. I don't know what it is, but I feel it deep inside." Her voice grew hushed, as if she were sharing a secret. "It's like a voice inside telling me I'm meant to do something special. Haven't you ever felt like that, Jake?"

His lips were nearly on hers now. "All I know is you've talked riddles like this since you was five years old. Only you're not a child anymore, Bethany Rose. You're a grown woman now, and it's time you talk and act like one. I've waited long enough."

He kissed her soundly, until she turned her head away and caught her breath. "Jake, we shouldn't! Let me go. It's too warm . . . I feel faint."

He took a step back and clasped her head between his calloused palms. He bunched her burnished hair in his two large hands and pressed his knuckles against her temples. "You're as pretty as the Hollywood stars in them magazines you read all the time, but you got the spirit of a prideful filly. Ain't no one gonna tame you, except maybe me."

"Not even you, Jake Witherspoon!" She wrenched away, but he caught her and pulled her back against him. His fingers pressed into the soft flesh of her upper arms. Just as he forced his lips down on hers again, she heard a voice behind them.

"Let go of my sister!"

Jake released her so abruptly she stumbled backward. Jake turned squarely and faced Luke Henry standing in the barn doorway. Luke was tall and rangy, with dark brows hovering over intense brown eyes and sharply angled features whittled in a narrow face. He was twenty-four and possessed a nervous, unpredictable edge that had intensified since the war. At nineteen he had fought at Normandy, scaling the bloody beaches and crawling over the broken bodies of his buddies. Sometimes Bethany had the feeling he was still fighting some terrible inner battle. But he was a devoted brother; he had always been there for Bethany, sometimes fussing and fretting over her more than Mama did.

His tone now was a mixture of irony and menace. "Okay, Jake, if you didn't come to see Bethany, maybe you came to see me. Is that it, Jake?"

"Go away, Luke," Jake warned, fists clenching. "This is between me and your sister. It's none of your business."

"You kissing Bethany Rose *is* my business, especially if she don't want your kisses."

Jake stood his ground. "She never complained before."

"You never kissed so hard before." Bethany wiped her lips with the back of her hand, but she still felt as if his warm mouth were on hers. "I better go inside. I've got chores."

Without a backward glance, she marched out of the barn, her long hair streaming behind her and her thin skirt sticking to her legs. Outside the barn she paused, trembling, and breathed in the alfalfa-scented air. Lightning bugs flickered like stars and crickets sang their ratchety song in the deepening shadows. After a moment she heard Luke and Jake coming up behind her, and Luke's stern voice. "Better go home, Jake. Maybe Bethany Rose will see you tomorrow; maybe not."

As Jake sidled past her, he bent close and cupped her chin in his massive hand. "Think about what I said, Bethany Rose. You could do a whole lot worse than me."

"Good night, Jake," she said coolly. Straightening her shoulders, she tramped through thriving sumac and spiky witchgrass to the sagging back porch. All of her life she had lived in this squat frame farmhouse with its raw timber and tar paper roof. All her life she had dreamed of waking somewhere else, of being someone besides the daughter of Tom and Laura Henry. But every morning she woke up here. Nothing changed. Nothing ever changed.

"And it wouldn't change even if I married you, Jake Witherspoon," she said under her breath. "I'd just have more of the same. I'd never see any place past Fort Wayne, past these gravel roads and endless fields filled with ragweed and thistles and dandelions."

"You talking to me?" Luke asked in a light, wheedling voice. He reached around from behind her and opened the screen door. It creaked on its hinges and clattered behind them when they entered the small kitchen. With half the screen missing, flies had invaded the room and were having a field day around the canister of bacon grease on the linoleum countertop.

Mama was sitting at the oilcloth-covered table, peeling a kettle of cooked beets. She was stout and plain-faced, her graying hair pulled back in a loose bun at the nape of her neck. In old photographs she had looked almost pretty at one time, but her smooth, finely etched features had long ago been swallowed up in loose folds of sun-baked flesh.

Mama's thick, stubby hands were stained to the wrists with red beet juice. Tomorrow she would be pickling beets in mason jars and the entire house would smell of vinegar. Without looking up she murmured, "Took long enough to look at a scrawny calf."

Beth opened the icebox and took out a jug of lemonade. "Jake stopped by," she said offhandedly as she poured herself a glass.

"What's that boy want now?"

"Same thing he always wants," said Luke. He helped himself to the lemonade and gave Bethany a sly smirk as he put his glass to his lips. "He just wanted a little kiss from Bethany Rose. And he got it too."

Bethany set her glass down hard on the table. "Hold your tongue, Luke Henry, or I'll smack you good!"

"Enough, you two. Sit down! Tell me about Jake."

Bethany and Luke sat down across from each other in the spindly white chairs on each side of Mama. "Nothing to tell," said Bethany.

Luke hooted. "That's not how I saw it. You two looked mighty cozy to me!"

Mama gave Bethany a long, scrutinizing stare. "Are you fixing to marry that boy?"

Bethany pressed her lemonade glass against her cheek, savoring its coldness. "No, Mama. You know better. I don't love Jake."

"Well, you better watch out. He's looking for a wife."

"Not me, Mama. I'd never marry Jake. I'd just be going from this house to his house. It would be hard work from sunup till sunset. I want more, Mama."

"Then you best not be kissing that boy."

"Why, Mama?" Bethany sipped her lemonade with a slow, languid detachment. "Don't you trust me?"

"I don't trust him. I don't trust you. I don't trust nobody when it comes to romancing." Her mother peeled the last of the beets and pushed the kettle aside, her hands veined with bright red streaks. "It starts innocent enough, but that's not how it ends. You take my word!"

Bethany felt the fine hairs on her arms bristling. "I'm grown now, Mama. I can take care of myself."

"I've heard that before."

"Then let it be. What are you afraid of, Mama?"

"I've seen the signs, daughter. I know what's coming."

"Say it, Mama. Say what you mean."

"You know. I don't need to spell it out."

"Yes, you do, Mama. You think Jake and I—"

"Don't matter what I think. Matters what you do."

Bethany's voice took on an edge of irritation. "Are you afraid I'll end up like you, Mama? That's it, isn't it? You're afraid I'll make the same mistake you did. I'll end up in a family way without a husband!"

Her mother's face blanched and her eyes flashed lightning. She slapped Bethany across the cheek. "Don't you ever talk to me that way, girl!"

Bethany covered her cheek with her hand. It stung, but Mama's anger hurt even more. She knew she should back down, but her own annoyance was flaring now. "But it's true, Mama. You let Papa have his way with you. You were nineteen—my age—when Papa came to the door selling his Fuller brushes. You didn't care that he was already married and had a family."

"I didn't know!"

"You never asked!"

"I trusted him, daughter. He was older and smooth-talking. I loved him. He said he loved me."

"You bore him two babies, Mama, before he married you!"

"Well, at least I married him."

"He was dying before we found out about his other family. Our whole lives are a lie, Mama!"

"Bridle your tongue, girl, or I'll do it for you!"

"I won't, Mama! I've kept silent long enough. For two years the shame of what Papa did has churned inside me like a poison."

"If you don't stifle yourself, Bethany Rose Henry—!"

"Even our name is a lie, Mama! Papa made up the name *Henry* so no one would tie him to the Herricks of Willowbrook."

"Your papa was trying to protect you. He never wanted to hurt you!"

"Really, Mama? How could we not be hurt? Luke and I have a brother and sister we never knew about until two years ago. Papa had another *wife*!"

Luke reached over and squeezed Bethany's hand. "Don't fight with Mama. It don't help matters."

"I'm not fighting. I just don't want her telling *me* what to do when she and Papa made such a mess of things."

Mama's faded blue eyes narrowed. She brushed a wisp of silvery hair back from her lined face. "I paid for my mistakes. I had only half a life with your papa; his other family had the rest of him. I can't change any of that now. But I'll give my dying breath to make sure you and Luke have a decent life."

Bethany's sarcasm deepened. "A decent life? You mean, like our brother and sister in Willowbrook—the wonderful, wealthy Herricks in their big, beautiful house? No, Mama. They're too good for us. I was a fool to think—"

"Think what?" challenged Luke.

"Nothing!"

"You thought Knowl and Catherine would welcome us like family," said Luke, his tone mildly mocking. "Just because we shared the same papa. But they haven't, have they?"

"No, they haven't," Bethany conceded, then volleyed back, "but admit it, Luke. You wanted it too!"

His thick brows furrowed, shadowing his eyes. "Okay, I did. Those days when I followed Catherine in secret, before I took her and brought her home to see Papa, I dreamed of living in the Herricks' fancy house. But that's all it was. A dream."

"It could have been different," said Bethany. She took a slice of blood-red beet from the iron kettle and put it to her lips. "When Catherine married that book editor, Robert Wayne, she invited us to her wedding. That had to mean something."

"I doubt it. Remember, she waited till two days before the wedding to invite us. She was just doing her duty for her 'poor white trash' relatives."

"Is that why you two didn't go to the wedding?" asked Mama, her tone still hard-edged.

"I would of gone," replied Luke, "but Bethany said no."

"I didn't want them looking down their noses at us, Mama. I don't need anybody's pity. If they cared a whit about us we would have heard something since the wedding. It's going on two years now, and not a letter, a card, or a phone call."

Luke looked at Mama and mumbled, "That's not exactly so."

Bethany's narrow brows arched. "What are you saying, Luke?"

"Be quiet, son!"

"What about the letter you got a while back, Mama?"

"There wasn't no letter."

"I saw it one day," Luke persisted. "I saw the Willowbrook postmark. I asked you about it, but you said it wasn't nothing."

"That's true. It wasn't nothing. Just a card."

Bethany stared at her mother. "You heard from the Herricks and didn't tell me?"

"I didn't want you upset, girl. I know how them people upset you."

"They wrote us? What did they say?"

Mama lowered her head, her small round chin lost in the thick folds of her neck. "Knowl Herrick offered us money," she announced matter-of-factly.

Bethany felt her mouth go dry. "Money? What for?"

With her index finger her mother wiped a beet stain from the red-checkered oilcloth. "It was last summer, after you graduated from high school, Bethany Rose." Her voice was slow and deliberate. "Knowl Herrick wrote and said he and his sister Catherine wanted to send you off to some fancy college or art school. Said he'd pay for everything. Wherever you wanted to go."

"College? The Herricks wanted to send me to college?"

"That's what the letter said."

"Why didn't you tell me?"

Mama's steel-blue eyes narrowed. "I didn't want you getting any big ideas."

Bethany was trembling. She could taste sweat on her upper lip. "I've been out of school a whole year. A *whole* year, Mama, stuck on this farm! What did you tell them?"

Her mother sat stone still, as if listening for some inner prompting. After a few moments, she ran her tongue over her dry, colorless lips and replied huskily, "I wrote back and told them we didn't need their charity."

The small kitchen felt charged with an electric silence. In the soundless vacuum Bethany wanted to scream at her mother, but the words remained in her head, forcing a pressure behind her brows. "Why didn't you tell me, Mama?" she said in a small, breathless voice. "Why didn't you let *me* decide?"

Her mother wiped her forehead with a corner of her apron. "You . . . you would have gone away and maybe never come back. You have a life here, Bethany. This is where you belong."

Bethany reached across the table and seized her mother's beet-stained hands. "You gave away my chance, Mama, my *only* chance for a real life. How could you do that to me?"

Her mother's thick fingers closed around Bethany's slender hands. "The Herricks took enough from me, daughter. They took your papa. They took the life I thought we had together. They took the last of my self-respect with their condescending airs."

"Papa did that to us, Mama. Not them! Papa robbed them and us with his deception."

"Maybe so, but the Herricks have plenty. I won't let them take you too! This is your place. My mama and papa lived and died forcing crops from this soil. And your papa worked this land—"

"No, Mama! He was gone more than he was here!"

"He was here as much as he could be, daughter. Don't you forget that. No matter what he did, he loved us. He loved this farm, same as I do. And someday I'll die on this land, and it'll be yours—yours and Luke's."

Luke shook his head. "Don't talk about dying, Mama."

Bethany jumped up and clutched the back of her chair, her words erupting in a burst of anguish. "I don't want this land, Mama. I've never wanted it. I hate it! And I hate you for trapping me here!"

She expected her mother to lash out at her again, or slap her, or retaliate with the same fury and vigor she poured into the dark, unyielding soil of her cornfields. But the silent, thick-jowled woman only settled lower in her chair. Her fleshy hands lay listless on the tabletop, stained with red. "I should have died with Papa," she said, the utterance more a guttural sigh than distinct words.

Bethany fell to her knees beside her mother's chair, clasped the warm, red-veined hands, and pressed them against her cheek. "Don't talk that way, Mama," she said, tears starting. "You've always been here for us. All those times Papa was away on his trips, you were here."

She laid her head on her mother's ample breast, the way she had done when she was a child. Mama's cotton housedress felt warmly reassuring against her cheekbone. Bethany savored the steady heartbeat, the rhythmic breathing, the faint, musky scent of Mama's flushed skin.

"I spoke out of turn, Mama," she whispered. "You were right. I don't want their charity. We'll get along just swell—just the three of us." She looked up at Luke, standing behind Mama's chair like a solemn-faced sentry. "Won't we get along, Luke?"

He nodded, his jaw set. "We'll get by just fine. I'll see to it. You don't need nobody else, Mama. Same with you, Bethany Rose. Luke Henry's here."

2

Bethany Rose stood in her sleeveless cotton nightshirt staring into the sallow mirror over her pine dresser. She hated the way she looked—tall and lanky as a broomstick, hardly a hundred pounds, her dark eyes and full mouth almost too large for her slender face.

She had long ago decided that her hair—the color of nutmeg and henna—was her only redeeming feature. Cascading in crimped tresses to her shoulders, it possessed a will of its own. Even when she plaited her auburn locks in a fashionable braid, she looked younger than her nineteen years; she could be mistaken for a child—fifteen perhaps—were she not so tall.

She moved her tapered fingers solemnly across her bony shoulders and chest. Mama called her willowy; it sounded better than *skinny*. Papa used to say she had the grace of a young sapling reaching for the stars. She liked that image because it captured exactly what she wanted to do. *Reach for the stars!* Someday she might even *be* a star, or at least fill out and look glamorous, like Lana Turner, or Barbara Stanwyck, or Lauren Bacall.

Or maybe it would never happen. She scowled at her somber reflection. What did it matter? Who of consequence would ever notice Bethany Rose Henry?

Here in her cramped bedroom she was captive of this muggy

August night; the air outside her screened window was as still as the air inside. It meant another sleepless night, enduring the tedium and lethargy that marked the dwindling days of summer.

Bethany turned on her bedside radio—an old Philco Papa had bought her that emitted as much static as music these days. Burns and Allen was playing. In her high singsong soprano Gracie was lamenting the misadventures of her scatterbrained aunt; George, sounding calmly bemused, was playing straight man. Bethany turned the dial, catching the fleeting voices of Horace Heidt and Fred Allen. She listened a moment to the smooth, deep tones of Edward R. Murrow announcing something about President Truman's Fair Deal legislation, then she settled at last on the sweet, melodic rhythms of Harry James and his orchestra.

Bethany pulled back her white chenille spread and lay down, stretching out her long legs on the hard, narrow bed. She fluffed her pillow under her head and stared up at the single overhead bulb in its milk-glass fixture. If she looked at the light long enough her eyes saw little sunspots amid the labyrinth of cracks on the ceiling.

Too much had happened tonight. Jake's kisses, Mama's deception, Knowl Herrick's offer of money for college. How could Mama have turned down a chance for Bethany to go to college, especially when so few girls—even the well-to-do—had such an opportunity? College was a man's domain, catering since the war to the brave soldiers who had served in the armed forces. After the war Luke could have gone to college under the GI Bill of Rights, but he had preferred to stay on the farm.

But not Bethany Rose. She yearned for an education, a way of escape.

Maybe the Herricks weren't as high and mighty and mean spirited as Bethany had assumed. And yet, there had been only the one letter in nearly two years. Why hadn't the Herricks made more of an effort to stay in touch since Papa's funeral?

All of her life Bethany had felt boxed in—by this room, by the farm, by poverty. In a constant state of expectancy, she had waited for someone, some great event, some door or window to open wide and let in a world she'd never seen before. There had to be more than this weathered farmhouse on a patch of green grass beside a dirt road a mile outside Fort Wayne. Beyond the horizon lay big, bustling cities like Chicago and Detroit and Indianapolis, but she had glimpsed them only in faded photographs and knew nothing of their vast colors and smells and sounds.

But one day everything would open up to her, and she wouldn't feel boxed in anymore. Fate would smile on her. She sensed it. She was a person whose dreams could be ignited and launched, if someone gave her half a chance.

Bethany gazed around at the four walls of her room, so familiar, yet so suffocating. She knew every inch by heart—where the chintz curtains were patched, where the paint was chipped, where Luke as a boy had carved his initials in the hardwood floor. This room was as much a part of her as her own flesh and bones. How could she ever escape?

She sat up and pressed her fingertips against her temples. *If I don't stop thinking, I'll explode,* she thought. She reached over to the nightstand and picked up a dog-eared issue of *Radio and Television Mirror.* She had read the articles a dozen times but was always drawn back, as if by memorizing random details of celebrity lives, some of their magic and charm might rub off on her.

Bethany knew the stories by heart. Dinah Shore and George Montgomery were celebrating their daughter Melissa's birth. Hal Peary—The Great Gildersleeve—and his bride were honeymooning in their glamorous Hollywood mansion. The Nat King Cole Trio was climbing the ladder of success, making an unbelievable $15,000 a week.

But what she liked best in this thumb-worn magazine—what she studied with an intensity that made her eyes ache—was a color photograph of comedienne Joan Davis helping her teenage daughter with her homework in their posh Bel-Air living room. Bethany thought about the popular radio star sitting on her lush green carpet in her red dress, leaning toward her daughter, smiling like she really wanted to be there—would always be there—and the girl stretched out on her stomach looking dreamy-eyed and content, as if everyone had a life like this and a mama who could fulfill any dream.

Bethany's mama had never helped with homework. She worked her knuckles raw doing chores on their tumbledown farm—chasing chickens, plowing fields, planting corn. She came in late with straggling hair and soiled clothes that smelled like the barnyard and ate whatever Bethany set on the table—macaroni and cheese or goulash or Spam, and she was usually too exhausted even to carry on a conversation.

Bethany fanned herself with the magazine, welcoming the momentary coolness. Hungry for the slightest breeze, she lifted her tousled hair and fanned the moisture at the back of her neck. She gazed around her room at the scant furniture—"piecemeal patched pine," as Papa once laughingly described it. She had adorned the yellowed wallpaper with her charcoal sketches of Hollywood stars and movie posters promoting *Gone with the Wind* and *The Best Years of Our Lives*. The room reflected a strange hodgepodge of extremes, from rank poverty to impossible dreams.

Yes, Bethany was a dreamer. Mama and Papa both said so; Mama meant it as criticism; Papa, as praise. "Don't let anyone take your dreams away," he had told her more than once. She wouldn't. Dreams were all she had.

About nine P.M. Bethany put aside her magazine, padded down the hall to the small, dimly lit bathroom, and peered inside the medicine cabinet. She had to find something to quash a pounding headache and help her sleep. She seized the bottle of sleeping pills

Dr. Hilliard had prescribed for Mama after Papa died. A handful of tablets remained. Did she dare take them? She sat on the edge of the rusted, clawfoot tub, shook two tablets into her palm, then swallowed an extra one for good measure.

She returned to bed, leaving her door open, hoping for a cool cross breeze. Within minutes she slipped into a drugged sleep. In her dream she was running somewhere, perhaps on her own weed-rimmed, rock-strewn road, breathless, chased by unseen phantoms. But the running took her nowhere; if anything it left her falling behind, exhausted, every pore pouring out perspiration as she gasped for air.

She awoke with a start, her mind groggy from the sedatives and the heavy dregs of dream-sleep muddling her thoughts. Where was she? What woke her? Her slim body was moist under her cotton nightshirt, her long russet hair limp as spun silk. The air was so still she was afraid to breathe.

In that ponderous silence she opened her eyes and gazed around her shadowed room. Through the doorway a shaft of light spilled in from the hall. There in that pale patch of light was carved the profile of a woman in a feather hat. Her features were sharply etched—a straight nose, long neck, prominent chin. The hat was wide-brimmed, with a generous plume that curled dramatically in the air.

The image seemed frozen in time, unreal, like the whimsical silhouettes of shadow puppets—birds and dogs and butterflies Bethany had made with her hands as a child. Before she could question whether the shadow was real or an illusion, her dreams intruded and bore her away so that the puzzling reflection became the substance of her nocturnal reveries.

Later—perhaps only minutes—she awoke again to the sound of voices in another room. Two women arguing. Her mother and someone whose voice was unfamiliar but filled with venom. A neighbor who couldn't sleep? Tempers always soared with the thermometer. She couldn't distinguish their words, only muffled patterns of sound rising and falling like undulating waves. Or perhaps it was only the radio. Again, she drifted into a drugged slumber.

Then—minutes or hours later, she couldn't be sure—she was jerked from her cozy womb of sleep by something dark and palpable. She sat bolt upright, heart pounding. Her eyes stung; her mouth was dry as sandpaper. She stared at the doorway. Smoke black as furnace soot was billowing into her room.

"Mama! Luke!" she screamed, but the sound died in her parched throat. She fought the paralysis of stark, numbing horror and rolled out of bed onto the floor. Covering her face with her nightshirt, she belly-crawled along the hallway to the living room. *Got to find Mama! Got to find Mama!* Bethany coughed, the heavy, acrid smoke already invading her nostrils and searing her throat.

Her eyes teared; the living room blurred in a deep surreal haze. Flames vaulted up wallpaper, coiling and swirling, crackling and popping. Tongues of fire pinwheeled from window to window, devouring curtains and spreading to the davenport and chairs.

"Mama!" she rasped.

A hazy orange glow whirled around her; flurries of embers sparked like fireflies. The fire fed on itself, hypnotic, mesmerizing. White hot flames danced like supple ghosts in a slow-motion ballet.

"Mama!" Bethany uttered again. She bumped something in the darkness—Papa's chair perhaps—and collapsed, seized by fits of coughing as the thick dark smoke stole her breath.

Then, as consciousness dimmed, Bethany felt herself hoisted up in Luke's strapping arms and swept through the smoke-clogged labyrinth of rooms outside to precious, clean night air.

Still coughing, she turned her face up to his and urgently mouthed the words, "Where's Mama?"

He held her tight. "Inside. It's too late!"

"No, no!" She pounded his chest and wrestled against his iron grip, but he held her fast as the firestorm devoured the small frame house—the only home she had ever known.

Days later, Bethany Rose would hear over and over how her brother had braved the inferno to rescue her and how fortunate she was to have survived such a conflagration. And she would hear the grievous laments and exclamations of despair over the fact that her mother had perished in the flames.

But Bethany said nothing. For two days she sat in a gray hospital room on a hard bed in a coarse backless gown. She sat in gloomy silence, unmoving, except for her frantic, fidgeting fingers. For hours she twisted the linen sheet, making a ragged snake that wore the skin off her knuckles and thumbs. She felt shell-shocked, her hold on sanity tenuous as filigrees of dew on tendrils of grass. She couldn't cry; she couldn't even bring herself to speak.

When she thought about the fire, the images were ghastly as phantoms and illusive as moths hovering at the edge of her consciousness. A grisly dream. She couldn't be sure it wasn't the same dream that startled her awake that fateful night. Perhaps she hadn't awakened yet. Perhaps her brother Luke hadn't carried her out of their burning house. Perhaps her mother wasn't really dead.

But reality had a way of intruding with a cold, relentless energy, exhausting her. Nothing she dreamed could erase this terrible onslaught of events that now defined her life. Her worst nightmare had invaded her days, and she would never wake up. Never.

Three days after the fire, Beth and her brother settled in at the Witherspoon farmhouse down the road. There was an odd sort of irony about moving in with the Witherspoons. The night of the fire Jake had talked about taking her home with him. *I'll marry you and take you home to my mama and daddy's farm. It's big enough for all of us.*

Jake's parents, Clive and Bertha Witherspoon, were a sturdy, hard-working, solemn-faced couple, plain and proper, and proudly straightlaced. In her last year of high school, while browsing through a book of paintings in art class, Bethany had discovered dead ringers for the Witherspoons in Grant Wood's painting *American Gothic*. Even the house behind the couple in the painting resembled the Witherspoons' farmhouse. It was rambling and old, cluttered but clean, the rough-hewn walls covered with hand-stitched tapestries and Norman Rockwell prints. The kitchen smelled of onions and garlic, the bathroom of lavender soap and Pine-Sol. It was a comfortable house, nicer than any Bethany had ever known. But it wasn't her home.

As the days dragged by, Bethany sat in the Witherspoon parlor in her robe and stared uncomprehendingly at pictures in magazines. *Modern Romances. Life. Look. Good Housekeeping*. The pictures, bright and colorful and filled with glimpses of other people's lives, had become the only reality she cared to know.

Jake and Luke fussed and fretted over her constantly; they brought her used shirts and frocks and dungarees from the Salvation Army store in Fort Wayne (only the nightshirt on her back had survived the fire), but she had no desire to get up in the morning and get dressed. Since she refused to join the family at the dinner table, Mrs. Witherspoon served Bethany meals of tea and toast or ham and eggs in her tiny attic room.

Bethany's desolation was more than Luke could tolerate. His anger flaring, he would badger her to react. "Get up. Do something. Are you just gonna mope around gloomy and moon-faced forever?"

Even Jake wouldn't let her be. When he and Luke came in from working the fields and found her sitting, staring into space, still in her robe and her hair uncombed, he would goad her, "Are you crazy? Don't just sit around like a zombie. You want them to cart you off to the loony bin?"

She began to feel a small, comforting power in not responding. Her self-imposed lethargy had become a protective wall between her and her own tempestuous emotions. She knew if she said the words out loud—if she admitted to herself that her mother was dead—it would become real. Final. She felt her emotions would surge out of control and drown her.

So she fixed her gaze on something remote and safe—the pictures in her magazines; or if she was outside, the moon, the ground, a rock, a tree. In her imagination she slid out of herself and became that hard, earthy, unfeeling thing. Only then did the pain ebb away.

But one week into the nightmare, Luke told her something that almost prompted her to break out of her passivity. "You're gonna be leaving Fort Wayne, Bethany Rose. You're moving to Willowbrook," he said matter-of-factly one evening as she sat at the small table in her attic room, finishing her cornbread and beans.

She stared defiantly at her brother. He might be older, but she was an adult too. He couldn't tell her what to do, especially something as improbable and outrageous as moving to Willowbrook. She shook her head and finally spoke. "No, I'm staying here!"

"No, Beth. You're going, and that's it." Luke, six feet of rangy, sinewy muscle, gripped her shoulders and stared her down, his dark eyes sharp as tacks. A shock of rust-colored hair had strayed over his high, ruddy forehead. "You pack what belongings you got, little sister. Whether you like it or not, tomorrow I'm driving you to Willowbrook."

"No!" She grabbed his hands and flung them off her shoulders, then stood and met his gaze with fire in her eyes.

"Look, Bethany Rose," he said, more gently now, "I'm trying to make this as easy for you as I can. It's for the best, believe me. It's no good for you to stay here anymore."

He turned away and paced the floor, his gaze darting restlessly around the room. "I talked on the telephone to Knowl and Catherine," he went on, speaking too fast, as if rushing through a memorized speech. "No matter how we feel about them, Beth, they're family—our brother and sister. They want you to come. It was their idea."

"No, Luke, I won't go!"

When her eyes continued to blaze defiance, he snapped, "For crying out loud, they're our flesh and blood. We had the same papa. With all their money and fancy homes, they owe us." He cracked his knuckles, one hand, then the other. His voice rose with a nervous agitation. "Catherine's husband—that Robert Wayne fella—fixed up the house that used to be Papa's. You could stay there."

She shook her head no.

"Or you could live with Knowl and Annie in that big old Victorian house on Honeysuckle Lane. Now there's a mansion for you. You could even take Knowl up on his offer to send you to college. Whaddaya say, Beth?"

She shook her head again. "I'm staying here."

Luke kicked the door, making the room shake. "You can't stay here anymore, Bethany. Don't you understand? The Witherspoons are making plans."

She stared up questioningly at him. "What plans?"

"I didn't want to tell you, but Jake's in on it too. They're planning a wedding. You and Jake. They figure it ain't proper for you to live under their roof unless you two tie the knot. They got their minds made up."

Bethany reached out and gripped Luke's shirt front. "You tell Jake I said no!"

Luke nodded. "Okay, Beth, I know you don't want to marry Jake. He's my best buddy, but he's stubborn and hot-tempered. I wouldn't force him on you. But if you stay here you'll get sucked into their plans, I know it. That's why I called the Herricks. This way you got a choice. You can settle down here with Jake or take your chances in Willowbrook."

Bethany blinked back tears. "What will you do if I go?"

"Don't worry about me, Beth. I'll stay here and earn my keep by working the Witherspoons' farm. I'll bring our animals over here, too. Whenever I can I'll work on our place and build the house up brand new. I'll bring you back home as soon as I can." He paused and cleared his throat. His voice came out raspy and uneven. "There's one more thing. It'll be at least another week before we can have Mama's funeral."

She stared at him in surprise. "Why?"

"We gotta wait till the police and the coroner finish their investigation." His voice wavered against a rush of emotion. He blinked and compressed his nostrils with his thumb and index finger. "It's like this, Beth. The authorities gotta find out how the fire started and how Mama died. We know it was just a terrible accident, but that's not enough for them. They gotta do an autopsy and poke into stuff that's none of their business. But it won't change anything. It won't bring Mama back."

This time it was Bethany's turn to kick the door. Hot tears rolled down her cheeks. "It's not fair!" She still hadn't gotten over Papa's death, and now Mama! She had never expected to lose Mama.

Luke pulled her into his arms and pressed her head against his chest. They held each other for a long time. She didn't want to let him go. Luke was all she had left. If she released him, she might lose him too.

"It'll be all right, Beth," he whispered. "I promise. The hurt will go away. You'll find a whole new life in Willowbrook."

But she didn't want a new life. She wanted the old one back—the hard, poverty-stricken life she had rued since the day she was born. She was willing to bargain anything to have Mama and their dowdy old house back the way it was before the fire. She was ready to do anything to survive, except go live in a house full of strangers.

3

The drive to Willowbrook in Luke's tumbledown pickup was a long, bumpy, teeth-jarring journey. The late-summer heat was stifling, drawing the sweat from Bethany's pores and soaking her ill-fitting gingham sundress. Drenched in humidity, her legs and back stuck to the cracked leather seats; her mouth and throat were parched and dry as desert sand.

Bethany's relief at escaping Jake Witherspoon's marriage plan was nullified by her terror at moving in with Papa's other family. She had met Knowl and Catherine Herrick during Papa's illness and at his funeral, but she had managed to push her half brother and sister to a shadowy corner of her mind, lest the reality of what Papa had done propel her to the edge of insanity.

Now, at last, she must face these people who were paradoxically both her closest kin and utter strangers. Every day, living among them, she would be reminded in a thousand ways that Papa had had another family—a wife, a son, and a daughter in Willowbrook—before taking up with her mama in Fort Wayne. She knew what everybody in the Herrick household would be thinking: The Herricks were the legitimate family; the Henrys were Tom's shamefully misbegotten spawn.

But she would show them. She had her pride, no matter what

Papa had done. She wouldn't let the Herricks treat her like the black sheep of the family; she didn't need their charity and didn't want their pity.

"Bethany, you okay?" asked Luke, glancing over at her from the driver's seat. "I know you've been down in the mouth since the fire, but today you're quieter than ever, hardly moving. You all right?"

She nodded and clasped her hands in her lap.

"I wish you'd talk to me, Bethany Rose. We got things to say to each other before I leave you in Willowbrook."

She looked at him with a solemn urgency. "I want to, Luke, but I can't. Not yet," she replied. She wanted to tell him how she felt about leaving him, about the gaping wound festering inside since losing Mama, about the misgivings that assailed her even now as they approached a town she had never seen, a house she had never known, and strangers who struck fear and resentment in her heart.

She wanted to tell Luke about the other terrors, too, that plagued her since the night of the fire, especially the horrifying shadow on the wall—the silhouette of the woman in the feather hat. But she couldn't be sure she hadn't dreamed the woman. Since that night that sinister shadow had invaded her dreams a dozen times, each vision more terrifying than the one before.

"Bethany," Luke went on in an oddly parental tone, "living with the Herricks won't be easy, them being strangers and all. But I know them better than you, and I'll tell you what I know. After that, I can't help you no more; you're on your own."

He paused and drew in a deep breath. His large hands clenched and unclenched the steering wheel. "Our sister Catherine is a nice sort. Feisty, smart, real keen on life. She's an artist and maybe she can help you with your drawing."

Bethany shook her head.

"Suit yourself. Now, our brother Knowl is a hard one to read. He's a proud, hard-working, tight-lipped man. Lives by the letter of the law. I got the feeling he don't like us one bit, but he feels like he's gotta do right by us. He gives with one hand and takes back with the other. I don't reckon he'll ever forgive us for being his daddy's misbegot offspring. So let him be; don't fret yourself over him and his lofty ways."

Bethany nodded, her gaze moving listlessly over the passing scenery—ripened cornfields, weathered barns, and snug little farmhouses like the one that had burned down. She had hated that house, had felt trapped by its cramped, confining rooms, and had for years yearned to flee her impoverished life; yet now she missed that ramshackle home as keenly as she missed Mama. Now, even what little she had was gone and she was forced to go live with rich relatives who surely didn't want her.

Why was it that those who had plenty prospered, while those who had little lost even what they had? Surely God had His favorites, and Bethany Rose Henry wasn't one of them!

"Now about Betty Herrick, Papa's other wife," said Luke, his tone turning dark, "she's the one to watch out for."

Bethany's interest perked.

"She's a drunk," Luke continued. "Been a drinker most of her life. Maybe that's why Papa left her and took up with our mama. The woman was in a sanitarium for years, but now she's back in Willowbrook, living with Knowl. She won't take kindly to you living there, Beth, but don't you pay her no mind, no matter what she says. She's just a crazy old woman."

By the time Luke had finished his advice, his rickety truck was trundling over the rough, red-brick streets of Willowbrook. The town looked smaller than Fort Wayne, but its buildings were handsome and well-kept and its grand old houses stood proudly on wide, green, manicured lawns shaded by towering oaks and majestic elms.

"We're almost there," said Luke as he turned onto Honeysuckle Lane. The cobbled street was lined with vintage estates surrounded by imposing wrought-iron fences. "Catherine and Robert live around the corner on Maypole Drive," Luke continued. "It was Papa's house, where Cath was raised. They've restored it, I hear, but it's not nearly as big and fancy as Knowl's place." He pointed out the window, his excitement mounting. "See, there it is, Beth! Herrick House!"

Bethany watched as the stately rose-colored mansion came into view—a maze of white gables and quaint cupolas, with delicate stained-glass windows and plenty of bric-a-brac trim. Lush green ivy grew bountifully beside the wraparound porch, climbed the lacy trellises, and cascaded over the steep slate-gray roof.

Its magnificence stole Bethany's breath and left her wrists feeling weak and tingly. Was it possible that she—Bethany Rose Henry—was actually going to live in this elegant old Victorian house? Heaven help her, she wouldn't know how to act or what to do.

A new thought struck her. Perhaps the Herricks had invited her here to serve as maid or housekeeper. Surely such a house had many rooms to clean. That had to be it. They would put her to work. Very well. She would do what she was told, and be as invisible as a gnat. No one would know she was there.

Luke's truck entered the open gate and rumbled up the long driveway to the house. The pickup jerked to a stop beside the porch, its tired engine coughing and sputtering as Luke reached for her valise and opened his door. He came around, opened her door, and helped her down. A slight breeze had risen and was cooling her moist skin even as she followed Luke up the wide steps to the paneled mahogany door.

Before Luke could knock, the door swung open and an attractive woman with shiny brown hair and gray-green eyes gazed out at Bethany. She was wearing a slim, mint-green sheath with big flap pockets. She smiled brightly and said with a hint of nervousness, "Hello. Welcome. You're Bethany Rose, of course. And Luke." She glanced from one to the other, her ivory face flushing. "I'm Annie, Knowl's wife. We met at your father's funeral."

"I remember," said Luke. "So does Bethany; don't you, Beth?"

She nodded and said, "Hello, Annie."

"Hello, Bethany. I'm so sorry about your mother and the fire. I can't imagine how difficult it must be for you both." Annie stepped back inside the foyer and made a sweeping gesture with her hand. "Please come in."

Luke entered first and Bethany followed, her scuffed saddle shoes clacking on the gleaming marble and jarring the cool, hushed atmosphere of the house. She gazed around at the polished mahogany tables and buffets, the tufted sofas and love seats of velvet and brocade, the antique lace curtains, the ornate paintings and exquisite wallpaper.

"Do you need help with your luggage?" asked Annie.

"No, she doesn't," said Luke. "There's just this valise."

Annie looked with surprise at the small satchel. "Oh, well, fine. I should have realized—your belongings—they were lost in the fire." She reached out and clasped Bethany's hand. "Don't worry, dear. We'll buy you some lovely new things."

Startled, Bethany drew back her hand, uncertain how to respond. Surely Annie was being nice out of a sense of duty.

"You'll have the rosebud room," Annie continued in a lilting voice. "It was my room when I was a child. It was my favorite room in the house. And your sister Catherine had the rosebud room when she lived here, before she married Robert Wayne and moved to . . . to . . ." Annie paused, flustered.

"Before she moved to Papa's house on Maypole Drive," supplied Luke. "It's okay. We know Cath is living in Papa's old house around the corner."

Annie smiled, relieved. "Bethany, would you like to go upstairs now and freshen up? The bathroom is just down the hall, and there are clean towels on the rack."

Bethany nodded.

"Fine," said Annie. "I'll take you up in a few minutes, but first let me go make a pot of tea and put some biscuits in the oven. You are hungry, aren't you?"

She shook her head.

"Sure she is," said Luke. "We both are."

Annie flashed a generous smile. "You'll stay for supper, won't you, Luke? I'm sure Knowl would like to see you. He's at work right now—our publishing venture—Herrick House. It keeps him terribly busy. He should be home by seven."

A baby's cry sounded from an upstairs room. "That's my sweet Maggie," Annie explained, still smiling, but sounding a bit breathless now. "Your little niece. The spitting image of Knowl. She's not quite two, but she's learned to make her wishes known, loud and clear."

Suddenly an older, silver-haired version of Annie appeared from another doorway—a graceful middle-aged woman in a blue silk dress and matching flat heels. "I'll tend to the baby, Annie," she said, her voice warm and mellow. "You take care of your guests."

Annie beckoned her over and said, "This is my mother, Anna Reed. Mother, this is Luke and Bethany Herrick—uh, I mean, *Henry*."

Luke flinched but shook Anna's hand with good-natured energy. "Nice to meet you, Mrs. Reed."

"Hello," Beth murmured.

The woman's smile lit up the room. She had to be at least fifty, yet her skin was clear and smooth as the tallow of candles. "I'm so pleased to meet you both. And please, call me Anna."

"Sure. Anna it is," said Luke politely. "Listen, my sister Bethany—she's still upset, you know. Not up to talking much. Just give her time and she'll be okay."

"Stop it, Luke. I'm fine."

Anna slipped a motherly arm around Bethany's shoulder. "After you've settled into your room, dear, would you like to join me for a little visit with my granddaughter? Maggie's such a precious girl. I know you'll love her."

Bethany managed a reluctant nod. "Sure, I guess so." So this was it. They'd brought her here to be a nanny. It didn't matter. She had no life of her own anymore.

Annie touched Bethany's arm. "Let me take you up to your room now." Together they climbed the immense, carpeted stairs. "I've invited Catherine and Robert over for dinner, and their precious little Jenny, so we can all be together on your first night here."

Bethany felt a wave of panic. She wanted to tell Annie she couldn't possibly face people yet, but the words wouldn't come. Bethany stayed in her new bedroom until supper time, examining every fragile knickknack and graceful article of furniture. The room was lovelier than she could have imagined, with fresh chintz curtains, a pale rose canopy bed, a cherry wood dresser and vanity, Tiffany lamps, and pink rosebud wallpaper. No wonder this was Annie's favorite room!

Shortly after seven a knock sounded on her door. It was Luke, grinning with excitement and warmth. "Come on. They called us to supper, Beth." He reached for her hand. "You should have joined Annie and me for a tour of the yard. Lots of trees and rose bushes and every kind of flower you can think of."

Bethany shrugged indifferently. "I've seen flowers and trees."

"Not like these. You'll love the garden, Beth, especially the gazebo. I almost wish I was staying too, except I'm no good rattling around in such a fancy house."

Hot tears stung her eyes. "I don't want you to go."

"Don't worry, I'll come to visit. And you'll do swell, Beth, once you get used to your new family."

She slapped his arm in protest. "They're not my new family!"

"Yes they are, Beth. And the sooner you realize it, the happier you'll be."

"Never!" Jutting out her lower lip, she grudgingly followed Luke downstairs and through the handsomely decorated rooms to the elegant dining room.

A tiered chandelier hung over a long, linen-draped table set with fine china, crystal goblets, and gleaming silver. A candelabra holding long-stemmed candles graced the center of the table. Anna Reed was setting down a steaming platter of fried chicken beside a heaping bowl of mashed potatoes. Bethany had never smelled anything so delicious in her life.

She turned her gaze from the table, startled, as her half-sister, Catherine Herrick, swept over and gave her a brief embrace. "It's good to see you again, Bethany Rose," Cath said, her green eyes vivid, her voice a bit too forced. Her red hair framed her rosy face in finely combed waves. "You remember my husband, don't you? Robert came to Fort Wayne to pick me up that time Luke drove me there to see Papa."

You mean the night Luke kidnapped you! Beth wanted to retort. She nodded faintly. It was a terrible memory; Papa was so ill, and Luke had brought home this stranger and announced that she was Papa's daughter too.

Robert—a ruddy, rough-hewn giant of a man with curly dark hair and crinkly eyes—was holding out his hand with a genial smile. "I'm sorry about your mother, Bethany."

"Thank you."

"Cath and I want to help any way we can. Please come visit us. We live just around the corner."

Bethany averted her gaze. She couldn't imagine visiting the house where Papa had raised his other family.

"Hello, Bethany." It was Knowl—Catherine's brother and Beth's half-brother—stepping forward, offering his hand with polite restraint. Tall, broad-shouldered, and brown-eyed, his wheat-colored hair impeccably styled, Knowl wore a dapper gray suit and wire-rimmed spectacles. "I hope you and Luke had a good drive."

"It was okay."

Catherine spoke again. "Bethany, this is my daughter Jenny." A young girl in a royal-blue taffeta dress sidled over to her. "Sugarplum, can you say hello to your Aunt Bethany?"

"Hello, Aunt Bethany," came the lyrical, singsong voice. The child looked about seven, with long, strawberry-blonde curls, round, freckled cheeks, and large, thickly lashed eyes. The impudence in her gaze made her look wise beyond her years and a bit formidable. But Beth sensed something familiar in the child's shrewd, imperturbable manner—a carefully protected vulnerability much like her own.

Bethany stooped down, took Jenny's hand, and smiled. "Hi, Jenny. You're pretty."

Jenny smiled back expansively. "So are you. Do you like to play hopscotch? I do."

Bethany nodded.

"Do you play cat's cradle or ring-around-the-rosy? Will you play with me? I'm very good at charades too."

Catherine laughed and squeezed Jenny's shoulders. "As you can see, Jenny's very outgoing. She has an opinion about everything. She'll talk your head off."

Bethany gave Jenny a lingering smile. This was the first person in the Herrick household she genuinely wanted to spend time with. The child had called her *Aunt Bethany.* It was true. As improbable as it seemed, Jenny was her very own niece!

"Take your seats, everyone, before the food gets cold," declared Anna, wiping her hands on her lacy apron. She looked at Knowl and added quietly, "I'll take a tray up to your mother and be back before you say grace."

"No, Mother Reed, you have enough to do here," said Knowl. "I'll take Mama her dinner. Especially tonight. She may be in one of her moods."

Bethany watched curiously as her half-brother slipped into the kitchen, returned with a covered tray, and disappeared down the hall. Wasn't Betty Herrick going to join them at the table? Was she ill? Or was she as reluctant to meet Tom's other children as they were to meet her? The others paid no attention to Knowl's brief absence. They were all sitting down, knowing their places without being told.

"Come sit over here, Bethany," said Annie, patting the chair beside her.

Reluctantly Beth sat down, but she would have preferred eating alone in her room, like Knowl's mama. She stared at the china plate surrounded by silverware. How did one know where to begin? With the fork? The spoon? Which fork? Which spoon? She reached for her linen napkin, then realized that Knowl had returned and everyone around the table was joining hands. Her face flushed as she realized they were waiting for her to complete the circle.

"We hold hands when we pray," whispered Annie.

Pray? Why? Are we in church? Bethany wondered.

When every head was bowed, Knowl intoned deeply, "Thank You, Heavenly Father, for this food and the hands that have prepared it. Thank You for all those You have brought together at this table. We don't always understand Your ways, but we know You work all things together for good to those who love You. In Jesus' name we pray, amen."

Luke met Bethany's gaze across the table, as if to say, *See? I told you! Our Willowbrook relatives are an odd lot!*

As the food was passed, only little Jenny persisted in talking nonstop to Bethany.

"Will you play house with me after dinner?" she inquired. "Mama Annie and Mama Cath are always too busy. Mama Annie writes books. Mama Cath paints pictures. Sometimes Mama Cath draws Snow

White and Cinderella for me, and I color in the lines very carefully. Would you like to color with me?"

Bethany broke into a spontaneous grin. "I like to draw."

Catherine reached over and patted Jenny's hand. "Aunt Bethany may be too tired to color tonight, sugarplum. We need to let her rest. Maybe tomorrow—"

Jenny shook her head, her long curls swinging around her face. "No. Aunt Bethany wants to color with me. She said so!"

Bethany nodded. "I'll draw you a picture, Jenny."

"See, Mama?" said Jenny triumphantly. "Aunt Bethany wants to play! She's nice!"

If nothing else, Bethany had made one friend in the Herrick household! For the rest of the meal, she and Jenny exchanged private smiles while the rest of the family engaged in what Bethany considered tedious conversation.

"Knowl, the paper says unemployment's up," noted Robert as he lifted a crispy drumstick to his lips. "At the four-million mark this month."

"That's about two-million fewer jobs than last year."

"Even people with jobs are having a hard time of it," said Annie. "I just hope President Truman has some answers."

Knowl nodded. "At least the House passed legislation to raise the minimum wage to seventy-five cents an hour, but it hasn't passed the Senate yet. Don't know that it will."

Anna shook her head. "Goodness gracious! What kind of future are we passing on to our children?"

"Some folks think the future lies in television," said Robert offhandedly.

"Don't say that," exclaimed Annie. "If people start watching television, they won't read the books we're publishing."

Anna patted a wisp of gray hair into place. "Television will never take the place of radio. It's unnatural. If you want to see a picture, go to the movies. Don't stare at a little box in your living room!"

"But look how television's grown this past year, Mother Reed," said Cath. "Even your daughter, Alice Marie, is singing on that new station in Chicago. She likes it, doesn't she?"

"That's what she writes in her rare letters home. But you know my daughter. Alice Marie managed to sound on top of the world even when she had to stop traveling with the big bands. Just as well. It was such a hard life."

"Music and people's tastes have changed since the war," said Robert. "Big bands aren't as popular anymore. But I'm telling you, television's coming in like a lion. Look at the radio stars going to television—Jack Benny, Bing Crosby, Arthur Godfrey."

Anna passed around a basket of hot, crusty rolls. "Well, even if my Alice Marie becomes a big star, I won't have one of those television contraptions in my home."

Knowl gave her a bemused smile. "Yes, you will, Mother Reed. Robert's right. The handwriting's on the wall. The Federal Communications Commission predicts in five years half of all homes in the United States will have television sets, with six to eight hundred stations on the air nationally."

"Maybe Herrick House should get on the bandwagon and figure out a way to capitalize on such a powerful new medium," said Robert.

"You mean promote our publishing house through television?" quizzed Annie. "Robert, they're like oil and water!"

"Not necessarily. If we someday want to survive we may have to learn to coexist. After all, we may even have a television station here in Willowbrook one day."

"It's possible," agreed Knowl. "The Bell System will be extending their network from South Bend to Fort Wayne next year."

Bethany Rose listened to the dreary dinner-table conversation with increasing dismay. Now that she had consumed every morsel on her plate, she longed for the sweet isolation of her room. She had no desire to hear about politics, economics, or something as remote and mystifying as television. She noticed that Luke looked just as uncomfortable. At least he would be escaping back to Fort Wayne after dinner, while she was doomed to remain in this huge mausoleum with these tiresome strangers.

Then she heard a word that drew her back into the conversation with a dizzying jolt. *Henry*. Her name. The name Papa had assumed when he moved to Fort Wayne and took up with her mama. She glanced curiously at Knowl, who had just spoken the name.

Seeing her sudden interest, he explained, "I was speaking of Reverend Henry, our minister at Willowbrook Christian Church."

Luke spoke up. "Is that where our papa got his name? From some preacher?"

"Apparently so," said Knowl, his tone uneasy. "Our father was born Tom Herrick, but he told your mother he was Tom Henry."

"All we ever knew was Henry," said Luke. "Tom Henry."

"It was all a terrible deception," murmured Cath, looking downcast. "I'll never understand why our papa did such a thing."

Maybe he couldn't stand living with your drunken mama! Beth wanted to shout, but she held her tongue.

"Dear, what were you saying about Reverend Henry?" asked Annie as she lifted her water goblet to her lips.

Knowl's voice still had a slight edge to it. "I was saying that the pulpit committee has found a man to take Reverend Henry's place when he retires in the fall."

"Really?" asked Anna. "Who?"

"A young fellow from New York. Todd Marshall. He's only twenty-six, but he has excellent credentials. A graduate of Columbia University and a prestigious New York seminary. He'll be coming next month to candidate at the church. And if the congregation approves, we'll have ourselves a new pastor."

"Goodness gracious," said Anna. "I can't imagine our church without Reverend Henry. He's been there since you children were babies."

"I don't envy the man who tries to fill his shoes," mused Annie. "St. Paul himself would probably face some ruffled feathers."

"Well, change is in the wind," said Robert. "It's a whole new world out there. And our church must be ready for it. Maybe we need a young man with a new vision."

"But does he have a family, Knowl?" asked Anna.

"No, he's single. I realize that may be a problem for some of our older members. They like a stable family man with lots of children and a wife who can play the piano and teach Sunday school."

"Well, I think the single ladies at church will take to him just fine," said Cath with a sly smile. "In fact, if he's as handsome as he is smart, he probably won't be single for very long."

Bethany sat tapping her toes restlessly on the carpet under the table. She had no wish to hear all this fiddle-faddle about some preacher coming to town. What did it have to do with her? Absolutely nothing. She leaned over and looked at little Jenny. The child sat listlessly, lining up her peas on her plate. *She's even more bored than I am!* Beth caught her eye and mouthed the words, "Let's go play!"

Jenny didn't have to be invited twice. She reached over and tugged on Catherine's arm and begged, "Please, Mama Cath, may I go play with Aunt Bethany now?"

With Catherine's nod, Jenny and Bethany Rose both pushed back their chairs and nearly bolted out of the dining room and down the hall, stifling laughter as they ran hand in hand.

4

For the next several days Catherine dropped Jenny off at Herrick House so that the child could spend time with Bethany. The two took walks in the garden, colored pictures together in the gazebo—Jenny colored the graceful fashion models Bethany drew—and played hopscotch on the sidewalk along Honeysuckle Lane. Bethany felt as if she had become a child again. In fact, she yearned to crawl back into the past and experience that sweet, trusting innocence.

But just when she thought she had blocked out the taunting ogres of pain and grief, the truth would strike home again in her heart like a pealing bell, jarring her back to reality. She was an orphan—first fatherless, now motherless.

Strangely, when she tried to resurrect her mother's voice, her gestures, her face, she could not unlock the images from her memory. Especially the face. The harder she tried to shape her mother's features, the more elusive they became. Why did her mind play such cruel tricks when memories were all she had left?

Bethany was thankful for little Jenny's company. The child didn't seem to mind that Bethany was at times sad and preoccupied; Jenny had plenty of energy and cheer for both of them. When they colored, she told Beth what colors to make Snow White's dress or what outfits to sketch on her statuesque models; when they played games, she delighted in explaining the rules, as if Jenny were the adult and Bethany the child. Bethany played along. She figured a child in two families of adults needed someone to boss around once in awhile, and baby Maggie was still too young to fill the bill.

Only once did Bethany oppose one of Jenny's wishes. They were sitting together on the back porch steps, cracking walnuts—Beth did the cracking while Jenny eagerly devoured the meaty little nuggets. Between bites, Jenny said, "Come home with me, Aunt Bethany. You can play with my dolls. I have Shirley Temple and Raggedy Ann and Andy, and a baby doll that says 'Mama.' Her eyes open and close just like mine too. Please, Aunt Bethany."

"I'm sorry, Jenny. I can't." Beth had no intention of ever entering her father's house; it would make his other, secret life too painfully real. But there was no way to explain her reluctance to a child.

When Jenny saw that Beth couldn't be persuaded, she pouted for a moment, then moved over close and patted her hand. "It's okay, Aunt Bethany. I like this house better too. I like Mama Annie best of all. She isn't my real mommy, but I pretend she is. She was my mama when my real mama was sick. But now she's got baby Maggie to love, so she doesn't need me to be her little girl anymore."

Bethany stared at the wide-eyed, rose-lipped child with her flaxen curls and ruby-red dress. Amazingly, at seven Jenny had her problems too. Shunted all her life between two homes and two families, she had too many mamas—and apparently not one she could call her own!

Impulsively, Bethany gathered the child into her arms and hugged her for a long, silent moment. She knew how Jenny felt, having lots of people around but not knowing where she really belonged, and not feeling truly connected to those who were supposedly family.

One week from the day Bethany arrived in Willowbrook, Luke phoned with the news that Mama's funeral would be held the following afternoon. At Annie's prompting, Knowl volunteered to drive Beth to Fort Wayne; Annie and Catherine agreed to go too.

It was a simple graveside service, all too painfully similar to Papa's modest funeral two years before. A handful of friends and neighbors, including the Witherspoons, clustered under a scorching sun while a clergyman Beth had never seen droned a few propitious words about a woman he had never known. Then, as the mourners drifted away, two husky men in bib overalls lowered the pine box into the dark earth beside Papa.

After the funeral the Witherspoons invited everyone back to their farmhouse for a picnic lunch in the backyard. While they all gathered around a redwood table brimming with barbecued chicken, potato salad, baked beans, and watermelon, Jake Witherspoon, dressed in his Sunday best, drew Bethany aside and said, "We gotta talk."

She followed him into the parlor inside the house and sat down on a tufted sofa while he took the maple rocker. Comfortable only in work clothes, he tugged at his stiff white collar, then pulled a handkerchief from his shirt pocket and wiped his glistening brow.

"I—I know how sorrowful you are, Bethany Rose," he said in a voice that rose and fell in nervous spurts. "I mean, burying your mama today and all. But I want you to know I'm ready now to take care of you right and proper. You just say the word and we'll tie the knot. My house is your house. This whole farm will be ours—ours and my mama's and papa's, long as they live, naturally."

Bethany felt a nervous tension erupt behind her eyes and travel around the back of her head and down her neck. She managed to shake her head and murmur, "I can't, Jake. Not now. Not yet. It's too soon. I don't know anything anymore—who I am, where I'm supposed to be, what I'm supposed to do."

"Sure, Bethany Rose. I understand. I don't mind waiting a spell—long as it's not too long."

"Bethany?"

She started at the sound of her brother's voice. Luke was standing in the doorway, eyeing Jake eyeing her. "You through with my sister, Jake? I got business to talk with her."

"Sure, Luke. Take as long as you like." Jake stood, gave Bethany one last, lingering glance, and shuffled out the door toward the picnic table.

Luke settled into the maple rocker and sat forward, his elbows on his knees. He met her gaze and came right to the point. "What's Jake want?"

"You know."

"You tell him you're not ready to settle down."

"I did."

"Good." His dark eyes narrowed. "You like living in Willowbrook?"

"It's okay."

"You seen Papa's other woman yet?"

Bethany shook her head. "That Betty Herrick's a strange one, Luke. Never leaves her room. Anna Reed takes all her meals up to her. They're all so secretive about her. I wonder what she's like."

"Leave her be. She's trouble."

"Do you think she's crazy?"

"Why else would they keep her hidden?"

"It gives me the willies, Luke." Lowering her voice, she confided, "I . . . I have awful nightmares about the fire."

Luke glanced around, the muscle in his jaw twitching nervously. "Listen, we gotta talk about that. I got news."

"About the fire?"

"Yeah. The police told me some things. Now they want to talk to you."

She stared open-mouthed at him. "Why, Luke?"

"About Mama. How she died."

"But she died in the fire. They know that."

"Not so." Luke cracked his knuckles. "They say she died before the fire."

"*Before*? That's impossible."

"I know. It's plumb crazy." Luke studied his hands. "They say Mama didn't have any smoke in her lungs. They say she . . . she died from a head injury, something called blunt head trauma."

"You mean, when the fire started she stumbled and fell down?"

"No, the police say Mama didn't fall. They have ways of telling these things. They say somebody hit Mama in the head or knocked her down."

Bethany clasped her hands over her ears. "I don't want to hear such a thing! It can't be!"

"They say—" Luke inhaled sharply and rubbed his thumb hard over each knuckle. "Listen, Beth. I'm sorry. There's more. I don't know how to tell you—"

"Tell me what?"

"The fire—they say it wasn't an accident."

Bethany stared at him in bewilderment. "Not an accident?" she countered, her voice too shrill. "Of course it was an accident!"

He shook his head. "They say it was set. Deliberate."

"No, Luke! I don't believe it. Who would do such a thing?" And then, as a grisly chill riddled her bones, she answered her own question. "The woman in the feather hat!"

"What?" asked Luke.

She realized she had spoken aloud. "I . . . I saw someone that night. A woman. I woke up and saw a woman's shadow on the wall in my room. And I heard her arguing with Mama."

Luke sprang from his chair and gripped her shoulders. "You heard someone? You couldn't have! You were sleeping!"

She had never seen his eyes so dark and riveting. "Yes, but I woke up, Luke. I saw a shadow. I fell back asleep. Then I woke again and heard voices."

"Who was it?" demanded Luke. "What did she say?"

"I don't know. I couldn't hear the words, only the sound, muffled, louder then softer, then louder again."

"You heard someone arguing with Mama and you didn't get up? You didn't try to help?"

Bethany choked back a sob. "I thought I was dreaming. I was upset. I took Mama's sleeping pills so I could sleep, and I couldn't wake up."

"It had to be a dream, Bethany. I never saw nobody. I never heard a sound!"

"No, Luke. I know now it was real. A woman in a feather hat was outside my room. I saw her profile, like one of those shadow puppets we made on the wall when we were small. Remember? She stopped for a minute outside my door, then she was gone."

Luke's brows furrowed with a new suspicion. "Was it Jake? Did you have Jake over that night? Did he light a match? Was he carrying a candle, looking for you?"

"No, Luke, I swear! I'd never sneak around with Jake!"

"Are you telling me the truth, Beth? You know how Mama was. She didn't trust Jake. Are you making up this story about a woman in a feather hat to protect Jake?"

"I wouldn't! Never! I'll swear on the Holy Bible!"

"I believe you, Beth. The voices you heard must have been the radio." Luke reached over and gently pushed Bethany's tousled hair back from her face. "Listen to me. What happened that night—the fire, Mama dying—it was all a terrible accident. That's all. Maybe heat lightning struck the house. I don't know. But the police want to make more of it. That's their way. If you start spouting nonsense about a woman being there, you'll just get them all worked up for nothing. They'll start looking for suspects where there aren't any."

He paused and his eyes narrowed as his voice took on a baneful urgency. "Or maybe they'll think you're crazy and cart you off to the loony bin. Don't let it happen, Beth. Don't let them lock you up!"

The idea of being sent to an insane asylum was appalling. But what if Luke were right? She had imagined the woman. Jake had set the fire. Had she blocked the truth from her memory? Was she losing her mind? The room suddenly swayed around her and she swooned back against the sofa.

"See how bad it upsets you?" said Luke. "That's why you gotta keep this to yourself, Beth. Don't say a word about a shadow on the wall or Mama arguing with some lady. Just tell the police the same thing I said. I slept through it all until the fire got way out of hand. I couldn't save Mama; I only had time to save you."

Bethany turned and gazed out the window at the folks milling around the picnic table. "When must I talk to the police?"

Luke's voice lowered a notch. "Today. I'm sorry, Beth. They're expecting you at the station now."

She whirled back around, facing him. "Now? I can't!"

"I'll drive you over and wait, then drive you back to Willowbrook when you're done. I already told Knowl."

Bethany blinked back tears. "I don't want to talk to anyone about that night. I just want to forget it!"

But there would be no forgetting. Bethany knew that the moment she stepped inside the gray, muggy station house and confronted the grim-faced sergeant sitting forward, elbows square on his cluttered desk. He had a scrunched, bulldog face with thick, bristly brows and carbon-black eyes that drilled her from ruddy pockets of flesh. "Sit down, Miss Henry. I'm Sergeant Kaminski."

Taking the nearest chair, she kept her gaze fixed warily on him. He was a big man with a neck so thick his head appeared to have erupted directly from his shoulders. The buttons on his uniform strained against his massive middle. Bethany could imagine them popping off if he ever let go with a big belly laugh. But he didn't look like a man given to humor.

On the wall behind him hung a sprawling map of northern Indiana dotted with shiny black thumbtacks, marking where crimes had been committed. Was there already one pegging her street? On another wall a bulletin board displayed a mishmash of newspaper articles, scrawled notes, and wanted posters showing front and side views of a mixed bag of fugitives and public enemies. A ceiling fan rotated languidly overhead, hardly stirring the air, while flies droned around the desk and probed a half-eaten bologna sandwich on a sheet of wax paper. Bethany wondered if she had interrupted the sergeant's dinner. Perhaps he would keep their conversation short so he could finish his meal. But she promptly dismissed that notion. There was something else in his eyes, and it wasn't hunger—a knowing, cunning, desolating expression. If only Luke had been allowed to join her!

The sergeant swatted a fly buzzing his head and drawled, "I guess you know we got us a problem here. Our investigation shows the fire that destroyed your house wasn't no accident. Somebody killed your mama and set the fire to cover up a murder. Now it's up to us to figure out who could've done such a terrible thing."

"No one would hurt Mama," said Beth. "It had to be an accident. Lightning maybe."

Sergeant Kaminski picked up a toothpick, put it between his teeth, and chewed thoughtfully. "Yeah, that's what we figured at first, but we was wrong," he said, his tone edged with sarcasm. "We even brought in some topnotch arson investigators from Indianapolis to give us their opinion. In a word, arson. So how about it, Miss Henry? Tell us what you know."

"Nothing. I was asleep when the fire woke me up."

He looked unruffled. "Okay, let's go over that evening step by step, moment by moment. Take it slow, Miss Henry. I got all the time in the world."

For two hours Bethany related the smallest, most tedious events of that fatal night. She even told him of her nightmares, omitting her conviction that the woman in the feather hat was real. Just when she was convinced she had told him every detail she could recollect, he would start the questioning over, with another approach, another round of inquiries. "Tell me again about the fight you and your mama had that night."

"It wasn't a fight, really. She had just kept something from me. A secret."

"And you were angry with her, weren't you, Miss Henry? Angrier than you'd ever been before."

"Yes, I was angry. I was upset. I was hurt." She began to sob. "But I didn't kill my mother!"

It was dark outside by the time Sergeant Kaminski told Bethany she could go. One or two lights had come on in the gray, airless room, cutting into the dusky shadows that stretched across the floor. The boozy redness in the sergeant's face had given way to a garish mask of bluish lights and inky shadows. He stood up and rustled several papers on his desk. "We'll keep in touch, Miss Henry," he told her, as if they were planning a social outing. "We can reach you at your brother's place in Willowbrook, right?"

Bethany nodded.

"Don't go anywhere else without letting us know."

She slipped her purse strap over her shoulder. "Are you saying I'm a suspect?"

"Everybody's a suspect, until we get our man—or woman."

"I'll never believe someone murdered my mother."

The sergeant cleared his throat and leaned forward as if confiding a secret. "Miss Henry, believe me, a murder was committed. Someone's out there. We don't know who. We don't know why. But the person struck once, and could strike again. Has it occurred to you that your life may be in danger?"

5

In the days following her trip to Fort Wayne for her mother's funeral, Bethany tried without success to block out the dark thoughts assailing her. Central in her memory, like an arrow piercing a bull's eye, was the police interrogation and the sergeant's veiled warnings. Bethany herself was a suspect in her mother's death. Just as imponderable, if she didn't do it, someone else did—someone who might want her dead too.

Someone's out there. Your life may be in danger.

The sergeant's words tolled in her mind like a death knell. Until now it hadn't occurred to her that her own life could be in jeopardy. Who would wish her harm?

The same person who murdered Mama and burned down our house! Although Bethany had slipped into the daily routine at Herrick House, appearing for meals on time, helping to care for baby Maggie and little Jenny, and sharing afternoon tea time with Anna Reed, her mind subsisted in the shadowed realm of her imagination. She constantly relived the night of the fire, replaying each incident, probing each detail for hidden meaning. Surely she had missed some clue that would unravel the mystery of that night. But always she returned to the same lamentable conclusion: too many pieces of the puzzle were missing.

One afternoon at tea, Anna Reed commented on Bethany's preoccupation. They were settled, just the two of them, on the orchid-rose brocade chairs in the parlor. Anna was serving tea in delicate porcelain demitasse cups when she paused unexpectedly, the flowered teapot poised over Beth's cup, and asked, "Aren't you happy here, dear?"

"Happy? I don't know," she said candidly.

Anna poured the steaming tea and set the pot back on the antique cherry wood table beside a bowl of pink hydrangeas. Her spun-silver hair swirled around her head in a loose bun. "I don't mean *happy* exactly. I know you're still grieving over your dear mother. I mean, are you content here? Have we made you feel at home?"

Bethany felt her face grow warm and her mouth dry. "You've made me feel at home, Mrs. Reed—Anna. You've been very kind."

Anna's eyes probed hers gently. "And what about the rest of my family? Have they made you feel welcome?"

Beth averted her eyes.

Anna sipped her tea and sat silently for a long moment. "Give them time, dear. They will come around."

Beth turned her gaze back to Anna. "Annie has been grand. She's like you, always concerned about others."

"Knowl and Catherine care about you, too, but they still have to make peace with the past. Healing will come, with God's help. And if there's one thing I'm sure of, whatever his mistakes, Tom Herrick loved all four of his children."

Tom *Henry*, Beth wanted to retort, but she held back the words; as much as she wanted Papa to be a Henry, he was born a Herrick. "I have wondered about something for weeks," she said, helping herself to one of Anna's warm sugar cookies. "Since I've been here I've never met Papa's other wife. She never comes out of her room. Is she sick?"

A rare frown creased Anna's brow. "Yes, dear. I suppose you

should know the truth. Betty Herrick has been ill for a very long time. In and out of sanitariums. She's had a problem with liquor for as long as I can remember, and it's affected her mind, poor thing. Sometimes she seems quite rational; other times she's in a world of her own making. Tragically unpredictable."

"Wouldn't she be better off in a . . . a hospital?"

Anna's lips pursed in vexation. "Knowl won't hear of it. He's a devoted son, very protective of his mother."

"It just seems so strange that she never comes out of her room."

"Oh, she's not locked in, dear. She can come and go as she pleases, although I must confess we never let her out of our sight. Mainly she just sits in that room rocking and listening to her radio. Hardly ever budges from that chair. But, oddly enough, she speaks often of going on a trip."

"Really? She's going somewhere?"

"Only in her mind," said Anna with a sad little smile.

"But every once in awhile Betty goes off on a tangent. Gets all agitated. Spruces herself up. Packs a suitcase. Says she's catching a train. Then after a while, when no one comes for her, she settles back in her chair and forgets the whole thing—until the next time."

"Does she know about me?"

"Yes, dear. Knowl and Catherine have told her you've come to live with us, but I'm not sure how much she understands."

"You mean she doesn't know who I am?"

"I really can't say," said Anna. "Would you like to meet her?"

Bethany felt a chill of apprehension. "I wouldn't know what to say to her."

Anna reached over and touched her hand. "You're not responsible for what your father did, child. You have nothing to be ashamed of."

"I'm not ashamed," Bethany shot back, indignant. "Papa must have been awfully unhappy with that woman to seek out my mama. My mama was the only one who made him happy, I know that much."

Anna began collecting the tea service. "I'm sure you're right, dear. Your mother must have been a very patient, kind-hearted woman."

"She was. Mama never owned nice things like Papa's other wife, but she worked hard and never complained."

"You loved her very much. You must have been a very good daughter."

"I—I tried to be. I would've done better, if only I'd known—"

"I'm sure she knew how much you loved her." Anna stood and walked to the doorway, balancing her tray of tea and cookies. "By the way, child, I almost forgot. We're having company for dinner tonight."

"Company?"

"Todd Marshall, the new minister. He'll be speaking in church tomorrow morning for the first time, and we want to welcome him with a home-cooked meal tonight. Of course, he's not our official pastor yet, but I think the congregation will approve of him. Knowl's on the pulpit committee. He's already heard Mr. Marshall preach and thinks he's quite grand. Besides, it's time to give poor Reverend Henry a rest. I'm afraid he's getting just a slight bit senile."

Bethany nodded. She had attended church twice so far with the Herricks. During one of the services the old minister got halfway through his sermon then lapsed back and repeated the beginning. Both Sundays the services were an extra half hour long. The last time the lady beside her complained that her pot roast had probably burned to a crisp.

"I guess a new preacher will make people perk up and take notice," said Bethany, making conversation—not that she knew much about the rites and rituals of a church service. Although Mama had attended Sunday school as a child, she and Papa had never made it a practice to take their children to services. Bethany never doubted that there was a God up in heaven, but she assumed He busied Himself with more important people than the Henrys. People like the wealthy, influential Herricks of Willowbrook.

"Bethany, dear, you'd better wear your prettiest dress and put a bow in your hair," Anna called back as she headed for the kitchen. "From what I understand, Todd Marshall is a very handsome young man, and quite eligible!"

Bethany answered politely, "All right, Anna." But as she trudged up the carpeted stairs, she thought to herself, *Why should I get all gussied up for some fancy preacher? He's probably as stuffy and boring as Reverend Henry!*

But Bethany Rose was as wrong as she had ever been about anything in her life. She knew it that evening, the instant Todd Marshall entered the marble foyer, clasped her hand warmly, and said, "I'm so pleased to meet you, Miss Herrick."

She didn't bother to correct him. Herrick, Henry—what did it matter? It was just a name. And Todd Marshall was much more than a name. He was six feet of lean muscle, broad shoulders, and solid arms. He had a full head of thick, wavy, umber brown hair combed back from his forehead and showing a slight widow's peak. His features were sturdy, yet precise; handsomely classic, with an earthy, unfinished edge.

As she gazed up into his clear blue eyes—eyes so riveting and direct they seemed to read her very soul—she sensed she had been waiting all of her life to feel this way about another human being.

"Hello, Mr. Marshall," she stammered, her heart pounding like a tambourine. "I mean, *Reverend* Marshall."

"Call me Todd," he said, his gaze still holding her fast. His brows formed a straight, narrow ridge over his eyes, casting a fine shadow that turned his pupils a deep royal blue and gave him a pensive expression.

If Knowl hadn't interrupted then, Bethany wasn't sure how long her eyes would have remained locked with Todd's. Was it her imagination, or had some secret, unspoken connection flared between them . . . a quickening, a stirring? The sensation broke when

Knowl put his hand on Todd's shoulder and said, "Shall we head for the dining room? Mother Reed has dinner on the table."

"It smells wonderful!" said Todd, his deep voice resonant. He offered Beth his arm. "May I escort you, Miss Herrick? Or may I call you Bethany?"

She nodded and looked away, flustered. During the meal she said little; she felt shy and self-conscious, but no one noticed her reticence. The family was too busy engaging their charming guest in conversation.

"Tell us about yourself, Reverend Marshall," said Annie as she passed him the glazed, clove-studded ham.

He helped himself to a thick, juicy slice and passed the platter on to Knowl. "Well, since Knowl's on the committee that invited me here, I suppose you know the important things from my résumé—where I received my university and seminary training."

"Knowl has said very little," said Anna, "although what he's said about you has been very favorable."

Todd smiled. "I hope you feel that way after tomorrow."

"Tell us what isn't on your résumé," prompted Annie. "About you, your family, what you like to do."

He grinned and tugged at his starched collar. "I'm twenty-six, an only child, born and raised in a small town in New York—you wouldn't know it unless you're a New Yorker. During my sophomore year at Columbia, I attended an evangelistic service and realized that God had a rightful claim on my life."

He gave Bethany a lingering glance. "That night I accepted Christ as my Savior, and everything changed for me. I had planned on becoming a lawyer or history professor, but now I knew God wanted me in the ministry." He tapped his fingers rhythmically on his water glass. "I haven't looked back since. I want to turn the world upside-down with the Gospel—or at least Willowbrook, God willing."

Knowl chuckled. "Willowbrook has many dear saints who have sat contentedly in their pews for decades. It'll take an extraordinary person to get them stirred up and out of their seats."

"We serve an extraordinary God." Todd looked at Beth again and said meaningfully, "Isn't that so, Miss Herr—Bethany? God works in mysterious ways, doesn't He?"

She gazed down at her plate. "Yes, Reverend Marshall. God has always been a mystery to me."

"Call me Todd, and I'll remember to call you Bethany." He paused and added, "You have a very special name, you know."

She looked at him. "Special?"

"Yes. Bethany's in the Bible—a village on the eastern slope of the Mount of Olives. Jesus had close friends there. Mary and Martha. It's where He raised their brother Lazarus from the dead. When I hear the name Bethany I think of Jesus' marvelous love for us."

Bethany's cheeks flushed. She wanted to tell the young minister to save his sermon for the morning; it was wasted on her. But she held her tongue.

When she didn't respond, Todd said quickly, "I'm sorry. I'm boring you with things you already know. Sometimes I forget I'm not in the pulpit."

"You were telling us about yourself, Reverend Marshall," said Anna. "Please tell us more. Is there a special lady in your life?"

His face reddened. "Yes. There's one special lady. My mother."

"I like that," said Anna. "A man who honors his mother."

"She's a remarkable woman. She raised me alone and worked hard to send me to the best schools."

"What about your father?" asked Annie.

Todd blinked several times. "My father died when I was seven. I . . . I don't remember much about him."

"And where is your mother now?" asked Knowl.

"At our home in New York. I may be single, but if I'm accepted for the Willowbrook pastorate, she'll join me here. She's quite able to take on the clerical duties a pastor's wife usually assumes. She plays piano rather well, has a knack for taking charge at social functions, and would keep the parsonage immaculate."

Anna smiled with a hint of mischievousness. "Singleness isn't a permanent condition, Reverend Marshall. Many deserving young ladies in our church would welcome the chance to charm the handsome new minister into marriage."

Todd blushed and cast Bethany another sidelong glance. "Only if God wills it," he said, clearing his throat.

"You sound like the man for us," said Knowl expansively.

Todd smiled. "Now if the rest of the congregation agrees!"

Later that evening, after bidding the rest of the family good night, Reverend Marshall drew Bethany aside in the foyer. "Tomorrow, when I get up to speak, I'll be watching for your face," he said with a quiet intensity. "Those eyes will give me courage. You'll be there, won't you?"

She lowered her lashes. "If you want me to be."

"I do. I've prayed that God has work for me to do in Willowbrook. Now I have another reason to hope He sends me here. I'd like to get better acquainted with you."

"I'd like that too," she said softly, meeting his gaze.

He lifted her hand to his lips and whispered gently, "Good night. Until tomorrow, Bethany Rose."

6

On September 26, 1949, Willowbrook Christian Church voted 159 to 23 to invite Reverend Todd Marshall to become their new pastor. A handful in the congregation—including, it was rumored, someone in the Herrick household—had reservations about accepting a minister so young and just out of seminary, especially a single man; but the majority felt the church needed the fresh vision and vigor a young man would bring.

Bethany was delighted that Todd Marshall would be coming to Willowbrook. In the weeks since his visit, she had thought of little else. Her preoccupation with Todd made her grief more bearable and tempered her lingering fears. If one believed in love at first sight, then Bethany was in love, and she hoped that Todd felt the same. Shortly after returning to New York he had written her a brief letter saying how much he had enjoyed meeting her, and added, "However the vote goes, I hope we can keep in touch." He had signed his note, "Yours in Christ." She wasn't sure what that meant, but it made her feel as if they shared a secret bond.

Although reveries of Todd filled Bethany's days, nights were different. She was still plagued by nightmares of the fire and the woman in the feather hat. Night after night she woke in a cold sweat with visions of that chilling silhouette branded in her memory. She began to feel that it was her lot in life to endure those grisly nocturnal visions; she even began to take them in her stride, until one night everything changed.

It was the first Tuesday in October, two days before Todd Marshall and his mother would be arriving in Willowbrook. Bethany had fallen asleep thinking of Todd, wondering if they could possibly have a future together. She slept fitfully for a few hours, then woke as usual in the dead of night, her skin wet with perspiration. Dark images of the mysterious woman clung like cobwebs at the edge of her consciousness. But something was different tonight. Usually her room was swathed in shadows so that even the furnishings were indistinguishable, but tonight her door stood ajar. A coldness like ice rippled down her spine. There on her wall was the shadow of the woman in the feather hat.

Surely she was still dreaming. She closed her eyes tight and opened them again. The shadow was gone. Her heart hammering, she sat up in bed and hugged her arms against her chest, shivering. Her nightmares were crossing over, invading real life.

Bethany tried to dismiss the incident, but it haunted her waking hours. Disturbing possibilities formed in her mind. If she could not tell whether the woman in the feather hat was real or imagined, how could she be sure she hadn't become embroiled in the events that led to the fire or her mother's death? Certainly she never would have set the fire or harmed her mother deliberately, but what if something had happened? What if Jake had come over? What if she had been caught up in a series of events so appalling that she had blocked them from her mind?

* * *

A week after Todd Marshall and his mother settled into the parsonage—a quaint Victorian house on Willowbrook's east side, somewhat in disrepair but still quite comfortable—Todd invited Bethany over to dinner to meet his mother.

Catherine and Annie were amazed. "Think of it, Bethany," said Cath as they searched Annie's closet for just the right outfit to lend her. "All of the single girls at church would love to get their hooks in Todd, but you're the one he's chosen."

"Just for dinner," said Bethany, reading between the lines. What Catherine really meant was, *Why would Todd Marshall pick you when he could have any girl at church?*

"Knowl and I saw how Todd looked at you that night he was here," said Annie. "We both think he has more in mind than dinner. Who knows? Maybe even matrimony."

Bethany laughed self-consciously. "Don't tease me, Annie."

"I'm not. I'm serious. Todd will need a wife one of these days. Some in the congregation feel the sooner the better; they expect him to settle down and become a family man right away." She held up a pink taffeta dress cinched at the waist with a flounce skirt. "Too dressy?"

They both nodded.

"How about this one?" Annie handed Bethany a silk organza jacket with a black silk skirt.

"It's beautiful," marveled Bethany, running her fingertips over the fine material. "You don't mind if I borrow this?"

"Of course not. It'll probably fit you better than it does me."

Bethany clasped Annie's hand. "I don't know how to thank you—for this, for everything you've done for me."

"We're glad to help. You're family."

Bethany noticed that Catherine didn't echo the sentiment.

"Just one thing," said Annie, catching Beth's arm as she turned to go. "About Reverend Marshall—"

Beth paused and met Annie's earnest gaze. "Yes?"

"The woman who marries Todd Marshall will need more than a

commitment to be his wife. She'll need a commitment to his church and the God he serves."

Bethany flashed an amused smile. "I'm only having dinner with the man, Annie!"

Todd picked Bethany up that evening in his noisy, rumbling Nash. "I'd like to buy one of those shiny new cars on the market," he told her, "but I won't be able to afford it for awhile on a preacher's salary."

"It's not so bad," she told him. "It rides better than my brother's tumbledown pickup."

"Don't look too closely at the house," he told her minutes later as he escorted her up the steps of the rambling gothic two-story. "Mother didn't want company yet—we haven't unpacked all the boxes and things are still out of place—but I told her it didn't matter. Not to me, and I hope not to you."

Bethany chuckled. "I don't care if there are chickens in the pantry and cows grazing in the kitchen."

He laughed. "What an interesting choice of words. But it won't be that bad. My mother would have a stroke if she found animals in her house!"

He opened the paneled door with its stained-glass window and showed her into the carpeted foyer. The house smelled of lavender and mint and old books and cedar chests. "We're here, Mother," he called.

He led Bethany to the parlor where her gaze took in a writing desk, a solid wall of bookshelves, flowered wallpaper, fringed lamps, a rattan rocker, and a hooked rug beside a stone fireplace. The room was attractive in a quaint, old-fashioned way—smaller than the parlor in the Herrick house, but certainly more elegant than the one in the Witherspoon farmhouse.

From the parlor it was only a few steps into the dimly lit dining room. A walnut table covered in lace gleamed with china and crystal. Beside it, a rosewood hutch held what Bethany supposed were

Marshall heirlooms—china teapots and vases, silver candlesticks and tea service, and several cut-glass canisters.

"Mother must be in the kitchen," Todd told her, "working feverishly, I suppose. I told her to keep it simple, but she's a perfectionist at heart. Fusses constantly, but I guarantee the food will be great."

"It smells delicious," said Bethany. She felt a tingly sensation in her wrists and her palms were clammy. What if Todd's mother didn't like her? What if she could see what Todd didn't—that Bethany Rose Henry was a poor farm girl without culture or breeding?

The kitchen door opened and a tall, stately woman emerged with a glass bowl of fresh fruit, which she set on the table. "Todd, darling, you're here already! I didn't hear you come in."

"You were working too hard to hear us, Mother," he chided, kissing her cheek. He turned to Beth. "Mother, this is Bethany Rose Herrick, Knowl's sister. Bethany, this is my mother, Eleanor Marshall."

Bethany smiled and offered a tentative hand, which the woman gripped firmly, her shrewd, gray-black eyes direct and unflinching. Bethany felt her mouth go dry and her words evaporate.

Eleanor Marshall was a stout, straight-backed woman with wide shoulders, imposing in her demeanor, with features that could have been carved from granite—a sturdy jaw, aquiline nose, and gray-brown hair swept up in an elegant roll at the back of her head. Her high forehead revealed a widow's peak just like Todd's. She wore a long, wine-colored silk dress with antique lace around the collar and sleeves and a delicate china brooch at the hollow of her throat. Tiny rimless spectacles perched just below the bridge of her nose.

At last Beth found her voice. "I'm happy to meet you, Mrs. Marshall."

"And I'm so pleased to meet you. Todd talks about you with fondness and enthusiasm. Come, dear, sit down. Everything's ready. I hope you like lamb chops."

"I'm sure I will." She had never tasted lamb in her life.

Todd pulled a chair out for her, but she turned to Mrs. Marshall and asked, "Can I help with anything? I'm real good in the kitchen."

"No, dear, you just keep my son company."

Beth sat down and gazed at Todd as he took the chair across from her. The spark that had ignited in her heart on their first meeting was still there, flaming even as his eyes met hers.

"I hope you didn't mind my inviting you to dinner without the rest of your family. I promise to return their kindness with a proper invitation very soon."

"They didn't mind. Catherine and Annie had a good time helping me pick out something to wear tonight."

"Their choice was excellent," he murmured as his gaze swept over her.

"This is fancier than I'm used to." She was about to mention that flannel shirts and bib overalls were her typical garb on the farm, then thought better of the idea. It occurred to her that Todd didn't know the real Bethany; he was captivated by a fanciful creation of his own imagination.

Eleanor Marshall returned with a platter brimming with thick lamb chops and small boiled potatoes garnished with mint leaves. She set the steaming plate down and took the empty seat.

"It looks wonderful," said Todd. "Let's thank the good Lord for what He's provided." He promptly bowed his head and offered a brief prayer.

When he had finished, Beth noted, "Nothing against the good Lord, but it was your mama who worked up a sweat in the kitchen."

Todd burst out laughing. "Well put, Bethany. Next time my mother will have a prominent place in my prayers of thanksgiving."

"I'm glad my efforts are appreciated," mused Eleanor, handing Beth a basket of crusty rolls.

They ate in silence for a few moments while Bethany scoured her mind for something clever to say to the sophisticated Mrs. Marshall. Finally she asked, "How do you like Indiana?"

Eleanor smiled faintly. "It's certainly not New York, is it? But I'm sure I'll learn to enjoy its country charm."

Bethany tried another tack. "I guess you're real proud of your son, being a minister and having his own church."

"I've always been proud of him," she said, patting his hand. "He's never disappointed me. Always studied hard and got excellent grades. He could have been anything he wanted to be—a doctor, lawyer—"

"Indian chief," Todd finished wryly. "But God had a higher calling for me, Mother."

"I know, dear. And whatever makes you happy makes me happy. But I told Todd he shouldn't have accepted the call to Willowbrook unless the vote was unanimous."

"A majority was good enough for me, Mother—one hundred fifty-nine votes."

"And twenty-three against," she pointed out. "If you ask me, that can only spell trouble."

Bethany squirmed. Had the Marshalls heard the rumor that a member of the Herrick household had voted against him? She looked across at Todd. He was smiling as he said, "I'm sure Bethany voted for me."

"I didn't vote," she murmured under her breath.

Eleanor Marshall fixed her gaze on Bethany. "Todd tells me your family is quite prominent in Willowbrook. He says your brother owns his own publishing house."

"Yes," said Beth, feeling uneasy under the older woman's cool scrutiny. "Knowl and my sister's husband, Robert, own Herrick House."

"And it's been a successful venture for them?"

"I believe so. Knowl's wife, Annie, is a writer. They published her book, and they say it's selling well. My sister, Catherine, is an artist, and she illustrated Annie's book and several others."

"My, what a talented family," said Eleanor. "And what is your gift, my dear?"

Bethany swallowed hard. "I . . . I don't know yet. But I like to draw, and I always dreamed of being a fashion model."

"Really? A fashion model?" said Todd, sounding surprised.

"It was just a dream," said Beth, flustered.

Todd smiled. "I was kind of hoping you played the piano."

Silence again as they concentrated on their food. Bethany ate slowly, watching how mother and son delicately cut their chops and speared small nuggets of potato with a casual grace. She watched how Mrs. Marshall politely dabbed her lips with her linen napkin and returned it to her lap with an air of dignity. As she did at the Herrick table, Beth watched which knives and forks and spoons they used and tried to imitate their gestures, right down to Eleanor's raised pinky when she sipped her tea.

After a while, Eleanor said, "Todd has told me about your lovely home, Bethany. He says it's one of the finest Victorian mansions he's ever seen. He says it reminds him of the house he lived in when he was a small boy."

Todd made a little sound low in his throat, not quite a cough. "I don't know that I went on that effusively, Mother, but yes, Bethany's family has a handsome estate. It reminds me of our first home, what little I remember of it." He looked at Beth. "We had to sell our house and move to a small brownstone when I was seven. That was the year my father died."

"But we won't talk about that, will we, son?" said Eleanor. "This is to be a pleasant evening, with only pleasant talk."

But there was little conversation after that. Bethany rehearsed a dozen comments or questions in her mind, but none of them seemed worth uttering aloud, so she remained painfully silent, convinced Todd's mother considered her a dunce.

When it was time for dessert, Eleanor appeared with a custard pie and announced, "You children take your pie into the parlor and relax while I clean the kitchen."

Bethany jumped up. "I'd really like to help, Mrs. Marshall."

"I won't hear of it," said Eleanor. "You take your pie and coffee and go visit with my son."

Beth nodded. Already she knew that no one dared argue with the eminent Eleanor Marshall.

Minutes later, she and Todd settled in the parlor side by side on a pink brocade sofa before a crackling fire. A basket of needlepoint sat on the coffee table along with a ceramic music box, several velvet pin cushions, and a large worn Bible.

"It's not really cold enough for a fire," said Todd, "but I love how cozy it makes the room feel."

"I like it too," she said, but quickly turned her eyes from the flames.

"I hope you didn't find my mother too intimidating," he said as he sipped his coffee.

Bethany forked a creamy wedge of pie. "She's a very elegant lady. I never met anyone like her."

Todd chuckled. "That's how most people feel. She comes on rather forcefully at times, but she's a remarkable woman. Strong, determined, indomitable. I couldn't have survived without her."

"Yes, you would. You're just as strong in your own way. Maybe even stronger."

"No one's ever told me that before. I like that." He looked at her with a long, searching gaze. "You know, I've never met anyone like you, Bethany Rose."

"Is that good?"

He laughed. "Yes, it's good. You're so candid and down to earth.

You say what you think. You don't put on airs. You're yourself. No pretenses. I like that about you."

"You really don't know me," she murmured in almost a whisper. What could she tell him? That she was the secret love child of Knowl Herrick's papa? The black sheep of the Herrick clan who didn't even carry the Herrick name? A poor, homeless orphan who police suspected of murdering her mother?

"But I *do* know you," he said lightly. "When I look into your eyes I see all the way to your soul. I feel as if I've always known you. I feel your kindness, your vitality, your passion for life. Am I wrong?"

"No, but—"

"See? I read people very well. I wish I could be like you, Bethany. I always try to project an image or meet someone's expectations. In college and seminary I had to be the best student. Now I have to be the best preacher, the best pastor." He grinned sheepishly. "I'm sorry to be rattling on like this."

"No. I like to hear you talk. Most men I know don't talk about feelings and ideas. They just want to know if the field's been plowed and supper's on the table."

He looked at her, amused. "Field plowed? What field? Is that an Indiana expression?"

She looked down at her hands. "No, just the facts."

He set down his cup and saucer and swiveled slightly, facing her. "Tell me about yourself, Bethany Rose. What you like to eat and what you do for fun. Your hopes and dreams, your worst day at school, your best birthday."

She laughed self-consciously. "That's not fair. You go first. Tell me everything about you."

He put his head back on the sofa and sighed deeply. "What do you want to know?"

She thought a moment. "Let's start with a hard one. Have you ever been in love?"

He sat forward, his wide forehead corrugated in a frown. "You're supposed to start with the easy questions. My favorite vegetable. Hobbies. Did I vote for Truman?"

She smiled. "I don't care about vegetables or politics."

He grew serious. "I was in love once. The summer before my sophomore year of college. But I went back to Columbia and never saw her again."

"You broke up?"

"Not exactly. She just stopped answering my letters. It was as if she dropped off the face of the earth. I don't know what ever happened to her."

"You sound sad. Do you still love her?"

"For a long time I thought I did. There's never been anyone else, before or since." He looked deep in her eyes. "But now I . . . I know someday I'll love again."

She felt her face grow warm and her pulse quicken. She wondered if he would pull her into his arms and kiss her. But he wasn't like Jake, bold and artless and unschooled. Todd was subtle, complex, analytical, with layers of meaning in everything he said and did.

"I have another question," she said with a hint of whimsy. "What were you like as a little boy?"

He chuckled. "I looked like Little Lord Fauntleroy."

"Who?"

"Or Buster Brown. You know. The fellow with the ghastly page boy on all those shoe boxes."

Bethany smiled. She had finished her pie, so she set the plate on the table. Todd leaned over and studied her face with mild scrutiny, then raised his hand until his fingers almost touched her lips. "Crumbs," he whispered.

She brushed them away and for a moment wished Todd had Jake's brazen abandon.

"I'm sorry," he said, "if I embarrassed you."

"You didn't."

"You were asking me about . . . about my childhood."

"Yes. Were you always a good boy?"

"Almost always."

"Were you happy?"

He turned his gaze to the flickering fire and was silent for so long she thought he hadn't heard her. "Were you happy?" she repeated.

"I was happy when we lived in the grand house with my father."

"Tell me about him."

"He was a businessman. Very successful, at least at first. He gave my mother and me everything we wanted, even things we didn't know we wanted. We were disgustingly rich. I thought everyone lived that way."

"You said he died."

Tears glinted in Todd's eyes. "I was seven. He left me with just a handful of memories. He brought home candy bars, and read me the funny papers on Sunday, and taught me how to polish my shoes. He told me a man never goes out the door without shoes he can see his face in. To this day I can't stand to have scuff marks on my shoes."

"How did he die?" Beth asked softly.

Todd sat forward and brushed at his eyes. He managed a guttural chuckle. "Listen, you've got me talking like a sinner at confession." He stood up and arched his shoulders. "I'd better get you home before the ladies at church decide they have something to talk about."

As they picked up their dishes and headed for the kitchen, Bethany felt a chill. Todd was keeping a secret. Something about his father. His father's death. The thought made her queasy, as if something dark and ominous had come between them. A knot of apprehension tightened in her chest. Her mother's death wasn't the only mystery casting a shadow over them.

7

At breakfast the next morning Knowl made a startling announcement. "Bethany Rose, I'm enrolling you in Willowbrook Community College for spring semester. Your classes start in January."

She stared at him in surprise. "You're sending me to college?"

"Yes, I certainly am," he said, helping himself to the scrambled eggs. "It's a good school. Close by. Started just after the war when all the vets came home wanting an education. In a year or two, if you keep up your grades, you can transfer to a university."

Beth's pulse raced. "I don't know what to say. How—how can I repay you?"

"By studying hard. Plan to spend your evenings on the books." He met her gaze and his eyes warmed slightly. "You may not know it, but I offered to send you once before. I wrote your mother, but she turned me down. But now you're living here with us, and I think it's time to think about your future."

"My future?"

"Yes. A career. Annie tells me you draw nearly as well as Catherine, so it seems I have two talented sisters. I'd like to see you pursue your art."

"You mean I can study drawing and painting at college?"

"And maybe someday when you've developed your skills, you can work for Herrick House and help us illustrate our books—if you'd like."

Bethany clapped her hands. "Oh, I would! I love Catherine's work. Especially the cover of your new book, Annie."

"Cath did do a wonderful job, didn't she?" Annie agreed, sipping her coffee. "Many bookstores throughout the country are carrying my book, in large part because of Cath's art work. People love her natural nostalgic style. She once did a *Saturday Evening Post* cover, you know."

"A portrait of Annie and baby Jenny," said Knowl.

"I didn't know." Beth didn't mention that she read only radio and movie magazines. But that would have to change, especially if she was going to become a college student.

"So you like the idea of college?" asked Knowl.

Beth nodded. "I've always dreamed of it, but there was no money. I never thought I'd leave home or be anything but a farm girl."

"Well, you're living here now," said Knowl. "You're part of this family. You need to act and think like a Herrick."

"But I'm not a Herrick; I'm a Henry," she protested softly.

"Call it what you will, you're a Herrick. You've got Papa's blood in your veins, and I know he wanted a good life for you. He's gone; I'm here. It's my place to take care of you." He gave her the smallest hint of a smile, but she knew he still wasn't comfortable in his big brother role.

"Have you heard from Luke lately?" he asked after a minute.

"No." Knowl rarely mentioned her brother. Luke was *his* brother too, but she sensed he didn't want to be reminded of the fact.

"Well, I'm willing to help Luke too," he said with a slight edge in his voice. "I know he wants to remain on the farm. The next time he calls, tell him I'll cover whatever it costs to rebuild the farmhouse."

"You're a very kind and generous man, Knowl Herrick. You're so much like Papa."

Knowl flinched and stabbed a morsel of ham. "I don't consider myself anything like Papa. God help me, I'll never be anything like that man!"

"Then you don't know what Papa was really like," she countered fiercely. "He was a good man, Knowl. He did wrong, but the wrong doesn't cancel out the good he did."

"Unfortunately, Papa wasn't around for me to see much of the good he did," Knowl shot back.

Annie handed her husband a plate stacked with pancakes. "Knowl, dear, try one of Mother's pancakes. They're delicious."

He speared one and doused it with fresh maple syrup, but the tendon along his jaw was still throbbing.

"Tell me, Bethany, how did you enjoy your evening with Reverend Marshall and his mother?" asked Annie, too cheerily.

Bethany drew in a sharp breath, her emotions still high. "I . . . I had a good time."

"What did you think of his mother?"

Beth weighed her words. "She's, uh, very elegant."

"Yes, she is. I talked with her briefly at church and she certainly has that New York sophistication. I hope she'll be satisfied here in Willowbrook." Annie turned to Knowl. "Dear, we need to invite the reverend and his mother over for dinner soon."

"Yes, we need to give him all the support we can," Knowl agreed, sounding composed again.

"Then I'll invite them. I'm sure it's quite an adjustment for Reverend Marshall—his first pastorate, new people, a new town."

Knowl sopped up a pool of syrup with his last wedge of pancake. "He's still getting used to the way we do things at Willowbrook Christian. Some of our long-term members can be a bit daunting to a young, inexperienced minister like Todd."

"But he's doing very well, don't you think? His sermon last Sunday was spirited and really quite profound." Annie cast a knowing glance at Bethany. "And, Knowl, he certainly seems taken with your sister."

Bethany blushed. "He's just being kind, that's all."

"No, there's more," said Annie. "Cath and I both see it. He's smitten, Bethany. And I have a notion the feeling's mutual."

"I like him just fine, but he's not courting me. He just hasn't got acquainted with the other girls at church yet."

Annie smiled. "Well, I wouldn't let him get too—"

"Excuse me, children." It was Anna in the doorway, looking unsettled. "Knowl, I took your mother's breakfast tray up to her as usual, but—"

"Is something wrong?"

"She seems especially agitated. You might want to go up and talk with her. See if you can calm her down. She's determined to catch a train somewhere. I can't reason with her."

He was on his feet immediately. "I'll be right back." He strode out of the room, the parlor door swinging behind him.

Anna took her usual place at the table and poured herself a cup of coffee. Her hand was trembling.

"Are you all right, Mother?" asked Annie.

"I will be in a minute." Anna sipped her coffee.

"It's too much for you, isn't it?" Annie pressed. "Having Knowl's mother here. You get the brunt of it, waiting on her, day in, day out."

"I don't mind that," said Anna. "But sometimes I think . . ."

"What? Tell me."

"I hate to say it, but sometimes I think that woman should be back in the sanitarium where they can give her the kind of care she needs. It's not natural, her living in this house like a hermit."

"I know," said Annie, "but Knowl won't let her go. She's the only parent he has left, and he's terrified of losing her."

"It's no life sitting alone in a rocker listening to the radio from morning till night."

"Does she ever come out?" asked Bethany, trying not to sound too inquisitive. She had a million questions about the elusive Betty Herrick, Papa's first wife. "I've never seen her. Not once since I've been here."

"She hasn't left this house in months," said Annie. "Not since we took her to see your father's grave. I think it was too much for her."

"Knowl made it all too easy for her to hide away," said Anna. "Last spring he converted the room next to hers to a bathroom, so she doesn't even have to go down the hall like the rest of us. If you ask me, Knowl caters too much to her."

"Does she stay in her room because of me?"

"No, Bethany," said Annie. "I don't think she even knows you're here."

"Even if she did, she probably wouldn't know who you are," said Anna. "Don't let her worry you, child. She's not your concern."

Knowl returned then, looking pale, his eyes troubled behind his wire-rimmed spectacles. He sat back down at the table, but pushed his plate away.

"How is she?" asked Annie.

He tapped his fingers on the table. "She's on one of her tangents. Wants Papa to come get her and take her to the depot. Says she's got to get to Cincinnati before nightfall."

"Cincinnati?" echoed Anna.

"She was born and raised there," said Knowl. "Claims her folks are waiting for her. I'm afraid she's delusional. No one's left. All her family are gone."

"It's sad," said Anna. "Sometimes she's clear-headed as a judge; other times she's as daft as a loon. Life can be very painful at times, can't it!"

Bethany nodded. She still felt a huge ache in her heart over her own mama's passing.

Knowl stood up again. "I need to get to work. Editorial is meeting this morning, deciding on several manuscripts. I promised Robert I'd be there by eight." He kissed Annie on the lips. "Sweetheart, if Mama gives you too much trouble, call me."

The telephone rang in the parlor. Knowl sighed. "I'll never get out of here today."

"I'll get it." Annie was back a moment later. "It's for you, Bethany. It's Luke."

"Tell him what I said about covering his expenses," Knowl called back, already out of sight down the hall.

Bethany hurried to the parlor and picked up the receiver. "Luke? Are you okay?"

"Surviving," he grunted.

"It's been ages since you called."

"I been busy working the Witherspoons' place. And I just started clearing the debris from our house."

"You just started?"

"Yeah. The police wouldn't let me touch the place until they finished prowling through the rubble."

"Why so long?"

"Who knows? I put up a fuss. Said they got no right to keep me off my own place. They didn't listen; just said keep out; it's a crime scene and they had work to do."

"But they're done now?"

"Yeah. So they say."

"What'd they find out? Do they know yet who set the fire and . . ." She let her words trail off.

"If they do they're not talking."

"I don't understand. Somebody must know something."

"They say they're still following leads. They've talked to all the neighbors, but nobody seen nothing." Luke paused. "Listen, Bethany, they're gonna wanta talk to both of us again. So don't be surprised if you get a visit one of these days."

"The police? Here?"

"They told me to tell you. It's crazy. They seem to think you might know something. I told them you were dead asleep that night and don't know nothing. But try telling the cops anything."

"I don't want to see them. I just want to forget the fire."

"You been having any more of them bad dreams?"

She swallowed hard. "Almost every night."

His voice grew tender. "I know how it pains you, Bethany Rose, losing Mama. It eats at me too."

"I think of her all the time, Luke. It's like she's with me somehow. When I wake up I hear her calling like she did when we were little. I keep my eyes closed tight and imagine her brushing my forehead with her gentle strokes, and I smell her skin with that sweet lilac perfume she bought at Woolworth's when Papa was alive. Remember?"

"I remember, baby. She wore it for Papa. He loved the smell of lilacs."

Beth was weeping now. "I keep thinking I'll walk into a room and she'll be there, Luke. I can't shake off the feeling of her. But that's all it is—a feeling, a dream, a shadow. I want her real. I want her back, flesh and blood, living and breathing, Luke."

He was silent for a full minute. She knew he was struggling with his own surging emotions. She was about to repeat his name when he said, "We gotta go on, Beth. Both of us. We can't die inside just because Mama did. You make a good life for yourself there, okay?"

"I will, Luke. I'm trying. But I miss you."

"I miss you something fierce too, Sis. Listen, if you can't sleep, maybe the doctor there can give you something."

She felt the receiver sweaty against her palm. "I don't want anything, Luke. Not ever again. It was Mama's pills that made me so groggy the night of the fire."

"Okay, sure. But tell me, are Knowl and Catherine treating you okay?"

"They've been real kind." She told him about Knowl sending her to college and offering to pay to rebuild the farmhouse.

Luke's voice brightened. "Sounds too good to turn down. Tell that brother of mine I'd be mighty indebted to him for any help I can get."

There wasn't much else to say. She didn't want to mention her dinner date last evening with Reverend Marshall. It might get back to Jake Witherspoon, and she didn't want him rushing to Willowbrook and stirring up trouble like a scorned suitor. So, after another long silence, she and Luke said good-bye.

As soon as Bethany hung up the phone, it rang again. This time it was Todd Marshall, asking if he could come over that afternoon. Bethany said yes without even asking Annie if she would mind having company.

In the hour before Todd arrived, Bethany bathed, dressed in a gold crocheted ribbon dress Annie had picked out for her, and brushed her hair until the long auburn tresses glistened like spun mahogany.

When she greeted Todd at the door, he looked approvingly at her. He was wearing corduroy trousers and a brown button-down sweater over a crisp white shirt and striped tie. "You look even more beautiful than you did last night," he said, his blue eyes dancing.

She felt a glow in her cheeks. "Thank you. Do you want to come in? Or, it's such a nice day this late in October. We could sit on the porch swing."

He glanced down the length of the sprawling, wraparound porch. "You're right. Not many sunny days left before winter sets in. Let's swing."

She slipped out the door and they settled comfortably on the wide

said she'd bring out some sweet cider and
n as she puts the roast in the oven."
rvel. Does she run the entire household as
l that wonderful dinner my first night in

a keeps everything going. She cooks all the
dy's where they're supposed to be on time,
k-and-span. I try to help with meals and
Maggie when Annie has to be away, but

said Todd.

ng things. This house was her home long
ught it, and I think she still considers it
ie was a Reed before she married Knowl,
ds have lived here for four generations."
ld turned slightly and slipped his arm
g, his hand not quite touching Beth's
boyhood home in New York was passed on
through several generations of Marshalls. I remember looking at old family portraits and feeling as if my forbears were still present in that house—their influence, their memories, their wisdom stockpiled somehow in those walls. I felt like a link in a long, unbroken chain." He paused and cleared his throat. "But, of course, the chain did break. We moved out of the house and left the memories behind."

For a few moments they were silent. A breeze rose, rustling the trees and sending dry leaves skittering across the porch. The hazy smoke of neighborhood chimneys and backyard bonfires gave the chill air a zesty aroma. Bethany shivered.

"Cold?" asked Todd, allowing his hand to settle lightly on her shoulder.

"A little," she said, vividly aware of his touch.

He looked at her, his intense blue eyes reflecting the cloudless aquamarine sky. "I had to see you today," he said with a sudden urgency. "I argued with myself. I told myself it's too soon to become involved with a woman. I reminded myself that I'm still on trial at the church. I don't know whether they're pleased with me or not, or whether the old-timers will even accept me; I'm young enough to be their son, their grandson. So I need to concentrate on my sermons and on discerning the needs of this congregation."

He wound a strand of her hair around his finger in a lazy, unconscious motion. "I spent this morning in the Scriptures," he continued, more softly now, "trying to work on Sunday's sermon. But I kept seeing your face, hearing your voice, and I knew I had to come over and make sure you were real. I was afraid I might have imagined the feeling I felt last night. But I didn't. I feel it this very moment, and you're real and every bit as delightful as I remembered."

She lowered her gaze, her pulse quickening.

"Tell me, Bethany Rose, do you feel it too—the rare, wonderful connection between us? Tell me it's not just wishful thinking on my part."

"It's not. I do," she stammered.

"Then may I court you? Be your beau?" He chuckled self-deprecatingly. "Goodness, is that too old fashioned? Do they even say that anymore? Things have changed so since the war. I'm not quite sure what's proper anymore."

"I'd like you to court me," she said in a small, breathless voice.

She waited for him to take her in his arms and express his passion in a kiss, but instead, he clasped her hand and pressed it against his lips. "God is in this," he murmured, his countenance bright and animated. "He brought me here to Willowbrook, to this church, this house, knowing we'd meet, knowing I'll need a helpmate. Do you see how God is working?"

She stiffened and looked toward the street. She didn't know his

God, but this didn't seem the time to tell him, so she said nothing, leaving him to draw his own conclusions.

He didn't seem to notice her reticence, so caught up was he in his own fervor. "I could say so much more, Bethany," he declared in an earnest whisper. "I feel so much, but it's too soon. I'm foolish even to say this much. Pray with me that God will reveal His will. Pray that we won't run recklessly ahead of Him."

To Beth's amazement, Todd bowed his head right there as he held her hand, and entreated the Almighty to bless their friendship. She had never heard such a sweet and gentle prayer, had never witnessed anyone talk to God with such simple, unswerving faith. She found herself wishing she believed as he did, with the same unshakable confidence of a child.

That night Bethany's dreams were filled with the handsome Reverend Marshall. They were in church together, standing at the altar, and she was wearing the most exquisite satin wedding gown. They were saying their marriage vows and, oddly enough, it was Reverend Marshall himself who was performing the ceremony. But then, when she looked back at her bridegroom, it was Jake Witherspoon smiling smugly, and her dear Reverend Marshall was pronouncing them husband and wife!

Bethany woke with a start, her heart pounding, all her senses acute. She felt as if she had been running. It was a nightmare, but at least not the usual one that plagued her dreams. She turned on her side, fluffed her pillow, laid her head back, and opened her eyes. The light of the full moon streamed in the window, bathing the room with a wash of incandescent white.

But, as Bethany's eyes focused on the wall nearest the door, a jagged black shadow cut into the expanse of whiteness with a horrifying silhouette—the woman in the feather hat!

Beth froze, her gaze riveted on the shadowy figure. *I'm not dreaming. This is real!* "Who's there?" she whispered, clutching her covers around her throat.

The apparition moved, then disappeared.

For a heart-pounding moment Bethany lay paralyzed, as if there were no connection between her mind and her limbs. Then, with a heady rush of adrenaline, she threw off her blankets and sprang from her bed. Her heart pummeled her chest like a jackhammer. The chill night air seeped through her long cotton nightgown as she padded barefoot across the room and peered into the hallway. All was quiet. She moved soundlessly over the carpet past Knowl and Annie's door and past Maggie's nursery, where the hall jutted off at an angle.

As soon as she turned the corner she saw it. Her stomach knotted in horror and revulsion. It couldn't be—her worst nightmare alive in this house! A woman in a feather hat and fur stole slipped into Betty Herrick's room and quietly shut the door behind her.

8

Bethany ran back to her room and sat on the edge of her bed, hugging herself, trembling. Already she was arguing with herself, insisting she couldn't have seen what she knew she'd glimpsed. But slowly it began to make sense. Of course Betty Herrick was the woman in the feather hat Who else had a reason to come and argue with her mother that night? Who else would have hated the Henrys for taking her husband away? Who else would have been crazy enough to kill her mother and set the house on fire with Laura Henry's children in it?

But Betty Herrick was a recluse who never even left her room. How could she have gone to Fort Wayne and accomplished such a grisly deed with no one the wiser?

Even as Bethany thought about the question, she heard Annie's voice in her mind saying, *She hasn't left this house in months. Not since we took her to see your father's grave.*

A fresh spasm of shock traveled Bethany's spine. Her father's grave was less than a mile from their farmhouse. Somehow Betty Herrick had slipped away that night, determined perhaps to see where Tom's other family lived. She and Mama had confronted each other for the first time in their lives. That's what Bethany had heard that night in her drugged stupor—Mama arguing with Betty Herrick. If Beth hadn't taken the sleeping pills, she could have come to Mama's aid; together they could have persuaded the demented woman to leave, and Mama would still be alive!

Hot, bitter tears pooled in Bethany's eyes. Why hadn't Luke heard the women arguing? Why hadn't he come to Mama's rescue? But he wouldn't have heard. His bedroom was at the back of the house, and he always slept so soundly.

Another realization began to dawn. Bethany had seen Betty Herrick's shadow more than once in her room here at Herrick House. Surely the deranged woman knew who Bethany was and that she was here, living in this house, occupying this room. Betty wasn't just a helpless old woman who didn't know whether she was coming or going; she was a conniving murderer looking for her chance to attack again and finish the gruesome job she had begun.

Bethany clenched her fists and dug her nails into her palms. *How can I protect myself? How can I tell Knowl and Catherine their mother is a murderer?*

There was nothing Bethany could do tonight, but tomorrow she would talk to Annie and learn what she could about their trip to Fort Wayne. And if only she could get her hands on the telltale feather hat that had haunted her dreams, she could convince Luke the stranger in their house that night was real.

Before she lay back down, she closed her door, wishing she could lock it, and finally pushed an old black trunk over to block the way.

At breakfast the next morning Bethany listlessly nibbled her oatmeal and toast while the rest of the family chatted amiably. On such a sunny morning her nocturnal suspicions seemed even more improbable. Perhaps she had dreamed the entire incident; that seemed more likely than the other possibility—that the unbalanced woman upstairs, the mother Knowl doted on—was a cold-blooded killer.

After Knowl had left for work and while Anna cleared away the dishes, Bethany inquired about Betty Herrick's trip to Fort Wayne. "Annie," she began awkwardly, "didn't you tell me Knowl's mama went to see Papa's grave?"

"Yes, I guess I did mention that, didn't I?" Annie was feeding baby Maggie applesauce and scrambled egg—first a spoonful of egg followed by a spoonful of applesauce to keep the egg down. When Annie wasn't quick enough, the egg would come spurting out of the toddler's puckered lips.

"When was that?" Bethany asked softly.

Annie shrugged. "Oh, goodness, I don't remember. Late in the summer. August, I think."

"What day?"

"Um, Friday, possibly. Yes, the second Friday of August."

Bethany sat still and cold as a glacier, taking in the meaning of Annie's words. *Yes, the second Friday of August. The night of the fire.*

"Why do you ask, Beth?"

"I just wondered."

"Oh."

"Tell me about it."

She missed the baby's mouth. "There's not much to tell."

"Please."

"All right. It wasn't a pleasant trip, but Knowl and I thought it might help his mother. Betty was in such doldrums. She had never had a chance to finish things with your father."

"Finish things?"

"There was the divorce years before and then, except for my wedding, Tom had simply disappeared from our lives. By the time Knowl and Catherine found him again, he was dying."

"It was my mama who sent Luke to Willowbrook to find Papa's other children," said Bethany.

"It was good of her to do that." Annie wiped Maggie's mouth, removed her bib, and handed her a spoon to play with. "Anyway, Betty was very bitter when she learned Tom had started another family even while he was married to her. She felt . . . betrayed. Evidently, she had always wanted to confront Tom and have it out with him, but then he died, and she grieved over never having her chance."

Bethany stirred, her emotions rising faster than she wanted. "You took Knowl's mama to Fort Wayne so she could tell Papa off over his grave?"

"That wasn't exactly our intention. We just wanted to give her a chance to say the things that had been bottled up in her for years. We hoped that making peace with your father would bring healing to her mind."

"But she's a sick woman! How could you let her go?"

"At the time she was quite rational. We thought she was improving. But we knew as soon as she started venting her anger that it was a mistake. Knowl had to constrain her and take her back to the cottage."

"The cottage?"

"Yes, we rented a little cottage—two actually, one for Knowl and me and one for his mother—at a tourist court just outside Fort Wayne. There was a Texaco station there, but the rooms were so drab. Just a couple of steel cots and straight-back chairs. And the heat that night—I'll never forget that heat!"

"I remember too," said Beth solemnly.

Annie nodded. "That's right. I suppose we weren't far from your home."

"Not far at all."

Annie reached over and touched Beth's hand. "I'm sorry. I'm stirring up sad memories with all this talk. I guess our trip to Fort Wayne couldn't have been many days before the fire."

Without replying, Beth stood up and gripped the back of her chair. "Will you excuse me, Annie? There's something I've got to do."

"Of course, dear. Run along." Annie scooped Maggie up and kissed her plump rosy cheek. The baby chortled and waved her fat, dimpled arms. Annie smiled. "Beth, if you need me, I'll be out in the yard with Maggie. You know how she loves to play in the leaves."

Bethany waited until Annie was outside before heading upstairs. The house seemed eerily silent as she made her way down the carpeted hallway to Betty Herrick's room. She listened a moment at the closed door. The radio was playing inside. It sounded like the Breakfast Club. She couldn't risk going in if Betty was there. But wait. From the bathroom she could hear the sound of running water. Good! Betty was occupied for at least a minute or two.

She tried the door. It opened with a faint creaking sound. Holding her breath, she peeked inside. The room—surprisingly large—was empty. Beth scanned its homey furnishings—a four-poster bed, love seat, rocking chair, dressing table, and bureau. On the nightstand sat a Crosley radio with a walnut finish. Don McNeill was announcing his next guest in his vibrant, cheery voice. Beside the radio stood an old framed photograph showing two children—surely Knowl and Catherine—standing beside Papa and a pretty young woman Bethany didn't recognize.

Swallowing her nervousness, Beth slipped inside and went directly to the closet. She rifled through several garments, then noticed an array of hats on the top shelf. She was about to reach for one when she heard the bathroom door open. She ducked behind several wool suits just as Betty Herrick shuffled over to the closet. Betty put on her fur stole and took a hat down from the top shelf and placed it carefully on her nest of gray hair. The hat was wide-brimmed with an enormous peacock plume curling from its center.

Bethany clasped her hand over her mouth lest she scream. The rustling sound caught Betty Herrick's attention. She made a guttural sound with an upward inflection, as if isolation had reduced her speech to mere syllables.

Bethany waited, holding her breath. Betty was obviously waiting too, for after a moment she said, "Who's there?"

"Me." Bethany eased gingerly out of the closet and stood face to face with a plain, dour woman with protruding cheekbones, angular features, and dark, insolent eyes. Years of boozing had carved a fine network of lines into her hardened face.

For a painfully long moment Betty stared dumbfounded at Beth, her grim mouth set over her jutting chin. At last she pointed an arthritic finger at Beth and blurted, "You're the spitting image of my Tom when he was young."

"I—I'm Tom's daughter."

"Tom's daughter? What's your name?"

"Bethany Rose Henry."

Betty's bristly brows arched warily. "You got his face and his eyes—especially his eyes. He was a handsome man when I met him."

"I know."

Betty gestured toward the love seat. "Sit a spell."

Bethany did as she was told. Betty sank down on the rocker facing her and demanded, "Why haven't you visited me before?"

Bethany shook her head. She was winging it now, without a script. "I didn't know you wanted me to visit."

"Of course I did! The others visit." Betty sat forward and peered at Bethany with a critical eye. "You look more like Tom than any of the others. You're Tom at his best."

"Thank you."

"He died, you know," Betty went on in a peevish, hard-edged voice. "Died too young."

"Yes, he did," Bethany agreed.

"But he knew how to live life. Lived too hard, too fast, but that man never knew a boring day. Traveled all over. Sold Fuller brushes, you know. He could give you his spiel and you'd buy the whole kit and caboodle."

Bethany smiled in spite of herself. That was Papa. He could charm the fuzz off a fly.

"You wait here long enough, you'll see him," said Betty.

"Who?" asked Beth.

"Tom. He's taking me to the train."

"The train?"

"I'm traveling to Cincinnati. My mama's plumb poorly." She adjusted her hat on her thicket of hair.

"I'm sorry." Beth kept her gaze off the hat and its vile feather.

"I promised I'd come. Soon as Tom fetches me."

Bethany started to rise, but Betty waved her down. "Stay. Keep me company. Say hello to Tom. Let him see how much you two look alike."

"I can't," said Bethany, standing. "I've really got to go."

Betty clasped Beth's wrist as she edged toward the door. "Child, do you know my daughter, Catherine?"

Beth's throat constricted. "Yes, I know her."

"Tell her to come visit me."

"Okay. I—I'll tell her."

Betty's eyes glinted and her tone grew urgent. "If she can't come, tell her I'm faring well. Tell her this is a nice place. The food is good. They take care of me."

Bethany was at the door now, turning the knob. "I'll tell her."

"You come back," insisted Betty. "Come see me. Land sakes, how you look like Tom. The spitting image."

Without answering, Bethany darted out the door and fled to her room. She threw herself on her bed and hugged her pillow. She was breathing too hard; her head was spinning. "Heaven help me, help me . . . ," she whispered over and over. She didn't know what to think or do. Was Betty Herrick a murderer? She seemed more like a sad, lonely old woman. Or was she putting on an act, fooling Bethany, trying to win her confidence so that she could murder her too?

She thought to herself, *If I tell Knowl and Catherine what I suspect, they'll think I'm crazy. They'll think I just want to hurt their mother. Oh, God—if You're there like You are for Todd—help me to know what to do!*

By supper time Bethany had decided she must tell her brother and sister their mother could be responsible for her mother's death. Catherine and Robert were coming to dinner, so everyone would be together. She would simply relate what she knew and let them decide what it meant.

But as the family settled around the dinner table, laughing and chatting happily, Beth knew this would be one of the hardest things she had ever done. Already her hands were clammy and her stomach was turning somersaults. As Knowl asked the blessing, she prayed God would give her the courage to speak out. Of course, it would be best to wait until the meal was over; no sense in spoiling everyone's appetite. That resolved, for the next half hour she sat in stony silence picking at the food on her plate while Knowl and Robert talked animatedly about the latest goings-on at their publishing company.

"I think the cover on the O'Hara book works quite well," Knowl said as he took a second helping of meat loaf. "Enough color to catch the eye, but subdued enough to show that it's a work to be taken seriously."

Bethany listened idly, her mind churning out the words, *Your mama's a killer, Knowl. What will you say to that?*

"I'm glad we made the title larger," Robert noted. "It stands out well. Underscores the importance of its subject."

"Absolutely," agreed Knowl. "It's the most incisive treatment I've read on the church and where it's headed in the second half of this century."

Between sips of coffee Robert mused, "I'm just afraid it'll be too liturgical for mainstream bookstores."

"Perhaps," said Knowl, "but we'll try it. The literary world is warming to spiritual issues. Religion's become a marketable subject. Look at the titles out this year by prestigious houses. Fulton Oursler's *The Greatest Story Ever Told*. Norman Vincent Peale's new book. What's it called?"

"*A Guide to Confident Living*. And don't forget Fulton Sheen's *Peace of Soul*," Robert added, his cup still raised to his lips.

Bethany tried to listen, but her heart was pounding too loudly. With the side of her fork she cut her meat loaf into little wedges, first four pieces, then eight, then sixteen. *None of us will know peace after tonight,* she thought darkly. *No one in this house will ever know peace again!*

"I'm reading Lloyd Douglas's new novel, *The Big Fisherman*," Annie interjected. "Did you know Douglas won't sell book club, movie, or serial rights, he's so confident the book will sell on its merits?"

"And on his name!" quipped Knowl. "And he's right!"

"It's a wonderful story," said Annie. "He makes Peter so real."

"I wish people would flock to buy our titles the way they buy his," said Cath.

Conversation swirled all around Bethany, but it seemed distant, muffled, of no consequence. Her mind was somewhere else. Methodically she mashed her meat loaf with the tines of her fork, turning it into a sickly brown paste. *In a minute, when I've had my say, everything will change,* she thought. *We can never go back.*

"So far, Knowl, our books have been aimed at a more academic niche," Robert said in his smooth, professional voice. "Frankly, I'd like to expand our readership, but it's a challenge, making the truth palatable without compromising its purity."

"I agree. Readers are hungry for spiritual truth, if we can just reach them. But too many want it sugar-coated. Watered-down."

"That's the problem," said Robert. "People are reluctant to read anything that may compel them to change. They want to feel comfortable in their religion, but they don't want the Holy Spirit transforming their lives."

"That's what we've come to after two world wars and a depression," said Knowl. "A society of lethargic Christians who plan to coast into the next millennium."

"Afraid so, old man. Aren't we all a bit guilty?"

Guilty? Bethany felt guilty. She pushed her meat loaf into a sad little mound. There must have been something she could have done that night. Surely she could have stopped Betty Herrick if she'd been awake. Knowl could have stopped his mother. Where was Knowl when her mother was dying?

Knowl forked up the last of his scalloped potatoes. "In other words, old man, we're in a sorry state."

"Exactly!" Robert set his cup on its saucer with a clattering sound. "Christians turned the world upside down in the first century. It's time to do it again. This could be the last century before Christ returns."

Bethany rocked slightly, tapping her fork on her plate, so softly no one could hear it at first. She tapped with a measured cadence. A pounding had started in her head, pressing painfully just behind her eyes. She rehearsed what she would say, how she would say it. *Knowl, Catherine, you'll find this hard to believe . . .*

Catherine was saying coyly, "You men have talked business and religion long enough. It's time for us women to talk about something frivolous."

. . . your mother isn't who you think she is.

"Bethany?" Cath was looking at her with a puzzled expression. "Don't you agree, Beth?"

An awkward silence crept over the room as Bethany realized all eyes were on her. "I'm sorry, what did you say?"

"I said, don't we girls have a right to monopolize the conversation for awhile?" Cath looked at her more closely, her brow furrowed. "Don't you feel well, Beth? You're terribly pale. Doesn't she look ill, Mother Reed?"

Anna craned her neck toward Beth. "You do look peaked, child. Do you have a fever? The influenza is going around this time of year."

Bethany raised her hands palms out, as if to deflect everyone's concern. "I'm fine. I'm not sick. I don't have a fever. I'm just a little . . . tired."

"Well, remind me, dear," said Anna. "Right after dinner I'll give you a good dose of castor oil. It's good for what ails you."

"Oh no, not the castor oil!" Annie stifled a laugh. "I'll never inflict that foul-tasting stuff on my children. Don't let her force it on you, Bethany."

Beth's lower lip trembled. "Mama always gave us castor oil when we were ailing."

"See? That settles the matter," said Anna triumphantly.

Robert wiped his mouth with his napkin. "Where's the frivolous conversation you ladies promised?"

"Annie and I did something quite daring today," said Cath with a hint of mystery.

"Don't keep us in suspense," Robert told her.

Cath's face glowed with mischievous pleasure. "Annie and I . . . we went out today and bought a . . . a television set!"

"It was a good buy, Knowl," Annie assured him. "Crosley has an easy payment plan. You put in a quarter and the set operates for an hour. The money is applied against the purchase price."

"I thought we agreed we wouldn't have one of those contraptions in this house," declared Anna.

"Mother Reed," said Cath, "imagine *seeing* your favorite stars, not just hearing them. Milton Berle, Arthur Godfrey, Jack Benny!"

Anna shook her head. "If I want to see my favorite stars I'll go to the motion pictures."

Bethany could wait no longer. "Listen," she said, but no one heard her.

"Where do you plan to put this television set?" asked Knowl.

"Listen to me," Beth said again, her voice sounding shrill in her ears. "Listen!"

Everyone stopped and looked at her.

"Are you feeling worse, dear?" asked Anna.

"No, I'm fine," she said, but she was far from fine. Her tongue felt thick in her mouth. "I have something to say," she said and then lapsed into silence.

Annie put a hand on Bethany's arm. "What's wrong, Beth? You can tell us."

Bethany realized that no matter how she phrased it the words made no sense. No matter what she said, no one would believe her.

"I'm going to be sick," she said, covering her mouth as she sprang from her chair and ran from the room. Her words were left unspoken, dangling in mid-air just beyond reach. *Your mother killed my mother . . . killed my mother!*

9

Later that night, while the rest of the household slumbered, Bethany Rose slipped downstairs and telephoned the Fort Wayne police. "I . . . I need to talk to someone," she whispered into the mouthpiece. "I have new information about my mother, Laura Henry's death."

The sergeant acted as if her call were routine. His tone impassive, his manner unruffled, he assured her he would send a detective to Willowbrook first thing in the morning.

Next, Bethany telephoned Luke and told him she had found the mysterious woman in the feather hat. When he reacted with skepticism, she haltingly related the entire story of her encounter with Betty Herrick.

Luke remained dubious until she told him Betty had been in Fort Wayne the night of the fire. "It can't be a coincidence, Luke," she insisted. "Somehow that woman sneaked away from the motor court and came to our house. She and Mama fought, she killed her and set the fire, and we never even knew. We slept right through it all."

"You haven't told anyone, have you?"

She kept her gaze on the darkened hallway, her ears alert to any sound from upstairs. "No. I tried at dinner tonight, but I couldn't do it."

"Good. No sense in rocking the boat just because the old lady looks suspicious."

"What do you mean, Luke? Are you saying I should keep quiet about this?"

"I'm saying you've got a good set-up there, Beth, but you start accusing Knowl's mama of murder and the Herricks will send you packing."

"Luke, don't you want the truth to come out about who killed Mama?"

"Sure I do. It eats at me day and night. But sometimes if you go poking around, you find a hornet's nest."

"I've got a hornet's nest either way. If that woman killed Mama, maybe she wants me dead too. I'm scared to go to sleep in this house, Luke."

"Listen, Sis, I really think the old woman's harmless."

"How can you say that? Mama's gone! Our house is gone!"

"I know, but accusing that crazy dame won't bring Mama and our house back." He drew in a ragged breath. "I'd hate to see you ruin things with Knowl and Catherine. They're giving you the kind of life I never could."

Tears stung her eyes. "It's too late, Luke. I've already called the police. They'll be here in the morning."

"Thunderation! You called the police?"

"They told me to call them if I had any new information." She bit her lip. "You sound angry."

"No, it's just—well, you get the police in this and there's no going back. You just ripped that hornet's nest wide open, kiddo."

She choked back a sob. "I didn't know what else to do, Luke. No matter what, someone's going to get hurt."

"Well, if you want my advice I'd tell the cops you were wrong; you don't have nothing new to tell them."

"I can't, Luke. In his sermon last Sunday Reverend Marshall said,

'The truth will set you free.' That's how I feel. I won't be free until I tell what I know."

"You're squealing because some preacher said so? Who is this guy?"

"Todd Marshall, the new minister. He's kind and polite, Luke. A real gentleman. He says he wants to court me. He's even had me over to dinner to meet his mother."

Luke returned an amused chuckle. "I bet he thinks you're one of the high-and-mighty Herricks, pompous pillars in the community. Or does he know you're the poor little black sheep of the family?"

Bethany felt a tightening in her stomach. "I don't know what he knows, Luke. But he cares about me. I can tell."

"Yeah? Well, see how long he cares when this whole murder business explodes in the news and he finds out you're disgracing one of Willowbrook's most established families."

She was weeping now, silently, so that her voice wouldn't carry down the dark hallway. "I can't help it, Luke. Can't you see? I've got to tell."

"Okay, tell the police, but you're gonna tear the whole family apart," Luke warned darkly, "and you're the one they'll blame."

Bethany heard a sound coming from upstairs—a toilet flushing. "I've got to go, Luke," she whispered. "Someone's up. I can't let them catch me on the phone."

"Do you want me to come to Willowbrook?"

"No, stay there. It's better if you're not involved."

After hanging up the phone, Bethany slipped back upstairs to her room, pushed the black trunk in front of her door, and crept back into bed. But sleep eluded her. In her mind she could hear Knowl and Catherine denouncing her for betraying them. Their words tolled in her head, heavy and mournful as a death knell. When at last she drifted off, her dreams rumbled in with a dark foreboding. Shadowy figures taunted her and whispered veiled warnings, gleeful in their torment.

She woke at dawn, exhausted and afraid to sleep, but even more afraid to get up. How could she face this day? How could she confront Knowl and Catherine with her accusations? Even more distressing, how could she remain in this house with what she knew?

At breakfast, when Annie inquired about Bethany's pallid countenance, Bethany forced herself to say, "I didn't sleep well. The truth is . . . I don't know how to say this, but I have something to tell you. It's important."

"It can't wait till tonight?" asked Knowl, swallowing the last of his coffee. "I have an early appointment."

"No, it can't wait," she cried, seizing his arm.

"Then tell us," he urged, pushing his cup aside. "What's wrong?"

"It's about my mama's death," she began, her throat already constricting. "And it's about your mama."

"My mother?" echoed Knowl, looking puzzled.

"It's about what happened when she came to Fort—"

The doorbell rang, once, twice, three times, insistent. Anna went to answer it and was back moments later with a troubled expression. "It's a police detective," she said. "From Fort Wayne. Here to see Bethany. Says she called him."

"I did," said Beth, flustered, "but I didn't expect him this early."

"What's this about?" asked Knowl, getting up.

"I showed Detective Stassen to the parlor," said Anna.

"Bethany, do you want to talk to him privately?"

She looked up at Knowl and brushed a wave of tawny hair back from her forehead. She was still in her housecoat and slippers. "No, I want you and Annie there. And Cath. She should be here too."

Knowl frowned. "Cath? What's she got to do with this?"

"You'll understand when . . . when I talk to the detective."

"Understand what?" asked Annie. "You're acting so mysterious, Beth."

"Let's just go meet the detective and get this over with," said Knowl, tightening his tie. "Mother Reed, call Cath. Tell her to come right over."

"I'm so sorry," Beth told them as they headed for the parlor. "I didn't want it to be like this. Please don't hate me."

Annie clasped her hand. "Hate you? Why would we hate you?"

Beth didn't reply. They were in the parlor now, and a tall, portly man in a rumpled suit stood gazing at the Monet prints over the fireplace. Bald except for a fringe of bristly hair around the back of his head, he had thick jowls, a bulbous nose, and pale gray eyes. "Nice paintings," he said offhandedly. "Always did like those Impressionists."

He wasn't what Bethany had expected. "Are you Detective Stassen?" she asked warily.

"Sure am." He showed his badge. "I guess you expected a uniform. I'm a plain-clothes investigator."

After a round of introductions, Annie suggested that everyone sit down and be comfortable. She offered coffee, which the detective waved off as he settled into the overstuffed chair by the bay window. Clearing his throat, he came right to the point. "You said you have some new information about your mother's death, Miss Henry."

Beth cast an anxious glance at Knowl sitting with Annie on the love seat across from her. She was about to destroy them with her words. She considered jumping up and fleeing the room, but where would she go? It was too late to escape. Everyone was watching, waiting. The truth had to come out, no matter its consequences.

"New information, Inspector? I wasn't aware—"

"Miss Henry phoned us last night, Mr. Herrick."

Knowl turned to her. "What's this all about, Bethany?"

Her heart drummed so fiercely she wondered if they could hear her voice over its thundering beat. "Your mama," she said thickly, meeting Knowl's gaze. "Your mama was at my house the night of the fire."

A heavy, tension-charged silence filled the room. At last Knowl sat forward and declared, "That's impossible. My mother's practically an invalid. She never leaves her room."

Beth was shaking now as she countered, "The fire . . . it happened the same night you took your mama to Fort Wayne to see Papa's grave. I saw your mama outside my room in her feather hat. I heard her arguing with my mama. She was there. I swear it!"

Knowl sat back, stunned. Annie covered her mouth with her hand. The detective remained silent, biding his time.

After a minute Annie gazed with sympathy at Beth and admitted, "We did drive Betty to Fort Wayne that night, but if you're suggesting she had anything to do with the fire or your mother's death, you're wrong. She was with us the whole time. I know how much you want to find your mother's killer, but you're grasping at straws, Beth."

"Barking up the wrong tree is more like it," Knowl retorted.

"I'm not wrong. I know she was there, and I can prove it."

Detective Stassen shifted in his chair and thrummed his fingers on the rolled arm. His doughy face seemed to tighten and glow with a keen, bright alertness. "Tell me about it, Miss Henry, every detail, right from the beginning."

With a slow, delicate precision Bethany told her story, starting with her glimpse of the woman in the feather hat outside her room the night of the fire. Her voice came out thin and tenuous as she described waking to hear two women arguing and later being jolted awake by crackling flames rolling into her room. She told of Luke's rescue and of her horror when she realized her mother hadn't escaped.

"That doesn't prove my mother was there," argued Knowl. "You're making her a scapegoat, Bethany, and frankly, I resent it."

"But there's more," she insisted. She told of seeing Betty just two nights ago outside her bedroom wearing the same wide-brimmed hat with the curled plume. And she told of visiting Betty's room and discovering that very hat in her closet. "I know she's the woman who was there arguing with my mama that night," she said, her voice rising to a thin treble. "I can't keep quiet when the truth is plain as day. I'm positive Betty Herrick killed my mama!"

Knowl stood up, strode over to the fireplace, and gripped the oak mantle with both hands. "This is the most preposterous thing I've ever heard. My mother a *murderer?* She's been blamed for a lot of things in her life, but this really takes the cake!" He turned back around, removed his glasses, and rubbed the bridge of his nose. "Detective Stassen, I hope you have the good sense to recognize a distraught, grieving, confused young woman when you hear one."

"I'm not confused," Bethany protested.

"Perhaps I should talk with your mother, Mr. Herrick," said the detective. "Maybe she can clear things up for us."

"No," said Knowl. "Like I said, my mother hasn't been well for a long time. I don't want her upset."

Annie joined Knowl at the fireplace. "Darling, maybe we could talk to her—"

"No! We should be able to clear this up without involving her."

Detective Stassen stood up. "I must warn you, Mr. Herrick, it's routine in homicides to question all suspects, however unlikely."

Knowl's ruddy complexion flushed crimson. "You won't go near my mother until I've conferred with her doctor and my lawyer!"

The raw tension in the room was defused momentarily by the sound of the doorbell. Seconds later Catherine marched into the room, wearing a pale green shirtwaist dress, her long, flaming red hair pinned back with gold barrettes. "Good morning, everyone," she chirped brightly. "Anna called and told me to come right over. What's up—a parliamentary meeting, or just a party?"

"More like a crisis, Cath," said Annie softly.

Cath glanced curiously around the room, her gaze settling quickly on Detective Stassen. "Oh, company. I'm sorry."

Annie made introductions, leaving Cath more perplexed than ever. "What's wrong?" she asked, her smile fading. "Why the police?"

Bethany pulled a hanky from the pocket of her housecoat and blew her nose. Her temples throbbed as Annie began in her polite, conciliatory voice, gently circumventing the issue.

But Knowl cut her off with a sharp, "Let's get to the point. It's absurd, Cath, but Bethany thinks . . ." He paused and rubbed perspiration from his forehead. "She thinks our mother somehow managed to kill her mother and burn down her house."

Cath stared from Knowl to Annie to Bethany. "Somebody tell me why she thinks this. Tell me!" She padded over and knelt beside Beth. "You can't really believe this!"

Bethany nodded.

Cath sat down in the nearest chair and listened as Knowl repeated the story, his tone heavy with skepticism. When he had finished, Cath looked back at Bethany. "There has to be an explanation, Beth. Granted, Mama's got a few bats in her belfry, but for that very reason she's not capable of pulling off a murder."

Beth felt a measure of courage returning. Catherine wasn't judging or condemning her for suspecting her mother! "I don't want to believe it was her, Cath," she mumbled, "but she's the woman I saw in the feather hat."

"But how would she have gotten from the motor court to your farmhouse?"

"Maybe she took Knowl's car."

"No, she doesn't drive," said Cath. "She always took taxis everywhere."

"Then maybe she took a taxi to my house."

Detective Stassen stood up and looked around. "Miss Henry, that's one idea I can check on right now. You got a phone handy?"

"There, on the desk," Annie offered.

He lumbered over and picked up the receiver. "I'm calling the Fort Wayne cab company," he informed them, dialing. "They've helped me out before. They keep a log of customers—names, dates, times. Hold on."

He adjusted the receiver and said in a confidential tone, "Hello, Charlie? Matt Stassen here. I need some info. Can you check your records for the second Friday of August? Yeah, this year. Did you send a taxi to the Fort Wayne Motor Court? The customer was a woman. Yeah, I'll wait." He drummed his fingers on the desk, a rhythmic rat-a-tat.

After a minute he said, "You did? Okay, what was the destination? You're sure? Did the passenger give her name? Is that a fact! Thanks, Charlie. Listen, I'll be in touch. And I'll want a full written report on that call. So long, buddy!"

He replaced the receiver and turned to Knowl with an expression of triumph and commiseration. "Looks like we got a case, folks. A woman at the motor court called for a cab that night."

"That doesn't mean a thing," said Knowl.

"There's more," said Stassen. "The cabbie drove her to the Henry farmhouse on Meadowlake Road. And here's the clincher. Make no mistake about it. The woman said her name was . . . Betty Herrick."

10

Detective Stassen turned to Knowl, his shaggy brows crouching over his pale gray eyes. "I'm sorry, Mr. Herrick, but this puts a whole new light on things. I'm afraid I'm gonna have to question your mother about her whereabouts the night Laura Henry was murdered. This morning."

Knowl looked visibly shaken. "I told you, she's been ill and confused. I don't see how she can help you."

"Just the same, I'd like to try."

"If this is an official interrogation, I want my lawyer present."

"Right now, Mr. Herrick, it's all informal. I'd just like to meet your mother and have a few words with her. Just a little friendly chitchat."

"I want to be there when you talk to her," Knowl told him.

"Me too," said Bethany. She met Knowl's dubious gaze squarely. "It was my mama who died. I need to hear what your mama has to say."

Bethany followed the two men up the stairs and waited behind them as Knowl knocked on his mother's door. After a minute Betty answered, wearing her fur stole and the unsettling feather hat. "Is Tom here yet?" she asked Knowl with an impatient whine. "I've been waiting all morning."

"No, Mama," he said, gently leading her back inside. "Papa's not here. But we have company. This gentleman would like to ask you a few questions."

She craned her neck at the detective, her small dark eyes narrowing with interest. "Do you know Tom? Is that why you're here?"

"No, ma'am, but I would like to talk with you. May I sit down?"

Ignoring his question, Betty looked past him to Bethany. Her thin lips broke into a spontaneous grin. "This one came back," she exclaimed. "Looks like Tom, if anyone ever did."

Bethany stepped tentatively into the room and managed a faint smile. "Hello, Mrs. Herrick."

Betty clasped Knowl's arm and shook it, like a child demanding attention. "What's her name, son? The girl. She's the spitting image of your papa."

"Her name's Bethany," said Knowl, urging his mother over to her rocking chair. "Bethany Rose Henry."

The detective sat down on the love seat and slung one arm casually over the back. "You seen Miss Henry before, Mrs. Herrick?"

Betty looked blankly at him for a moment, then nodded.

"When, Mrs. Herrick?"

Betty offered a faint smile. "I watched her when she wasn't looking. Watched her sleeping. She looks like my Tom when he was young. Just like my Tom."

Bethany hugged herself until her fingernails dug painfully into her arms. So, she hadn't been dreaming! Betty had come to her room. Her skin felt crawly; she wanted to bolt from the old woman's presence, but she forced herself to remain motionless and listen.

Detective Stassen sat forward attentively now. "Where were you when you watched Bethany Rose?"

Betty ran her tongue over her dry lips. "I was right here. Just walked down the hall and looked in on her."

"How did you know she was here, Mrs. Herrick?"

Lowering her gaze, Betty smoothed her fur stole with thin, knobby fingers. She tilted her head and hummed a familiar refrain. It sounded like *Sentimental Journey*, but no, it was something else. Bethany had heard the tune before; it was from one of Betty's radio shows, but she couldn't recall which one.

"Did you hear me, Mrs. Herrick?"

Betty looked up in surprise, as if just realizing she had company. "Were you talking to me, Mr.—?"

"Stassen. Yes, Mrs. Herrick. I asked how you knew this young lady was staying here."

Betty glanced covertly at Knowl and whispered, "It's a secret. Sometimes, when no one's upstairs, I go out on the landing and listen. I listen for Tom, but sometimes I hear people talking. One day I saw this girl and when I looked at that lean, handsome face, I thought it was Tom coming for me."

Detective Stassen planted his large hands squarely on his knees. "Mrs. Herrick, this is important. Did you ever see this young lady before she came to this house?"

Bethany flinched as Betty stared hard at her. "Yes, I saw her before."

"Where?"

"I don't know. Not here. At another house."

"Whose house, Mrs. Herrick?"

"I don't remember."

"What was she doing when you saw her in that other house?"

Betty pressed her cheek against her stole. "Sleeping."

"She was sleeping?" repeated Detective Stassen.

"Yes. Sleeping."

"When was that, Mrs. Herrick? Try to remember."

Betty shook her head.

"Was it summertime?"

She nodded. "It was hot. Hot as hades."

Carefully the detective asked, "Was it the same night you went to see your husband's grave, Mrs. Herrick?"

Betty scowled. "I went and I told him off real good, I did, but it wasn't enough. He was dead and buried. I had to tell someone who could hear me."

"Who did you tell? Was it another woman?"

"Yes, it was that horrid woman! I told her she had no right to my Tom. She just laughed and said Tom loved her, not me." Betty looked urgently around the room. "It's not true. When we were courting, my Tom adored me. He was a handsome man, he was. A real looker, like a movie star." She glanced toward the door. "He should be here any time now. He's taking me to the station, you know. I'm catching the train to Cincinnati. Staying a spell with my mama. She's been feeling poorly." She groaned up out of her rocker, her hands still gripping the arms. "I hear him at the door. Someone go get the door for me."

Detective Stassen reached out and placed his hand over Betty's. "Mrs. Herrick, I need to know what happened the night you visited that woman, the one who said Tom loved her. Do you remember that night?"

Knowl broke in with a terse rebuke. "That's enough, Detective Stassen. No more questions until I've talked with my lawyer and my mother's physician."

"Just a few more minutes—"

"No! You're putting words into my mother's mouth."

"Mr. Herrick, I could take your mother into custody today if I wanted to. She's as much as admitted she was at the scene of the crime."

"Don't you say another word to my mother until my lawyer gets here."

Stassen sat back and drew in a breath, his gaze on Betty. "I won't as long as you promise to deliver her to the sanitarium tomorrow for a full psychiatric examination. I warn you, don't let me regret my generosity. I want that evaluation on my desk as soon as possible."

"But aren't you going to finish questioning her now?" urged Bethany. "She was just about to tell you what happened!"

Detective Stassen stood up and arched his back. "Don't worry. We'll talk to her again, Miss Henry. We'll get the whole story." He turned and said a polite good-bye to Betty, then lumbered out of the room, with Bethany right behind him.

Knowl stayed a moment with his mother, then joined the others on the landing. He started to speak, but the words knotted in his throat. He removed his glasses and cleaned them with his handkerchief. His eyes were moist, red-rimmed. "I . . . I'm sorry," he mumbled, but Bethany wasn't sure what he was sorry about.

As they headed downstairs, Detective Stassen said, "I'll see myself out, Mr. Herrick." Knowl gave him a cool nod; then he and Bethany joined Annie and Catherine in the parlor.

Knowl strode directly over to Annie and hugged her, then embraced Cath. "It doesn't look good," he murmured.

"What happened, Knowl?" asked Cath.

Knowl looked brokenly from one to the other. "She had moments of confusion, but she didn't deny being at the Henry farmhouse the night we drove her to Fort Wayne." He gazed at Bethany, tears glazing his eyes. "If it's true—if my mother did this horrendous thing—I don't know what to say to you. I don't know how to ever make things right."

Bethany stood motionless, her hands loose at her sides, her gaze downcast, tears blurring her own vision. She could think of nothing to say either. Knowl had spoken the truth. Nothing anyone said or did could alter the past or make things right. Her private pain had grown to include all of Herrick House, perhaps all of Willowbrook. Her grief had touched and changed everything, everyone. It seemed there was nothing else on earth except this sweeping, radiating hurt, encompassing them all in its dark, deadly vortex.

Knowl sank down in the nearest chair and massaged his hands. "I have to take Mother to the Hillsdale Sanitarium this afternoon." He seemed to be speaking to himself now. "I've endured my mother's alcoholism and my father's philandering, but I never thought I'd see a day like this. Better I'd never been born; better my mother had never been born." He put his head in his hands and made a muffled sound in his throat, a low sob.

* * *

That evening just before dinner, Bethany was in the nursery rocking baby Maggie when she heard Knowl's car pull up in the driveway. She put the slumbering baby back in her crib and slipped downstairs, eager to learn what the sanitarium doctors had said.

As she approached the parlor, she heard Knowl's voice, sounding ragged, on edge. "I'm really sick at heart, Annie. I don't know what we're going to do."

Bethany paused outside the door and pressed her cheek against the varnished woodwork. She listened, hardly daring to breathe. Whatever Knowl was about to say, he might not be so candid in her presence.

"Did it go badly?" Annie's voice.

"Not exactly. Mother was no trouble. She liked the idea of going somewhere. Thought she was visiting her sick mother."

"Then why are you looking so grim?"

"It was the whole idea of leaving her there again. She was still wearing her stole and feather hat, fidgeting in a rocker, worried about missing her train, when I left. I started to empty the valise you packed for her—but I couldn't. And then I had a long talk with Dr. Falkenburg."

"Who?"

"Hillsdale's resident psychiatrist. He's familiar with Mother's case. He evaluated her two years ago when she . . . when she . . ." His voice wavered as the words fell away.

"Oh, Knowl, does he see a connection between Laura Henry's death and that terrible night your mother took Jenny?"

"He believes there is a pattern of erratic behavior. He said Mother had to be mentally disturbed the night she took Jenny hostage and fed her sleeping pills."

Annie's voice caught with emotion. "I still have nightmares. Our darling little Jenny! She could have died."

"And the house," Knowl continued unevenly. "Mother practically set fire to her own house. She and Jenny could have burned to death if Cath and Robert hadn't found them in time."

"Are you saying . . . your mother—?"

Knowl made a low groaning sound. "Annie, with her history of unsound behavior, who can say Mother didn't kill Laura Henry and burn down *her* house?"

Listening at the door, Bethany felt a shuddering chill. Knowl was practically admitting his mother was guilty!

"Oh, Knowl, you believe it's true?"

"What else can I believe?"

"What if the police find out about the night she took Jenny?"

"It's in Mother's medical records. The doctors will say it's privileged information, but the police have their ways of finding out such things."

"What happens next?" asked Annie.

"Dr. Falkenburg agreed to observe Mother for several weeks before determining her sanity. He suggested I talk to our lawyer about the legal ramifications, so I stopped by and chatted with Arnold Kraslow."

"Why not John Russell, our regular attorney?"

"John recommended Kraslow. He's in criminal law. He told me what to expect if the police press charges against Mother."

"Tell me," said Annie.

"The court would set a date for a preliminary hearing."

"A hearing? What does that mean?"

Knowl's voice darkened. "A grand jury would decide if there's enough evidence to bring charges against Mother. If there is, she'll be arraigned and a trial date will be set."

In the doorway Bethany held her breath and strained to hear Annie's response. "Oh, Knowl, a murder trial?"

"Incredible, isn't it?" Anger colored his voice. "We'll all be on trial, you know. The whole town will be watching, the whole state, maybe the whole confounded world! None of us will know a day of peace until this thing is finished."

"Don't think that way, Knowl. We've got to take this one day at a time."

"How can I, Annie? It's a no-win situation. We've spent years building an impeccable reputation in this community. We've poured our lifeblood into producing Christian literature of excellence and integrity. A scandal like this could ruin the publishing house."

"Knowl, I'm not thinking about the company. I'm thinking of our family. A murder trial could tear our family apart!"

"It already has." Knowl's voice broke with a despairing edge. "How can we all live under one roof with my mother on trial for killing my half-sister's mother?"

Bethany had heard enough. She slipped back from the door, made a scuffling sound on the carpet, then entered the parlor. She fixed her gaze on Knowl. "You're right. We can't all live under the same roof."

"What are you talking about?"

"I'm not staying here. I'm going back to Fort Wayne. I'll call Luke.

He'll come pick me up. You can take back the fancy clothes you bought me. I won't need them on the farm."

Both Knowl and Annie stared at her. "You can't go, Beth," said Annie. "School will be starting soon."

"I don't need school."

"Yes you do." Knowl's forceful tone softened. "I'm sorry you heard what I said. I was speaking out of frustration."

"But it's true. I don't belong here."

"Yes you do. This is your home now."

Beth kept her gaze unflinchingly on Knowl. "You don't want me here. You never did."

Knowl removed his glasses and rubbed his eyes. "This isn't about what I want or don't want. It's about what's right. No matter what happened between our mothers, you're my sister, and neither God nor Annie would let me rest if I let you walk out that door."

Annie came over and clasped Bethany's hands. "He's right, Beth. We're all caught in a terribly painful situation, but somehow we've got to get through it together. Please stay."

Beth looked back at Knowl. "Even if I beg God to let your mother rot in prison for what she did to my mother?"

Knowl replaced his glasses and adjusted them on his nose. His ruddy forehead glistened and his eyes looked pale and weary behind the glinting lenses. "We all want justice, Bethany. Justice tempered with a little mercy. But, in this instance, only God knows what justice is."

11

During the first week of November the *Willowbrook News* broke the story about the Laura Henry murder investigation. *Reliable sources report that police are about to make an arrest. . . . The suspect is reportedly a long-time resident of Willowbrook.* While the article fell short of revealing actual names, rumors were already running rampant around town that the suspect was a member of the prominent Herrick family, owners of Herrick House Publishers.

On Thursday, November 10th, Knowl announced at breakfast, "I've made a decision." He tapped his fingers on the newspaper beside his plate. "We can't quell the rumors anymore. Any day now Mother may be arrested, and our entire family will be in the headlines. If she goes on trial, I won't let her stand alone. I've got to be there for her."

"Of course, dear," said Annie, sipping her coffee.

"There's more." Knowl cleared his throat. "We need the support of our pastor. As a deacon, I consider it a matter of honor and integrity to inform Reverend Marshall of our situation."

"Is that wise?" Anna set a linen-draped basket of hot biscuits on the table. "This is a family matter, not something to be aired in public."

"The newspaper *will* make it public, Mother Reed. It's better if the news comes from us first." Knowl glanced at Bethany. "That's why I've asked Todd to stop by for breakfast this morning."

Bethany's fork clattered on her plate. "You're going to tell Todd about my mama and papa—the whole story?"

"Tom Herrick was *my* father too."

"I still don't think it's necessary to air the family's dirty linen," said Anna.

Bethany bristled. "My mama was not dirty linen."

Anna patted her hand. "Dear, you know I didn't mean—"

"Knowl, maybe Mother's right." Annie handed little Maggie a piece of melba toast. "This ordeal we're facing—why place such a great burden on a young, inexperienced minister?"

"I have no choice."

"You can't!" cried Bethany. "When Todd learns I'm not a Herrick he'll think I lied to him. He won't want to court me anymore."

"Let's hope we're all underestimating him," said Knowl. "We need his prayers and support—at church and in the community."

"We'll know how he reacts soon enough," said Anna, wiping her hands on her apron. "There's the doorbell." She left and returned moments later with Reverend Marshall, looking debonair in a gray pinstripe suit and navy tie.

"Good morning," he said brightly, his cheeks ruddy from the cold. He rubbed his hands together, warming them. "I see you're at it again, Anna. It smells like a bakery in here. Hope I'm not too late."

"Just in time, Reverend. Sit down and I'll bring you a plate of ham and eggs."

Taking the empty seat beside Bethany, he offered a bright, nervous smile. "I have a feeling this is more than just a social occasion. Is something wrong, Knowl?"

Knowl drummed his well-manicured fingers on the tablecloth. He looked grim, as if he were conducting a meeting at the publishing house and announcing the demise of the company. "I'm afraid we're in quite a dilemma."

Anna handed Todd the biscuits. "Can I get you some jam—strawberry jam, Reverend Marshall?"

"We already have preserves on the table, Mother," said Annie. "You do like orange marmalade, don't you, Reverend?"

"Yes, jam, marmalade—either one is fine." Todd buttered a biscuit. "Is this about me, Knowl? If it's about my work at the church, perhaps we could meet alone to discuss it."

"No, Todd. This has nothing to do with the church—except for the gossip that's been going around lately. Maybe you've heard. This is about my mother—and Bethany's mother."

"Now I'm confused. You and Bethany are brother and sister."

"Knowl's my *half*-brother," said Beth, her lower lip trembling. "I'm not a Herrick. I'm Bethany Rose *Henry*."

"Henry? You're related to Reverend Henry?"

"No." Tears burned in her eyes. "My papa made up the name. He didn't want anybody to know about Luke and me."

Todd shook his head. "Now you've really got me baffled."

"It's a long story, but it's time you knew." As Knowl divulged the painful truth about Papa's two families, everyone at the table picked silently at their food. Bethany sat unmoving, her spine rigid, feeling stiff and cold as a dead branch in the snow. Every wrenching detail from Knowl's lips felt like another nail hammered into Papa's coffin.

"Now," Knowl concluded solemnly, "my mother's implicated in the murder of Bethany's mother. We're all devastated. Our family is struggling to survive the emotional upheaval engendered by this deplorable predicament."

After a long moment of silence, Todd said, "Thank you, Knowl, for trusting me enough to confide in me. You know I'll do whatever I can to help." He looked at Bethany. "You could have told me. I would have understood."

But seeing the disenchantment in his eyes, she wasn't sure. Words came easily; actions were another matter. Only time would tell whether her relationship with Todd could survive.

On Sunday Bethany's doubts surged. As the congregation filed out after the service, Todd shook her hand and greeted her with a formal, "Good morning, Miss Henry."

Henry, not Herrick.

And before she could reply, he was gripping the hand of the parishioner behind her. That was it. *Good morning, Miss Henry.*

For the next five days she heard nothing from Todd. He was either avoiding her or too busy with his church duties to phone. For a man of the Word, he had few words for her these days.

Then, on the third Saturday of November, Todd telephoned and invited her over for dinner to celebrate his twenty-seventh birthday. She accepted, her emotions running the gamut between panic and euphoria. It would be their first time alone since he had learned the truth.

When he arrived to pick her up, she sensed the same lack of composure he had exhibited at church. He didn't quite meet her gaze, didn't even comment on her emerald green cardigan and plaid wool skirt. His gestures seemed restrained and his voice too carefully modulated to be natural.

As he drove her to his house, she wondered why he had even bothered inviting her over. Perhaps just as a token of kindness before revealing he no longer wanted to court her.

"I should confess," he said as he accelerated his vintage Nash over the red-brick pavement, "I've been avoiding you."

"I know. It's because of what Knowl told you, isn't it?"

"Yes, and I'm not proud of it. But I was so flabbergasted by it all. A minister should be able to hear anything and help his parishioners, but I didn't know what to say or how to help. I still don't know what to say. At times like this I realize how inexperienced I am. I imagine old Reverend Henry would have known just how to respond."

"I never knew Reverend Henry," said Beth.

"That's right. But your father took on his name." He glanced over at her as he turned onto his street. "I don't blame you for not telling me, Bethany. You were trying to put the past behind you and start a new life."

She gazed at her hands. "I haven't done very well so far."

"But that's not your fault. You can't help what other people do. Sometimes another person's actions—or even your own—change your entire life and you're caught in the maelstrom. You live in the shadow of it for the rest of your life, and only God can deliver you from the tides of darkness."

Preaching. He's always preaching! She listened quietly, bewildered by his words and yet comforted by his earnest, urgent tone.

"I'm prattling, I know. I'm sorry."

"Don't be. I like listening to you." *I like being with you, even when you're preaching.*

"My mother keeps telling me I shouldn't bother you. She says you've got enough to worry about without me intruding on your life. Am I intruding, Bethany? If I am, say so."

"No. You're not. I'm glad you invited me over."

"Good." He pulled into the driveway and turned off the engine. "I should warn you. Mother was against this little party. She says I'm being insensitive to expect you to take part in festivities at a time like this. Tell me if she's right. I'll understand. Frankly, I've never liked birthdays myself."

"I thought everyone liked birthdays."

"No. I've dreaded every one since I was seven. I figured if I had to celebrate another birthday, I wanted to spend it with you. Maybe a party will chase away the gloom for both of us."

"A party? Who else is coming?"

"No one. It's a party of three. You, Mother, and I." He grinned. "Usually it's a party of two."

Bethany groaned inwardly at the prospect of spending an evening with Eleanor Marshall, but as Todd escorted her inside, she chided herself for such unkind musings. After all, the woman *was* a devoted mother and had sacrificed a lot for her son.

But as soon as Eleanor Marshall swept into the living room, looking elegant in a black crepe dress with fleur-de-lis buttons, Bethany felt a familiar chill. The woman was daunting and unbending, with her tight, cold-eyed smile, the aloof way she offered her hand, and the rigid carriage of her stout frame.

"My dear, welcome to our little party. It was so sweet of you to come, considering . . ." Eleanor's words trailed off as she gestured toward a flowered settee with ball-and-claw legs. "Sit down and visit with Todd while I finish setting the table."

Bethany hesitated. "I'd be pleased to help you in the kitchen."

"Thank you, but everything's ready—a rump roast, brown potatoes, and carrots. And birthday cake, of course." Again she flashed her brittle smile. "A party's not complete without a cake, is it, dear?"

"No, Mrs. Marshall." Why did this woman unnerve her so? No matter how much Eleanor smiled, she seemed to be saying something else with her eyes, her silences, her inflections.

Annoyed, Bethany sat down and smoothed her plaid skirt over her legs. She had dressed with the elegant Mrs. Marshall in mind and was wearing silk hose and flat black pumps that felt too tight. Her toes curled painfully in their cramped space. On the farm she wore bobby sox and saddle shoes or leather boots that allowed plenty of room to flex her toes.

Oddly Bethany felt as if she herself were trapped in a cramped space and couldn't move freely. She sat so stiffly on the settee her back ached. Todd sat across from her, his rangy frame looking ill at ease in a Queen Anne chair. Until moving to Honeysuckle Lane, she hadn't known a Queen Anne from a Chippendale; chairs were just chairs—basic, ordinary, unadorned.

Todd unbuttoned his tweed jacket and inhaled sharply. "Would you like a cup of tea?" When she shook her head, he said, "Well, well! A lot has happened since you were here last."

She nodded and gazed around at the dark, raised-panel woodwork, the massive mahogany tables with ginger jar lamps, and the heavy red velvet drapes. It was a handsome, imposing room, but she missed the homey atmosphere of the Marshall parlor.

More than that, she missed the sweet, easy camaraderie she had felt with Todd the last time they were together. What had happened to that closeness?

"Perhaps Mother was right," said Todd, loosening his tie. "This wasn't a good idea. The party, I mean. We've both got our minds on other things."

"No," she said quickly. "I like parties. I want to help you celebrate your birthday."

"Good. Because Mother will probably have hats and horns and little mint cups beside our plates. An embarrassing carry-over from my boyhood. But I draw the line at playing 'Pin the Tail on the Donkey.'"

She laughed lightly. Clearly Todd wanted her to have a good time; he hoped as much as she did to break through the awkwardness that immobilized them. Perhaps they just needed this time alone together to recapture the magic spark between them.

But at dinner Bethany felt more tongue-tied than ever. She ate in silence while Eleanor chatted about Willowbrook's upcoming holiday events. "I'm sure all the parties will be quaint and charming," she purred, lifting her pinky as she sipped her tea. "If only the ladies of Indiana could see how we celebrate Christmas in New York, with charity balls and gala black-tie affairs!"

Bethany broke her silence at last, the words spilling out like a fountain. "We Hoosiers are real good at celebrating Christmas too. On the farm my papa used to take Luke and me out to chop down the biggest tree in the forest. If it was too big for the house, we'd set it up in the barn and decorate it with candles and popcorn and cranberries. And Papa would hook up the horses to an old sleigh and take us riding through the snow in the moonlight. Sometimes we'd go to neighbors' houses and he'd leave little gifts—combs and brushes from his big sample case. And he'd shout 'Ho-ho-ho,' so the little kids would think it was Santa Claus."

Eleanor sipped her tea. "How quaint, dear."

"Those are wonderful memories," said Todd with feeling.

For a moment Bethany thought he was mocking her; then she realized he was choking back tears. "What about your memories, Todd?"

"Like Mother said. Grand parties, fancy dinners, Christmas caroling, candlelight services at midnight. There's no time of year like Christmas!"

Eleanor set down her tea cup and gazed solemnly at Bethany. "Dear, I'm just sorry it won't be a happy holiday for your family this year."

Todd's fork clattered on his plate. "Really, Mother! We agreed not to bring that up."

"Bethany knows what I mean, Todd, darling. With all their troubles, her family will certainly find it difficult to enter into the spirit of the season. I want her to know we're praying for her."

Bethany managed a curt, "Thank you."

They finished dinner with a minimum of conversation. As Eleanor gathered the plates, she paused by Bethany's chair and said with a note of conspiracy, "Would you like to come help me in the kitchen?"

"Why, yes, I would." Bethany jumped up, cleared the table, and carried the soiled dishes to the kitchen. She stacked the delicate china beside the deep enamel sink while Eleanor stood at the counter, spreading fluffy mounds of white icing on a three-layer chocolate cake. When the icing was smooth, she squeezed out a tube of blue frosting and wrote Todd's name in fancy scrolled letters.

"The candles are in the drawer," she told Bethany. "Would you like to place them on the cake?"

As Bethany began inserting the small wax candles, Eleanor hovered close, watching. "May I give you a little piece of advice, dear?"

Bethany nodded. Was she placing the candles too close together?

"Stay away from my son."

Bethany looked up in confusion. "What did you say?"

"You heard me, dear." Eleanor's tone was venomous. "Stay away from my son. He doesn't need trouble like yours. He's not as strong as you think. You want someone to rescue you and take care of you. Todd can't be your knight in shining armor."

"I don't want a knight—"

"Yes, you do. I see it in your eyes when you look at my son. You've invented a hero from storybooks. You don't know Todd—his needs, his flaws, his failings."

"I haven't seen any flaws."

"Exactly my point. Todd is working hard to make a success of his life. He can't be embroiled in controversy. I wouldn't have chosen Willowbrook for him; the church didn't even give him a unanimous vote. But now that he's here, I intend to see that he establishes an impeccable reputation for himself. He can't do that with a girl like you, Bethany Rose *Henry*."

"That's not true."

"It is, dear. I'm sure you want the best for my son. There will be other, bigger churches in his future if he stays on track and doesn't put down his roots too deeply here."

Anger warmed Bethany's cheeks. "You can't tell Todd what to do. He's a grown man. He makes his own decisions."

Eleanor raised a deprecating eyebrow. "I'm sure he likes to think he does. But as strong as he pretends to be, I know how fragile he is at heart. Like his father, poor darling. Believe me, if you knew him as I do, you'd go away and let him be."

Bethany plunged the final candle so forcefully into the cake, a layer of frosting stuck to her hand. Eleanor handed her a tea towel and smiled thinly. "Think about what I said, dear. Now, shall we take my son his birthday cake?"

If Bethany still had doubts about Eleanor Marshall's possessiveness toward her son, they were dispelled as she watched her serve his cake. "Make a wish and blow out the candles, son. Wonderful! You got every one!"

Bethany watched, perplexed. It was as if Todd were still seven years old. Didn't he feel smothered by such fawning attention? No wonder he didn't enjoy his birthdays.

Bethany sighed with relief when Eleanor finally excused herself and, with one final, withering glance at Bethany, went upstairs to bed. Todd looked relieved too. He poured two cups of steaming tea and handed her one.

"No, it's getting late. I really should go."

"What's wrong? You've looked preoccupied ever since Mother brought in my cake. And you hardly ate a bite."

"Nothing's wrong. It's just . . ."

He led her over to the settee. "How about a little music?"

"No, Todd, I really can't—"

"Would you like to see our new television set?"

"Television?"

"It's quite the rage these days, you know."

She smiled relentingly and sat down beside him on the settee. "I know. Annie bought one a few weeks ago."

"What's the verdict? Will it replace radio?"

She made a face. "Only if you like watching a little screen with people moving around in a blizzard of snow."

"Yes, I've noticed that. But I've already grown fond of *The Life of Riley* and Milton Berle's *Texaco Star Theatre.* Not to mention the boxing matches."

Beth stirred a spoonful of sugar into her tea. "Annie's mama calls television 'that newfangled contraption.' She says it's just a fuzzy jumble of puppet shows, wrestling matches, and test patterns, and she'll keep her radio, thank you!"

Todd laughed. "Let's forget television. I have an excellent record collection—the latest by Schoenberg and Bernstein, and tunes from current Broadway musicals—Cole Porter's *Kiss Me Kate* and Rodgers and Hammerstein's *South Pacific*. Shall we go to the parlor and have a listen?"

"All right." Bethany had never heard of Schoenberg and Bernstein and was only vaguely familiar with Broadway musicals, but if Todd liked them, so would she. Maybe they could still have a pleasant evening together in spite of his mother.

Todd carried their teacups to the parlor and set them on the coffee table beside the old family Bible. While she sat down on the pink brocade sofa, he removed his tweed jacket, folded it, and laid it over the rattan rocker, then pulled his tie from around his button-down collar. "Hope you don't mind if I get comfortable."

"Sure, if I can kick off my shoes."

"Be my guest." He knelt beside the hearth and stoked the hungry flames in the massive rock fireplace, then put on a stack of records, adjusted the volume, and joined her on the sofa. "Now I'm enjoying my birthday!"

"Me too." She sipped her tea and wondered what he would say if he knew what his mother had said to her. But the mood was too nice to spoil with such disagreeable talk.

"This is my favorite room," Todd was saying. "It's where I relax, pray, study, meditate. I never had a room like this in our New York brownstone."

"What about the house you lived in with your dad?"

"Oh, yes, all the rooms were huge, but I was too young to appreciate them. And too young to appreciate my father."

Bethany drew her legs up under her plaid skirt. She felt pleasantly lulled by the toasty heat radiating from the fireplace. "You always get that faraway look on your face when you talk about him."

"My father? I suppose I do. I've never stopped missing him."

"You never told me how he died."

"I don't talk about it, Bethany. Words make the memories too vivid."

"Sometimes talking about sad things makes the hurt go away. That's what Annie says. She always listens when I talk about Mama."

He nodded. "Annie's a very compassionate person, I'm sure, but it takes more than talking to heal some wounds."

"Annie says that's what friends are for. Talking things out. The hurtful things. Are we still friends?"

He looked at her. "Of course. Why do you ask?"

She ran her thumb over a broken fingernail. "Once you told me we were courting, but since you found out who I am, it feels like that's changed."

"Not true, Bethany. I care about you. I want us to be good friends, more than friends. But I'm a man of the cloth. I'm trying to, uh, exercise proper restraint."

She met his gaze. "I don't know what that means. I just know I . . . I want to be close to you."

He looked away. For a while he sat twisting the gold cuff link on his starched cuff.

"You've never even held my hand, except on Sunday morning when you shake hands with everyone." She ran her fingertips over the downy hair on the back of his hand. "Are you afraid of me?"

He turned his hand over and clasped her long fingers. "Not of you. Maybe I'm afraid of my own feelings."

"I trust you, Todd."

"I'm not sure I trust myself."

She studied his sturdy, chiseled profile. "You're so different from the men I know—Jake back home, my brother Luke, even my papa, God rest his soul."

"Different how?"

"If Jake were courting me, he'd be stealing kisses all the time. I'd have to shoo him away with a fly swatter."

Todd smiled wryly. "Don't think I wouldn't like to steal a few kisses."

"Then why don't you?"

He pressed her hand against his lips. A delicious warmth rushed to her cheeks. "Just my hand?" she murmured. "Why not more?"

He shook his head, his face reddening.

"Are you thinking about the girl you loved? The one who stopped writing?"

"I suppose so, but not in the way you think."

"Do you still love her?"

"Love her? I'm not sure, but I can't forget her."

"Tell me about her."

The muscles along his jaw tightened. "I drove her away. I didn't mean to. I was young and foolish and hadn't experienced Christ's redemption yet. God has forgiven me, but I'm not sure I've forgiven myself."

"Did you try to find her?"

"Yes, but she had moved and left no address. It was as if she simply vanished from the earth." He pressed Bethany's palm against his, matching finger with finger. "Let's not talk about lost loves tonight."

The grandfather clock chimed the hour. They listened in silence, counting. Ten o'clock. "I didn't realize we'd been talking so long," said Todd. "I'd better get you home before your brother comes looking for you."

"Which brother?"

"Both!"

"First, tell me."

"Tell you what?"

"The secret about your papa."

Todd's face blanched. "Who says there's a secret?"

"I can tell. It makes you sad. I see it in your eyes when you talk about him."

He was still holding her hand, cradling it between his two large hands. "You're trying to comfort me, but I should be comforting you. I suffered my loss two decades ago. For you it's been just a few months."

"We both hurt. It helps me to help you. Tell me."

Todd lapsed into silence. He doubled his fist and pressed it against his mouth, as if physically holding back the words. Bethany watched a tendon flex from his temple to his jaw. His ruddy forehead glistened with a patina of moisture. She sensed an emotional battle raging inside him. A melancholy song was playing in the background, muted and scratchy, weaving its spell in their hearts. *Now Is the Hour*. The title said it all.

Todd sat forward and rubbed his temples. Bethany put her hand on his shoulder as a gesture of comfort. After a minute Todd looked at her. The struggle had gone from his face. "All right, I'll tell you about my father."

She sat motionless, hardly breathing as he spoke.

"My father was very wealthy and successful, a powerful man with great influence in our community. I learned that later, after his death. When I knew him, he was just Dad, the man who slipped me penny candy before dinner, rode me on his shoulders playing horsey, and read me the funny papers at bedtime. He spoiled my mother and me. Until the year I turned seven, the year the stock market crashed."

"That's what started the Depression, right?"

"Yes. It was Black Tuesday, October 29, 1929. My father lost everything. For weeks he tried to salvage enough to save the house, but on that cold November day—November 19th, my seventh birthday—the call came from Papa's attorney. Everything was gone. We were left penniless."

"Is that why you hate your birthdays?"

"That was only the beginning, Beth. After the phone call, my parents started arguing. It was just before dinner. I was sitting at the table waiting, my mouth watering for the birthday cake my mother had baked. Finally they came to the table and we ate as if nothing were wrong. My father even cracked jokes and laughed. I thought everything was fine.

"We had cake and I opened my presents. Then my father called me to his side. He took off his gold watch and put it on my wrist. He told me to keep it; it was mine now. He embraced me and whispered, 'Be a good little man. Take care of your mother.' I had no idea what he meant. I just felt an overwhelming sense of pride and duty."

Bethany moved her hand to Todd's wrist. "Was this your father's watch?"

He nodded and fingered the band, as if just realizing it was there.

"What happened after he gave you the watch?"

Todd's voice grew husky. He sat forward, his elbows on his knees, his head lowered. "After dinner my father excused himself, went to his study, and shut the door. A few minutes later we heard a gunshot. Mother ran to the door, but she wouldn't let me go in. She just stood there screaming. In my mind I can still hear that long, shrill, agonized wail."

For a long minute neither spoke. The room was silent, except for a phonograph record spinning out the doleful sound of a soprano sax.

Bethany moved close to Todd and whispered, "Hold me."

He slipped his arms around her. They rocked back and forth, as if they were at sea, buffeted by dark winds. They were still holding each other when the clock struck eleven.

12

If Bethany had expected her courtship with Todd to blossom after the tender moments they shared at his birthday celebration, she was quickly disappointed. At church on Sunday morning he was polite, even friendly, but on a deeper level he seemed to hold her at a distance. Had she offended him last evening? Was he embarrassed to have confided so much of his personal life to her?

After the service Annie, at Beth's prompting, invited Todd and his mother to Thanksgiving dinner. His face clouded. "Mother just accepted another invitation this morning."

Isabel Clarenton, the church organist—thirty if she was a day and plain as a mud fence, as Beth's mother would have said—sashayed up at just that moment and possessively clasped Todd's arm. "Dinner will be at two sharp on Thursday, Reverend Marshall. My mama said to tell you to be sure and bring a big appetite."

Bethany was livid. She clasped Todd's other arm and sputtered in his ear, "I thought we were courting! Last night you said—"

He gently disengaged himself from both ladies and stepped back with a heavy sigh. To Isabel he said, "Thank your folks for their kind invitation. Mother and I will see you on Thursday at two sharp." Turning to Bethany he said, "Please understand. It's just Thanksgiving dinner, and the Clarentons have been very supportive of my work here."

Bethany turned on her heel and ran outside to Knowl's car. They rode home in silence, Bethany inwardly fuming and resolving to put all thoughts of Todd Marshall out of her mind. As Thanksgiving Day approached, she threw herself into the hustle and bustle of holiday preparations. She helped Anna bake pumpkin and mincemeat pies, took Jenny for walks to gather autumn leaves, drew fat turkeys and smiling pilgrims to decorate Jenny's house, and prepared the guest room for her brother Luke's upcoming visit to Willowbrook—a visit she herself had instigated.

Two days before Thanksgiving she had persuaded Knowl to phone and invite Luke for the holidays. He did so halfheartedly and Luke warily accepted. Beth knew there was bad blood between the brothers, especially with Knowl's mother under investigation for their mother's murder. But if Bethany had managed to maintain cordial relations with the Herricks, why couldn't Luke do so as well? Whatever happened, she was determined to make Luke feel welcome at the Herrick house.

Luke arrived on Thanksgiving eve, bringing shiny gourds and a basket of Indian corn. "These are for Jenny. Enough for her to decorate her house and this one too."

When they were alone in his room, Beth asked Luke if he had heard any more news about the investigation. A shadow crossed his face; he turned away and started unpacking his worn valise. "The police are looking for the cabby who drove Betty Herrick to our house that night."

"They can't find him?"

"Naw. He moved out of state. Nobody knows where."

"But they need him as a witness. He's the only one who can prove Betty was there that night."

"Don't worry. They'll track him down."

"But when? How long will this whole thing drag out?"

"Don't get riled. The cops got other cases to solve, Bethany."

"I don't care about other cases! I care about this one. Don't you, Luke? How can you be so unconcerned?"

"I just put the whole mess out of my mind, that's how." His expression brightened as he said, "Listen, Beth. Jake said to say hello. He misses you. Wants you to come home. But, to tell you the truth, I figure you got a better life here in Willowbrook than marrying Jake and working that farm for his ma and pa."

She hung one of Luke's flannel shirts on a hanger and placed it in the narrow closet. "I do have a swell life here. They treat me good, Luke."

He handed her another shirt, red plaid. "They better treat you good, or they'll answer to me. Don't let 'em talk down to you because you grew up poor."

"They don't, Luke." She returned to his valise and removed the last few items—underwear, socks, a red checkered handkerchief—and tucked them in a bureau drawer. "I'm learning so much here," she continued avidly. "What all the silverware's for at the table, how to hold my pinky in the air when I'm sipping tea, and how to wear fine lady's dresses instead of flannel shirts and bib overalls."

"I can see the difference in you, Beth." He clasped her shoulders and turned her toward him. "Yeah, you're prettier than ever. I like the way you fix your hair now, the curls waving around your face and over your shoulders like one of them fancy actresses in your movie magazines. Just don't change too much, okay? You're still my little sister, the one I used to cart around in a wheelbarrow, remember?"

She laughed. "You always spilled me out on the ground!"

"All right, so I was a mite clumsy. I always picked you up again, didn't I?"

She gave him a spontaneous hug. "You were always there for me, Luke. Even when Papa was gone and Mama was too busy."

"And I'm here now—now and always—and I'm right proud of my baby sister!"

She clasped his arms with excitement. "Just think! I'm starting college in January. Me, Bethany Rose Henry, going to college!"

"So you're really happy here? Even with that Betty Herrick dame running loose?"

"She's under observation in a sanitarium, Luke. You know that. When the police gather enough evidence against her, she'll go to jail, or maybe to a mental hospital. She has to be crazy to do what she did to Mama."

"Don't get your hopes up about them putting her away."

"Why? They'll find the proof against her."

"Don't be too sure. I got a feeling we'll never know what really happened that night."

She looked him in the eye. "I won't give up until we know what happened to Mama. I don't care how long it takes!"

He swung her up in his arms. "Simmer down, little sister! I don't wanna talk about fretful things tonight. Thanksgiving's just the other side of midnight, and I'm ready to celebrate!"

She playfully tossed back her deep auburn hair. "Don't hurry it along, Luke. I got a hundred things to do before Anna puts the turkey on the table tomorrow. I may even tie an apron on you and put you to work!"

"Just try," he teased, tickling her ribs. "I promise you one thing. I'll make real short work of that turkey!"

She stifled her laughter. "Just you be good, Luke. I want to make it through the day without trouble."

"Don't you worry, Sis. I'll be a perfect gentleman—like our brother Knowl."

Indeed, Thanksgiving dinner went surprisingly well, considering there was such a variety of people around the table. Knowl, Annie, and baby Maggie were there, of course, and Robert and Catherine came with little Jenny. Bethany helped Anna serve the mashed potatoes, gravy, cranberry sauce, and green bean casserole. Luke was on his best behavior, as promised, and everyone did their best to make him feel at home.

The only glimmer of sadness came when Beth thought about Todd missing this glorious dinner. Isabel Clarenton, who had been looking for a husband nearly a decade, would be serving Todd his dinner today. Would he find her more suitable than Beth? Would he decide to court her instead?

Bethany kept her misgivings to herself while conversation around the table flowed as freely as the coffee and apple cider. Knowl and Robert were talking shop as usual. "Can you believe it? The Nobel Prize for literature won't even be awarded this year," said Knowl, brandishing a crispy, brown drumstick. "No candidate received a majority vote! A fine state of affairs, if you ask me."

"At least it was a good year for Pulitzer prizes," said Robert. "Arthur Miller's *Death of a Salesman* topped the list."

"A good year for plays, but not so good in other ways," mused Anna. "Look at Korea."

Luke's eyebrows shot up. "Korea?"

Anna nodded, her thin lips pursed. "If we're not careful, we'll be in another war—as if we haven't lost enough of our boys in the last one. My son Chip died for freedom. Have people already forgotten? How many more will have to die?"

Catherine reached over and patted Anna's hand. "No one's forgotten Chip. We see him every day in my sweet Jenny's face. He'll always live on in her and her children."

Jenny tugged on Cath's arm. "Are you talking about my soldier daddy—the one in the picture at home? The one who was very brave at Pearl, um, Pearl—"

"Harbor," said Cath. "Yes, sugarplum. Daddy Robert was there too, and he was just as brave as your other daddy."

Jenny looked over at Beth and said proudly, "Daddy Robert got shot in the leg. That's why he limps. He was very brave."

"My brother Luke was in the war too," said Beth, "at Normandy."

Luke raised his hands, palms out, in a protesting gesture. "The war's been over a long time. Let's forget it, okay?"

Robert frowned. "How can we forget it when the Communists have taken over North Korea and are threatening South Korea?"

"You're right, Robert," said Knowl. "With U.S. forces withdrawing last June, anything can happen now."

"We should stay out of it," said Anna. "Let the Koreans fight their own battles."

"And let the Communists take over the world?" said Cath. "We'd all lose our freedom then. Chip's death would be in vain."

Luke forked up a mound of mashed potatoes. "I wouldn't mind going to Korea. Maybe I'll just reenlist."

"You will not," said Bethany sharply. "What would I do without you?"

Luke chuckled. "Maybe settle down with that preacher boy you've got eyes for."

Bethany groaned inwardly. She didn't want to be reminded of the aggravating Todd Marshall, who stirred her deepest emotions one day and turned a cold shoulder the next. "I don't have eyes for any preacher I know of," she protested, and bit her lip at the lie. Even if Todd Marshall took up now with the prim and proper Isabel Clarenton, there was no way she could ever stop loving him.

Or could she?

For the next two Sundays Todd remained aloof when he greeted her after services. He spoke politely, of course, and offered a tight little smile as he wished her a pleasant week. But his forced kindness and genteel manners only seared her heart and left her feeling betrayed. What had happened to the sparks of passion that had flashed between them just a few short weeks ago? This stiff, bland, courteous man was a stranger now.

Worst of all, rumors were already circulating that Reverend Marshall was courting Isabel Clarenton. For the past two Sundays Todd's mother was seen sitting with the elder Clarentons in the front pew, and Beth couldn't help noticing that Isabel lingered in the vestibule after church, obviously waiting for Todd.

By the third Sunday of December—a cold, blustery, sleet-driven day, Bethany had had enough. When Todd shook her hand at the door, she held on tight and said, "Why are you doing this?"

He looked back blankly. "Doing what?"

"*This*," she insisted. "Acting like nothing ever happened between us."

He looked flustered. "Nothing did, Bethany. We were friends, nothing more."

"There was more. We felt it. Why did you stop calling?"

He lowered his voice. "This isn't something we can talk about here, Bethany."

"When?"

"Later. I don't know. I'll call you."

"No. Tell me now."

He glanced around, his face reddening. Several parishioners were waiting to greet him. "Wait in my office," he said at last. When he joined her minutes later he looked pale and a bit ruffled. "We can't talk here, Bethany. It wouldn't look proper."

"Then where?"

"Somewhere public. Perhaps the park by your house?"

"It's snowing out."

"That's all right. We're both bundled up in our warm, heavy coats. Do you have gloves?"

She nodded and pulled a pair of white mittens from her deep, nubby pocket.

"Good. My car's just outside."

She hesitated. "What about your mother?"

"The Clarentons drove her home."

As they stepped outside into the brisk, biting air, snow flurries whirled and danced around them, blinding them with a vivid whiteness. He took her arm and they crunched through fresh frosty drifts to his car. The air inside the vehicle was as cold as the air outside. Bethany hugged herself, shivering, as Todd turned the ignition and sighed as the engine coughed, sputtered, and died. After several more attempts, the engine wheezed and shuddered but kept running.

They were both silent as he pulled out of the driveway and chugged gingerly over icy pavement corrugated with dirty, brown snow. Driving even the short distance to the neighborhood park was treacherous. Several times the wheels veered off to one side or the other, seemingly with a mind of their own. Each time Todd seized the wheel and strained forward, peering out the snow-glazed windshield.

At the park he pulled off to the side of the road and turned off the engine. Immediately the chill began to seep in through every chink and joint of the automobile. Todd swiveled slightly in his seat, facing Beth. His cheeks and nose were ruddy with the cold, his eyes bluer than she'd ever seen them—a cold, icy blue.

"I'm sorry, Beth," he said in a throaty, emotion-filled voice. "So sorry. I should have talked with you before. It's my distaste for confrontation. I didn't want to hurt you."

She searched his eyes, feeling herself drawn into their cold azure depths. "What did I do wrong?"

"Nothing," he said quickly. "It's nothing you did. It's me. I've prayed about this. I've agonized over it. And God's voice is clear."

"Agonized over what? I don't understand."

"It's a spiritual battle." He ran his gloved hand over his lips. "The truth is, Bethany, it's not God's will for us to be together."

She felt a sinking in her stomach. "You mean, God doesn't want you to court me? He said this to you?"

"Not in so many words, of course, but I've felt it in my heart."

Beth's eyes glistened. She was hurt. More than hurt. Angry. With Todd. With his capricious God. "Does He say I'm not good enough because I'm poor? Because of what my father and mother did?"

He winced. "No, Bethany, it has nothing to do with your background. I just felt—"

"Maybe you felt wrong. Maybe you didn't hear God right."

He looked away and ran his hand over the steering wheel. "This is why I didn't want to get into this with you. I knew you wouldn't understand."

"I understand this much. God wouldn't do this to me. Not the God Annie talks about."

"Please, Bethany, I've spent years studying theology; I've dedicated my life to the ministry. I can't violate God's standards. I can't go against His clear teachings. When He tells me something, I must obey."

The words caught in her throat. "Why did He tell you to stop being my friend?"

Todd drummed his gloved fingers on the steering wheel. "Bethany, my mother brought something to my attention the night of my birthday party."

"What? About me? I was there. I would have heard her."

"No. I had already driven you home. I came back and found Mother sitting at the kitchen table drinking warm milk. She said she couldn't sleep, that something had been bothering her for some time."

Bethany frowned. "What did she say?"

"She told me she was quite certain you weren't a believer."

"A believer?"

"A committed Christian. I was stunned. I had just assumed you had made a profession of faith in childhood. After all, your family is a pillar of the church. Then she pointed out that you hadn't been brought up in the church, that you likely had no spiritual training whatsoever."

"I go to church now."

"I know, but my mother feels you've been misleading me. Tell me, Bethany. Is my mother wrong? Are you a believer?"

"I—I believe. Everything I know about God I've learned from you and the Herricks."

"Then you've accepted Christ as your Savior?"

She gazed down at her mittened hands. The coldness had turned her fingertips numb, and yet she felt a nervous warmth in her cheeks. "I don't know how. I want to someday, when I understand better."

Todd reached over and put his gloved hand over hers. "Someday isn't enough, Beth. God makes it clear in His Word that light can't mix with darkness, that a man and woman should not be unequally yoked."

She felt cold tears sting her eyes. "I don't know what that means."

"It means two people must be committed to Christ and serve Him together. They need to be of one mind, one heart, one purpose."

Beth trembled. The chill had invaded her skin, her very bones. Her nose felt cold, her lips stiff, as if she had to concentrate to form the right words. "I'm not smart like you. I could never be good enough. I couldn't serve God like you do."

He shook his head in frustration. "I'm not saying this right. It's not a matter of being good enough to serve God. None of us can earn God's favor. We've all come short of His glory. He asks us only to confess our sins and accept Him as our Savior."

"All right. I will."

"You will? Do what?"

"Do what you just said. How do I do it?"

"We . . . we pray together, but—Bethany, you don't invite Jesus into your heart just so you can marry the preacher. Do you understand? Don't do it just to please me."

"I will do it, and whoever is pleased, that's fine with me."

"I'm serious, Beth. You must come to Him for the right reason. Not just because you expect me to court you again."

"But if I do what you said, we will be—what you said—equally yoked?"

Todd heaved a sigh. It was so cold now she could see his breath in the air. "I've never been in quite this predicament," he confessed. "I blame myself. I was so drawn to you, I wanted to believe you had settled things with God. Now I feel I'm influencing you for the wrong reasons. I'm not sure how . . ."

She shivered again. Her toes were numb now. "Don't you want me to know God like you do?"

His aqua eyes probed hers. "More than anything in this world, Beth. But if you do it just to please me, it won't work."

She shook her head. "I'm confused, Todd. Should I do it or not?"

"I don't want to hold you back from the kingdom, Beth. I just want you to consider your motives. Make sure they're the right ones. Make sure your decision is between you and God, not between you and me."

"How can I be sure?"

He rubbed his gloved hands together. "It's getting too cold to sit here in the car. I'd better get you home."

"But what should I do?"

"Ask Annie for her Bible. Study the books of John and Romans in the New Testament. Search your heart, Beth. If you're ready to accept Christ regardless of whether we have a future together, then call me and we'll pray together. Or, I'm sure Annie would pray with you."

For the next several days, Bethany spent every spare moment reading and rereading Annie's worn, well-marked Bible. She lingered over the words of Jesus in the Gospel of John. *Except a man be born again, he cannot see the kingdom of God. . . . Ye must be born again. . . . For God so loved the world, that he gave his only begotten Son . . . whosoever believeth in him should not perish, but have everlasting life. . . . whosoever believeth . . . whosoever believeth!*

In Romans she studied Paul's words. *There is therefore now no condemnation to them which are in Christ Jesus. . . . all things work together for good to them that love God. . . . For whosoever shall call upon the name of the Lord shall be saved.*

On Sunday morning Bethany sat in the front pew beside the Clarentons and Todd's mother as Todd spoke on Jesus healing the leper. As he gave his closing invitation, he said, "Remember, beloved, before you ever accepted God, He accepted you—unconditionally, as you are. He reached out and touched the leper when no one else would. Who in our congregation today needs a touch of the Master's hand?"

Bethany stood up, her head high, walked to the altar and clasped Reverend Marshall's outstretched hand. "I want Jesus in my heart," she told him.

"Wonderful!" he declared. "The angels in heaven are rejoicing over another soul in the kingdom!" But privately he whispered to Bethany, "Are you doing this for the right reasons, Beth? Not just for me?"

"I don't know," she admitted quietly. "Maybe I'm doing it for all of us—you, me, and God. I just know God told me to walk up this aisle and get saved. He'll have to sort out all the reasons why I'm doing it."

13

"Annie, what should I wear? My cashmere sweater and velvet skirt or my corduroy dress with the patch pockets?" Bethany held up one outfit, then the other as she stood before Annie's full-length bedroom mirror. It was December 17th—a brisk, snowy Saturday morning.

"A sweater sounds nice and toasty on a cold morning." Annie sat at her dressing table brushing Maggie's cornsilk curls. The two-year-old, in a knit shirt and denim rompers, fidgeted, reaching for the talcum decanter and bottles of cologne as Annie struggled to fasten a gold barrette in her downy hair.

"Hold still, babykins. No, don't touch. Those are Mommy's pretties." Annie handed her daughter a stuffed Minnie Mouse doll and sent her scooting with a love pat on her padded derriere, then looked up at Bethany. "So, what's the special occasion?"

"Choir practice this afternoon. It's our last weekend to practice for the Christmas cantata."

"There's more to it, I'm sure. Your eyes are dancing."

"Afterward," Beth said, flashing a pleased smile, "Todd, um, I mean Reverend Marshall invited me over to help decorate his Christmas tree."

"I see. Sounds like fun."

"It's a party. With eggnog and cookies. And Christmas carols around the fire."

"Romantic!"

"It would be if it was just the two of us."

"Don't tell me. His mother too?"

"And Isabel Clarenton, among others. It's a party for the choir, actually. That's why I want the prettiest outfit."

"Then I'd definitely wear the cashmere and velvet." Annie gathered a handful of Beth's burnished ringlets on top of her head. "Tie back a few curls with a red velvet bow and let the rest cascade down your back. Todd won't be able to take his eyes off you."

Beth clutched the sweater and skirt to her chest. "Thanks, Annie. You always say the nicest things."

"I mean every word, Beth. Tell me, is Todd picking you up?"

"No, Cath is. She has to drive Jenny over to the church for her rehearsal anyway."

"That's right. Jenny's an angel in the children's Christmas program."

"The prettiest angel of all."

Annie smoothed the sleeve of the cashmere sweater. "In this outfit Todd will think you're the prettiest one of all."

"I hope so."

"You really care about him, don't you, Beth?"

"I—I think I love him, Annie."

"Does he know?"

"I haven't told him. He says we should just be friends. But I see something more in his eyes when he looks at me."

"You've spent a lot of time together since your baptism a couple of weeks ago. Was it his idea for you to join the choir?"

Beth nodded. "Now that I'm a member he wants me to be involved in the church. He wants to help me understand the Bible too."

Annie scooped Maggie up in her arms. "I'm glad Todd has taken you under his wing, but I can't help thinking . . ."

"What, Annie?"

"No, I shouldn't say anything."

"Please, tell me."

"All right. I can't help wondering if he's grooming you to become a . . . a minister's wife."

Beth's pulse quickened. "Do you really think so?"

"He's young and single, and he's taken on a big responsibility pastoring our church. I'm sure he's looking for a wife to share his ministry." Annie shifted Maggie from one hip to the other. "But it would be a very demanding life, Beth. A minister's wife needs to feel a calling from God just as her husband does. Without that calling it could be a disaster."

Bethany pressed her cashmere sweater against her cheek. "You don't think I'd make Todd a good wife, do you, Annie?"

"I didn't say that, Beth. It's just that you're a new Christian. I don't want Todd pushing you into a mold just to suit his purposes."

"He wouldn't do that."

"Not deliberately. But he may not even realize he's doing it. Give yourself time to get to know God without added pressures from Todd."

Bethany tried not to think about Annie's words as she rode to church with Cath and later as she reluctantly caught a ride to the Marshall home in the Clarentons' roomy Packard. Under her beaver coat Isabel was garbed in her frilliest dress and lace petticoats; her mousy brown hair was done up in a nest of tight ringlets and a spot of rouge dotted each pale cheek. She twittered endlessly about how pleased Reverend Marshall was that she was playing piano for the Christmas cantata. Bethany sat in the back seat staring out the window, watching the afternoon sun hover listlessly in a metallic gray sky. She closed her ears and gritted her teeth, lest she utter a naughty retort to the endless prattle of the annoying Miss Clarenton.

Several tedious minutes later, Bethany and the Clarentons were met at the Marshall door by Todd's mother, who beamed at Isabel and glowered at Beth. Seeing them, Todd broke away from several guests and greeted them with an expansive smile. "Come in, come in!" he urged. But as Bethany slipped off her heavy wool coat and handed it to an unsmiling Eleanor Marshall, she knew this wasn't going to be a pleasant occasion.

Still, as Bethany made her way to the parlor, her spirits lightened. The room was festive with bouquets of poinsettias, an enormous Christmas tree in the corner, pine wreathes in the windows, clouds of angel hair on the mantle, and Bing Crosby crooning "White Christmas" on an old Victrola. Todd handed her an eggnog and privately squeezed her hand, as if they shared a special secret. This party might be fun after all.

Beth's gaze lingered as Todd moved on, but even as he mingled with other guests, he glanced back at her and winked. He cared. Yes, he obviously cared. She relaxed, greeting others around her and letting herself enter into the frivolity and activities of the moment—tying red velvet bows on pine cones, stringing popcorn and cranberries for the tree, and adding her clear soprano to the carolers around the crackling fire.

But, later, as she paused by the silver tray brimming with sugar cookies, snicker doodles, and macaroons, Mrs. Clarenton sashayed over and said confidentially, "You will be needing a ride home after the party, won't you, Bethany Rose?"

"Thank you, but I don't think so."

"Oh, you already have a ride?"

"No, but I'll find one." She wasn't about to tell Mrs. Clarenton, but if she had her way Todd would be doing the honors.

Mrs. Clarenton ran a fluttery hand over her thinning brown hair.

"You realize, Bethany Rose, we drive right by Honeysuckle Lane. It's no trouble for us to drop you off."

"Thanks, but I'll be fine."

"If you change your mind . . ." Mrs. Clarenton selected a snicker doodle and held it poised near her thin red lips. "Tell me, dear, when do you start classes at Willowbrook Junior College?"

Beth helped herself to a red Santa cookie, thick with frosting. She bit off Santa's stocking cap. "Next month."

"How nice for you. I'm sure you'll enjoy college. My Isabel did. She studied music education at Purdue, you know."

Beth nodded, taking another bite, polishing off Santa's beard.

"And now she's teaching at Willowbrook Elementary," Mrs. Clarenton continued in a high, lilting voice. "Three years already. And such a way with children! She'll make some young man a fine wife someday." The plain-faced woman drew close to Beth and added with a conspiratorial air, "I think our Reverend Marshall has taken quite a shine to my Isabel. Wouldn't surprise me to see him courting her one of these days."

Beth slipped her last bite of cookie—Santa's boots—into her mouth and chewed slowly. Under her breath she murmured, "It would surprise me a whole lot!"

"What, dear?"

Before Beth could repeat herself, Todd sidled over with a basket of apples, oranges, fruitcakes, and candy canes, and said, "Come on, everyone. We're putting the finishing touches on the tree; then we're wrapping little gifts for the youngsters in the children's program."

With a parting nod at Mrs. Clarenton, Beth turned and followed Todd as he joined the others around the mammoth blue spruce in the far corner of the parlor. The thick, lush branches already glittered with red and gold bulbs, white tapered candles, red velvet Santas with cotton beards, silver garlands, and shimmery icicles. Stepping on a footstool, Todd reached up and placed a crystal star on the top of the tree.

By late afternoon the tree was trimmed, presents were wrapped, and Christmas cookies devoured. As guests began to leave, Bethany wondered how she'd get home. Please, Lord, not with the Clarentons! But who else would take her? Todd was the only one she wanted.

As she reached for her heavy wool coat on the hat rack, Todd appeared and whispered, "Don't rush off. I'll drive you home."

Stifling a smile, she returned her coat to the rack and watched with satisfaction as Isabel Clarenton, casting a longing glance at Todd, made her departure with a parent on each arm.

After all the guests were gone, Eleanor Marshall busied herself in the kitchen while Todd walked Bethany to the entryway and helped her on with her coat. He shrugged into his own overcoat and reached for the doorknob, then paused and looked up at the arched doorway. "Look, Bethany."

She gazed up at a green sprig of mistletoe above the door. Before she could reply, Todd bent down and grazed her lips with a kiss. They stood for a long moment, transfixed, neither one moving, their gaze locked. It had been a sweet kiss, like the flutter of a butterfly's wing, but Bethany yearned for more—for the warm, close embrace of the man she loved. Then, as if his desires matched—yes, even surpassed her own—Todd swept her up in his arms and kissed her soundly. Reluctant to break the spell, he pressed her face against his chest and held her in the circle of his arms. At last he released her, his breathing labored, and murmured, "You don't know how long I've wanted to do that."

"You don't know how long I've waited," she said breathlessly.

He drove her home over the icy, snow-clogged streets, but she saw only the spangled glitter of stars over a wintry wonderland. All the dreams she'd ever gleaned from her movie magazines, all the hopes she'd hidden in her heart, all the sweet fantasies spun in her imagination seemed possible tonight. She was Jennifer Jones romanced by Laurence Olivier or Lauren Bacall with her devoted Humphrey Bogart. This was better than the movies; this was real; Bethany Rose Henry was the young starlet and Todd Marshall her handsome leading man. The moment was complete except for the grand swell of an orchestra serenading them; but no, she had even that. The music swelled from her heart, crescendoed in her emotions.

"I've had a wonderful time," Todd told her as they walked through the drifting snow to her door. "I'll see you at church in the morning."

"I can't wait," she murmured, facing him, watching the moonlight glint in his eyes.

"After the choir sings, come sit in the front pew so I can see your eyes and your smile as I deliver my sermon."

She felt the color rise in her cheeks. "I'll be there." *And I won't take my eyes off you, either!*

As she stepped inside the Herrick house and closed the door behind her, the clean, spicy scent of Todd's skin still lingered in the chill air. She leaned against the heavy, carved door and closed her eyes, savoring the taste of his lips on hers. So vivid was the memory, she hardly heard the telephone ringing until Anna appeared in the hallway and said, "Bethany, you're just in time. The phone's for you. It's your brother Luke."

"Luke?" She hung her coat hurriedly on the coat rack and took long strides to the parlor. Luke hardly ever called. Maybe he wanted to make plans for Christmas. He would have to come here. Surely Knowl wouldn't mind. She felt breathless as she put the receiver to her ear and said hello—breathless over Todd or from hurrying, she wasn't sure.

"Bethany? Is that you?"

"Of course it's me. Who else?"

"Listen, Beth—" Luke's voice sounded strange, like someone had tied a clothesline around his neck and was tightening it.

"What's wrong, Luke?"

"I'm in big trouble."

Her skin bristled. "What happened?"

"I—I'm in jail, Bethany."

"Jail?"

"Here in Fort Wayne."

"Why? What'd you do?"

"Nothing! I done nothing, Beth."

"Then why—?"

"These fool cops. They . . . they think I killed Mama!"

The blood in Beth's veins turned to ice. "Mama?"

Luke was almost blubbering now. "They came in their big black car and dragged me off the farm. They booked me like a lowlife thug and stuck me in a stinking cell. You tell them, Bethany, I wouldn't hurt Mama. I'd never hurt Mama!"

"Luke, listen to me. I don't see how—"

"They just come and got me, Beth. They put handcuffs on me and put me in a lineup and somebody picked me out—said I was at the farmhouse that night. Sure I was. I lived there, but I was asleep. No matter what I say, the crazy fools are gonna charge me, Beth. They say they got evidence!"

Beth was trembling now. This was a bizarre mistake. "What can I do, Luke?"

"Tell Knowl. Tell him to call his fancy lawyers and get me out of here. Help me, Beth. Ain't nobody else I can call!"

"I'll talk to Knowl, Luke. We'll come soon as we can. You just hold on."

"I'm not going nowhere, Sis. Just get here pronto!"

Beth hung up the phone and sank down on the tufted sofa. Her head was spinning. Nothing Luke had told her made sense.

"Bethany? Are you okay?" It was Annie, standing in the doorway with baby Maggie. "Is something wrong? My mother said Luke called."

She nodded. Her throat felt too tight to speak.

"Is he okay?"

"No." Beth stood up shakily. "Where's Knowl?"

"He just got home. He's washing up for dinner."

Beth wrung her hands. "I need to talk to Knowl right away."

"Talk to me about what?" Knowl ambled into the parlor, still dressed in his navy pinstripe suit. He loosened his silk tie and removed his gold cufflinks, his gaze focused all the while on Bethany. "What's going on, Beth?"

"It's Luke," she said in a wail of anguish. Then the words tumbled out, what little she knew of Luke's appalling, improbable account.

Knowl looked stunned. He removed his glasses and rubbed the bridge of his nose. "He's in jail? Charged with your mother's death?"

"He didn't do it, Knowl. You know he didn't. You know it was your mama—"

"No, Bethany, I don't know that." He replaced his glasses. "No one knows exactly what happened in your house that night."

Bethany crossed her arms. "It wasn't Luke. I know that much."

Knowl walked over to the phone and picked up the receiver. "We'd better get the story. What was that detective's name who paid us a visit?"

"Staats? Stanton? Something like that," said Annie.

"Stassen," said Knowl. "Detective Stassen." He dialed the operator. "Connect me with the Fort Wayne police department, please. Thank you. Yes, I'll hold." He drummed his fingers on the tabletop.

"Luke needs a lawyer," Beth whispered urgently.

"A lawyer? First let's find out what trouble he's in." Knowl turned his attention back to the phone. "Yes, officer, I'm calling from

Willowbrook. The name's Herrick. Knowl Herrick. I'd like to speak to Detective Stassen. Oh? When will he be there? Okay, I'll—"

Bethany clasped Knowl's arm. "Find out about Luke!"

Knowl nodded. "Officer, I received word tonight that my brother was arrested. Luke. Luke Henry. That's right. I'd like to know what the charges are. . . . You're sure? Would you tell him his sister and I will be there tomorrow to see him. Tell him to hold tight. We'll be there."

Knowl hung up and turned to Beth. "I'm sorry. Everything Luke told you is true. He's being held for questioning in connection with your mother's death."

"No, no!" Beth seized Knowl's jacket lapels and collapsed against him, burying her face against his chest.

He held her for a long moment, then released her. "You'd better get some rest, Beth. We have a long day ahead of us."

They left for Fort Wayne the next morning, Knowl's DeSoto rumbling over the mud-streaked, snow-rutted highway. All the way through the gray, gloomy countryside Bethany numbly replayed her conversation with Luke, trying to make sense of it all. The harder she tried, the more implausible it seemed.

"I can't believe this is happening," she told Knowl as they entered the Fort Wayne city limits. "My brother in jail!"

Knowl slowed his speed. "I know, Beth. I felt that way when the police accused my mother. All we can do is try our best to find out the truth and trust God to see us through it."

"It's a terrible mistake."

"Let's not despair until we hear what Detective Stassen has to say."

They entered the modest station house and spoke with one sergeant, then another. No one had information about Luke Henry. Finally an officer told Knowl and Beth to take a seat and Detective Stassen would speak with them shortly. Exchanging private grimaces, they sat down and waited on a hard bench in a smoke-filled room beside a wall of windows smudged with grime. A half hour passed before Detective Stassen emerged from another room and lumbered over to them in the same rumpled suit he had worn to Willowbrook.

He stuck out a beefy hand and offered a faint smile, his thick jowls swelling against his unbuttoned white shirt. A loose tie hung around his neck like an afterthought. "Nice to see you folks again," he said, as if this were a social call.

"I want to see my brother," Beth said evenly, her clammy hands clenched at her sides.

"Your brother? Oh yeah, that's right. Luke Henry. He's here, all right."

"Why is he here?" asked Knowl sharply.

Detective Stassen massaged both his chins. "Now that's a real interesting story. Maybe we all better go sit down in my office and chat a spell."

They followed him into a dreary cubicle where fresh air was at a premium and thin sunlight strained through small, smudged windowpanes. Knowl took the narrow ladder-back chair and Beth claimed the squat one with a cane seat.

Detective Stassen lowered himself into his swivel chair and reached for a ceramic mug on his desk. "You two want coffee? I'll get you some. It's a bit tepid now, but it's a hearty brew. Made it myself."

"No, thanks," said Knowl. "We just want some answers."

The corpulent detective took a leisurely swallow from his mug and wiped his mouth with the back of his hand. Bethany sensed that he enjoyed playing center stage. "It took us a while to put the pieces together," he said, eyeing Bethany. "But it looks like we've got our man." He picked up a toothpick, placed it between his lips, and chewed thoughtfully.

"What pieces?" said Knowl with an edge of impatience.

"I'm getting to it. Like I said, it's a long story. Took us months to track down the cabbie who drove your mother to Meadowlake Road that night."

Knowl sat forward. "The cabbie?"

"Yep. He moved outta state late last summer. No forwarding address. We finally found him in a little one-horse town in Georgia. I drove down myself and questioned him. Took his statement. Brought him back here. Had him take a look at a lineup."

"But if he drove my mother to Laura Henry's that night, how is Luke involved?"

"He drove her, all right."

"Then answer us," insisted Beth. "Why have you arrested Luke?"

"Here's where the story gets interesting." The ruddy-faced detective leaned forward on both elbows. "For a long time now we've known Betty Herrick couldn't have killed Laura Henry. That's why we haven't brought her in for questioning—that and the fact that she's not all there upstairs."

Knowl sprang to his feet and planted his hands squarely on the desk. "You've known that my mother's innocent and you haven't said a word to us? Great Scott, man, what kind of law enforcement officer are you?"

"Hold your horses, Mr. Herrick. Your mother's involved, all right, but we know now she couldn't have done the actual deed. Laura Henry died when her temple struck the corner of a heavy metal chest. She didn't fall against it; she was thrown hard. Betty Herrick is too small a woman to exert such force. It had to be someone strong and powerful, someone like Luke Henry."

"You don't know it was Luke," Beth protested. "A stranger could have broken in—a thief, anybody!"

"That's right. That's why we had to get the cabbie's story. And that's just what we did."

"What'd he tell you?" demanded Knowl, sitting back on the edge of his straight-back chair.

Detective Stassen ran a stubby forefinger over his thick, bristly brows. He picked up a sheet of paper on his desk and scanned it, although Bethany suspected it had nothing to do with this case. Finally his pale gray eyes met Beth's. "Here's the story. The cabbie drove Betty Herrick to your house that night. She told him to wait in the driveway; she'd only be a few minutes, so he sat there, the meter running. It was a hot night; all the windows were open in the house and in the cab. He heard some arguing—two women shouting at each other. He started watching the screen door with a real eagle's eye, thinking there might be trouble and not wanting to get caught up in it."

Detective Stassen reached for his mug and took a long swallow. Bethany could smell the coffee on his breath clear across the desk. Cupping the mug in his brawny hands, he leaned back in his chair, inhaled deeply, and went on with his story. "After about twenty minutes the screen door opened and Betty Herrick came striding out. She was upset, spewing a stream of vile words as she got back in the cab."

"That proves it," said Beth. "She was mad enough to push my mother down. I've heard people have superhuman strength when they're angry."

"Just one problem, Miss Henry."

"What's that?"

"After Mrs. Herrick came stomping out of your house, the cab driver saw two people through the screen door—a man and a woman. He swears the man was your brother Luke and the woman was your mother. So, you see? Laura Henry was still alive when Betty Herrick left. And the fire—well, the cabbie was dropping Mrs. Herrick off at the motor court about the time the fire started."

The balding detective turned his mug in his hands, round and round, as if playing a game. "That brings us back to the scene of the crime, doesn't it? We have one victim, your mother, and right now one suspect, your brother. Of course, you were there too, weren't you, Miss Henry? But with your slight build you couldn't have pushed your mother any more than Betty Herrick could have. So it all comes back to Luke."

Tears brimmed in Beth's eyes. "He wouldn't hurt Mama. He'd never hurt her. He loved her more than anybody on earth!"

Knowl stood up and cleared his throat. "You think you've got it all worked out, Detective, but the evidence is entirely circumstantial. Luke hasn't confessed to anything, has he?"

"That boy? No, not a word. Says he won't talk till you get him a lawyer."

"Well, that's just what I intend to do. How much is his bail?"

"That'll be set at his preliminary hearing. You can bet it'll be steep. We're talking arson and homicide. And if the district attorney brings in an indictment of first degree murder, there won't be no bail."

"When is the hearing?"

"Don't know. That'll be up to the district attorney. Maybe a week, ten days."

"Then I want you to set Luke free until the hearing."

"Let me give you a friendly little warning, Mr. Herrick. That brother of yours is a loose cannon. We'd like to keep him under lock and key until the hearing."

"In that case, I'll talk to my attorney and find out just what rights Luke has."

"Then again, maybe we could remand him to the custody of someone with plenty of power and clout, somebody who can keep a lid on that boy and make sure he doesn't skip the state."

Knowl's brows arched. "You're suggesting I take Luke home with me?"

"May be the only way."

Bethany seized Knowl's arm. "Please, Knowl! Luke's your brother. Please help him!"

Knowl patted her hand, but his brow remained deeply furrowed. "Let me talk with my lawyer and see what he advises."

"Fair enough." Detective Stassen stood up. "You wanna see your brother now?"

"Yes," said Beth. "Please!"

"He's in lock-up. Just so you know the procedure, you'll be searched; guards will remain in the room. You'll have to talk to your brother through a mesh screen. No touching, just talking. You going in too, Mr. Herrick?"

"If Luke wants to see me."

"Fine and dandy. Come with me. And keep it brief, okay?"

Bethany and Knowl were ushered into a cold, drab room partitioned by a long utilitarian table with a metal screen stretching all the way to the ceiling.

"One at a time," said the stony-faced guard, thumbing Knowl back.

Beth crossed the room, sat down gingerly on a primitive pine chair, and waited as a guard on the other side brought Luke in, garbed in seaweed-green coveralls. His thick, dark hair was disheveled, his lean face looked haggard, and his handsome mouth was twisted in a grimace. "Oh, Luke!" she cried as he sat down and turned sullen, despairing eyes on her.

"They framed me, kiddo," he drawled. "They gotta pin this rap on someone, and that's me."

"Knowl will help you, Luke. He promised. He's calling his lawyer tomorrow."

"Can he get me outta here?"

"He'll do his best. Detective Stassen says the judge might release you into Knowl's custody. You'd have to come to Willowbrook until your preliminary hearing."

Luke sneered. "Go live with my big brother in his fancy house? You gotta be kidding."

"It may be the only way, Luke."

"I bet that's got my brother dancing for joy. Luke Henry strutting around Honeysuckle Lane like a rich boy."

"Don't spoil it, Luke. Knowl's trying. Talk nice to him, please!"

"I don't want him doing me no favors."

"Then you'll rot in jail, Luke. Is that what you want?"

The mockery drained from Luke's face. "I want outta this rat hole, Bethany Rose. They got nothing to hold me on. I need fresh air and the big outdoors, not a dingy closet with bars." He lowered his head and cupped his hands over the back of his neck. "Thunderation! How'd I get into this mess!"

She leaned forward, her mouth only inches from the screen, so close she could smell the tarnished metal, and whispered, "What happened that night, Luke? You told me you were sleeping, like me. But the cab driver says he saw you in the house with Mama. Tell me the truth."

"The man's blind, Beth. He didn't see nothing. He just told the cops what they wanted to hear."

"But he identified you, Luke. You were in the lineup and he picked you out."

"I tell you, it's a frame-up. The cops wanna close this case; they gotta finger somebody. I'm their stooge."

Bitter tears welled again in Beth's eyes. "You wouldn't lie to me, not about something like this. Not about Mama and the fire. I know you wouldn't hurt Mama. You'd never burn down our house. I know that, Luke."

He pressed his long fingers hard against the screen, as if by sheer will he could reach beyond the net and caress Bethany's face. "Convince the rest of the world, little sister, and I'll be home free."

14

On Tuesday, December 20th, Knowl and his attorney, Arnold Kraslow, drove to Fort Wayne and made arrangements for Luke to be released into Knowl's custody. That evening, when the brothers arrived back in Willowbrook, Bethany greeted Luke with tears of relief. "It's going to be okay," she promised. "You're safe now."

He looked weary and careworn as he gave her an enormous bear hug. "I hope so, Sis. I'm sure glad to be outta that cell."

"It's not over," said Knowl, loosening his tie. "Luke's hearing is set for the first week of January."

Beth clasped Luke's hand. "What happens then?"

"He'll be officially charged, bail will be set or denied, and he'll enter his plea."

"Not guilty!" declared Luke. "Those blockheads are crazy if they think they can pin this rap on me!"

"Save it, Luke," said Knowl. "Your attorney's going to need your full cooperation, so keep a clear head. You and Kraslow have your work cut out for you."

"Knowl's right," said Beth. "This could be the most important battle of your life, Luke."

He slammed his fist against his palm. "Man alive, I already fought a war! Now I gotta fight for my life all over again!"

Bethany gave him a consoling embrace. "Don't think about it now. It's Christmas and you're with family. Let's try to have a good time."

From the corner of her eye she caught Knowl's dubious expression. She knew he had taken Luke in against his better judgment and would be watching him with hawk eyes. "Everything's going to be all right, won't it, Knowl?" she prompted.

He sighed, his eyes solemn as he gripped Luke's shoulder, then turned away. "Yes, Lord willing, all will be okay!"

In the days that followed, no one in the Herrick household seemed to know exactly what to do with Luke, or how to treat him, except for Anna, who fussed over him like a mother hen, and little Maggie, who took to him with a toddler's unabashed delight.

Only Catherine expressed outright dismay over Luke's temporary sojourn. She told Bethany, "Don't expect me to come around much while he's there. We may be related, but I'll never forget the way he kidnapped me. I'll never trust him again."

Luke seemed to sense he was on trial, not only before a court of law, but also with the Herricks. With a minimum of complaints he accompanied the family to Sunday services, the Christmas cantata, the children's program, and Wednesday night prayer meeting. When Knowl offered him a temporary job in the shipping department at Herrick House Publishers, loading cartons of books on trucks, Luke grudgingly accepted. It was as if he knew his time in Willowbrook was the peace before the storm, or maybe he was already steeling himself to face a prison term.

During the holidays, as Bethany fretted over Luke's future, she found hope and solace in the arms of Todd Marshall. Together they prayed for Luke and sought God's guidance for their own lives. In his gentle expressions of comfort and goodwill, Todd seemed to be offering something more—an unspoken promise to watch over Bethany and protect her from life's harsh realities. He never pledged such promises aloud, but she read them in his eyes, in his touch, in his fervent tone when they prayed about their future.

During the communion service on New Year's Eve, the congregation of Willowbrook Christian Church celebrated a new year, a new decade, and the twentieth century's halfway mark. As the steeple bells rang in the first moments of 1950, Bethany sat, head bowed, holding her wafer and tiny cup of grape juice and asked God to let Todd be the man He had chosen for her. A deeper question loomed in her heart, but she pushed it away, feeling guilty for entertaining such a thought when she held the elements of Christ's Last Supper in her palm. As she placed the wafer on her tongue, the unsettling question crept back into her consciousness: Would she still choose to serve God were Todd Marshall not part of the package?

On January 3rd Bethany started classes at Willowbrook Junior College and quickly discovered a thirst for learning she hadn't experienced in high school. Perhaps her new motivation sprang from her blossoming love for Todd. He enjoyed delving into books—theology, historical tomes, the classics—and exploring new ideas and other worlds. He would want the woman he loved to possess that same hunger for knowledge.

But beyond that, Bethany felt her own inner stirring, an awakening of her heart, her mind, her soul. She realized she wasn't satisfied to live vicariously through her movie magazines anymore. The lives of Hollywood starlets and leading men seemed remote and irrelevant these days, especially when her own life was brimming with wonderful possibilities.

The only cloud hanging over her head was Luke's preliminary hearing. Would he be charged and brought to trial? Would a jury find him guilty and send him to the penitentiary? He had survived a world war, but could he survive prison? Beth knew the answer. Luke had grown up on a farm, free to stretch and grow in the wide open spaces of Indiana's lush heartland. He wasn't the sort of man to live behind bars.

The day before the hearing, Luke's attorney stopped by to report that the district attorney's office had requested a two-week delay to complete their investigation. "These boys mean business," Kraslow told Knowl. "I was hoping they'd settle for a charge of involuntary manslaughter, but I got a feeling they'll be pushing for a murder conviction. Maybe even first degree. If that's the case, you'd better bring in a defense attorney from Indianapolis. I can handle the smaller stuff, but Luke's going to need someone with solid experience in murder trials—a big-time lawyer with lots of success stories. I can recommend a man named Kimbrough. Most of his clients have been found innocent."

"Then call him, Knowl, please," Bethany begged. "Don't wait until the hearing. Call him now, so we'll be ready, whatever comes—because if there's one thing I'm sure of, it's Luke's innocence."

"All right, I'll give this fellow a call tomorrow," Knowl agreed, adding privately to Bethany, "I just wish I had the same faith in Luke you do."

She gave Knowl a quick kiss of gratitude. "It's okay. I have enough faith in Luke for all of us!"

It was true. In her heart of hearts she knew her brother would never lay a hand on their mother. Granted, with his fiery temper he had had his share of brawls and fist fights, but he had never manhandled a woman. And yes, he could be impulsive and foolish at times; he had been stupid enough to kidnap Cath and drag her off to Fort Wayne to introduce her to her father's other family. But that hadn't been his only motivation; it went deeper than that. He had done it for Papa, out of a misguided desire to reunite a daughter with her dying father.

A son who was that devoted wouldn't harm his mama, wouldn't

burn down the house of his childhood. There had to be another explanation. Knowl's mama had been the logical suspect. How was it possible that Betty Herrick had been at the house that night and wasn't guilty of the crimes?

Several days later, when Bethany asked Luke about that night, he refused to discuss it. When she asked how the cab driver could have seen him in the house with Mama when he was supposedly in the back bedroom sleeping, he just shrugged his shoulders and turned away. When in a fit of frustration she came right out and demanded, "Did you hurt Mama? Did you burn down our house?" he looked her in the eye and answered, "What do you think?"

Bethany always came back to the same thought: The Luke she knew and loved would never do such grisly deeds. And that's what she had to hold on to for her own peace of mind.

On the second Saturday of January Bethany celebrated her twentieth birthday. Anna prepared her favorite dinner—fried chicken and dumplings—and invited Cath's family and Todd Marshall over. Catherine agreed to come as long as she didn't have to sit beside Luke.

After dinner everyone gathered in the parlor and sipped hot cider while Beth opened her gifts. The first present was a collection of records by Bing Crosby, Nat King Cole, and Peggy Lee.

"These are wonderful! Now if only I had something to play them on!"

"And you do." Knowl set a large, mysterious box on the rosewood table. "From us to you. Open it."

She tore off the wrappings and read the bold black letters on the box. *Capehart three-speed automatic phonograph. Plays standard 78s, plus sensational new long-playing 33-1/3 and small 45 rpm discs.*

"Oh, Knowl. This is grand! I love it! Thank you!"

Cath handed her a long, flat, foil-wrapped box and said with a hint of mystery, "This is to wear when Todd takes you out on the town."

He laughed. "Uh-oh. I'm in trouble now."

"Maybe, maybe not," Beth teased. Everyone strained to see what was inside the tissue-lined box. Beth gently held up a black taffeta sheath dress with a white flared cape—the most elegant outfit she'd ever seen. "Oh, Cath, it's perfect!"

"I'd better take her to Chicago or Detroit," said Todd with a grin. "There's no place in Willowbrook sophisticated enough for a dress like that."

Amid a ripple of laughter, Todd broke in again. "Before we all get entirely off track, I have a gift for the birthday girl." He handed Beth a foil-wrapped package the size of a shoe box.

"Should I shake it and guess what it is?"

"Only if you want it in a million pieces."

"I know! It's the world's largest jigsaw puzzle," teased Cath.

Bethany opened the box carefully. "Whatever it is, it's breakable." She lifted out a satin music box with a crystal ballerina on top. She wound it and set it on the table. The delicate dancer revolved to the tune of "Let Me Call You Sweetheart." She blinked rapidly and smoothed back her crimped curls with both hands. "It's beautiful!"

Todd tugged at his shirt cuff. "It reminded me of you."

She reached over, clasped his hand, and whispered, "I love it," but she really meant, *I love you!*

For a long moment no one said anything, and Beth began to wonder if she'd said the words aloud. Todd's eyes were on her, loving and tender, crinkling at the edges with a hint of merriment. He was reading her heart as surely as she read his. "I hate to be a spoilsport," said Cath, standing up, breaking the spell, "but it's getting late, and I'm bushed. Robert, we'd better get home."

"I'll go upstairs and get Jenny," he said, standing too.

"She's asleep in Maggie's room," said Annie. "I tucked them in right after dinner. The two were all cuddled up together. Why don't you just let her stay the night, Cath?"

Catherine looked doubtful. "I don't know, Annie. I like having my daughter close by, so I can peek in on her in the night. You understand."

Annie nodded, her smile fading. "Yes, I know. Only too well."

Robert slipped a protective arm around Cath's waist. "Listen, honey, Annie's right. Let's just let Jenny sleep here tonight. We'll get her in the morning. Besides, you can use your beauty rest."

Knowl ambled over to Cath and gently pinched her cheek. "Your husband's right, Sis. You look like you could use a good night's sleep. You've been a little pale lately."

Catherine and Robert looked at each other with a knowing smile.

"Is something going on here we don't know about?" asked Annie.

Cath let out a little sigh. "You all might as well know." She patted her middle. "Robert and I are expecting a baby this summer. A little baby brother or sister for Jenny."

Annie went to Cath and gave her a hug. "That's wonderful!"

Cath looked over at Beth. "I didn't mean to break the news at your party and steal your thunder."

"I'm glad you did. Nothing's more special than a baby." Beth stole a glance at Todd and wondered what it would be like to be his wife and have his baby. The idea turned her face crimson. Surely Todd noticed, because when he met her gaze he averted his eyes as quickly as she did.

It was after ten before everyone said good night and headed off for home or bed—Cath and Robert to their house around the corner, Knowl and Annie upstairs to their room, and Anna to hers.

"I think I've overstayed my welcome," said Todd, ambling over to the fireplace to warm his hands.

"Don't go yet," said Beth. "It's my birthday. Stay a little longer."

"All right. A few more minutes." He sat down beside her on the love seat and swung his arm lightly around her shoulder.

She moved closer to him and nuzzled his neck. She wished she was wearing the new outfit Cath had given her instead of her simple laurel-green knit dress. "When do I get my birthday kiss?" she asked, only half teasing.

He smiled with a glint of amusement, then tilted her chin up to his and kissed her gently on the lips. "Happy birthday, Bethany Rose."

"Don't stop," she whispered.

He kissed her again, with a slow, simmering urgency. Between kisses, she gazed into the azure depths of his eyes and thought, *I worship you*, then thought with chagrin, *It's not right to worship a man!*

He pulled away from her and ran his hand through his thick chestnut hair. "I'd better go, Bethany."

"Why? Did I do something wrong?"

"No. I'm leaving before *I* do something I regret."

"You think it's wrong to kiss me?"

He faced her again and took her hands in his. "Please understand. I care too much to risk hurting you, Beth."

She pressed his hands against her lips. They were strong hands with sturdy, tapered fingers, a man's hands and yet smooth and clean and perfectly manicured, not like a farmer's rough, calloused hands with dirt embedded in the creases. Not like Jake's hands. "You won't hurt me, Todd. You could never hurt me. Just don't go."

"I've got to." He gently withdrew his hands. Something dark and frightening moved in the shadows of his face. She felt the distance growing between them. "I pray for peace about our future together," he said, speaking out of an anguish she couldn't comprehend. "I've agonized over this with the Lord. You have no idea how I've pleaded for guidance, for direction, for confirmation. But I don't have the answers yet, Beth. Don't you see? I don't dare take from you what's not mine to have, what might never be in God's plan for me."

"You're not taking," she said, touching his wrist just below his starched white cuff. "I love you, Todd." There, she had said it. It no longer hung like an unspoken question between them.

"I love you too," he said after a long, uneasy moment, but not with the dulcet tones she wanted to hear. He said it, not joyously, not with the sweet abandon of romance, but as if it were a burden. It was clear. He loved her, but he didn't want to love her.

A heaviness settled inside her, cold and hard as a rock. "Why do you always do this?" she whispered, near tears.

"Do what?"

"Make me want you, then push me away. You kiss me, then you stop and pick everything apart. You make everything hard, and complicated, and confusing."

"Because it is, Bethany. I'm a man with huge responsibilities, a man who must answer to God and his church. If I'm to serve Him faithfully, my life must be without blemish."

"Am I a blemish?"

"Of course not."

"Then why can't you serve God with me? Why can't we serve Him together?"

Smiling, he drew close to her again and rubbed a tear from her cheek. "That's my prayer. But God may be testing me, to see whether I love you or Him more. I must be true to Him first, and if He would give me you, I would be of all men most glad."

She blinked; huge tears dotted her lashes. "You are a fine, upstanding man, Todd Marshall. The most honorable man I ever met. I wish I could please God the way you do."

He chuckled self-consciously. "I'm no saint, believe me."

"But you are, Todd. You are to me. You're a good, good man."

He lightly kissed the top of her head. "If I'm to remain a good man, I'd better say good night." He stood up, straightened his tie, and buttoned his jacket.

She walked him to the door and stood in the silent, marble entryway as he pulled on his heavy wool overcoat. He brushed a kiss on her lips, clutched a handful of her curls, and gently knuckled her ear. Then, with a graceful sweep of his arm, he put on his hat and snapped the brim as he cocked it on his head. "Good night, birthday girl. Sweet dreams."

She felt a sudden inrush of icy wind as he opened the door and stepped out onto the sprawling porch with its frosty veneer of new-fallen snow. She shivered and closed the door after him, and pressed her face against the solid, carved mahogany. "Good night, Todd," she whispered. "I'll always love you."

But the chill in the air lingered inside her. She knew, with a swift, cold certainty, no matter how much she loved him, she would never be good enough for a man like Todd Marshall.

15

On January 18th, two days before his preliminary hearing, Luke called Bethany into his room and shut the door after her. He placed his hands squarely on her shoulders and said softly, "Little sister, I'm leaving. I won't be seeing you for a while."

"Leaving?" she echoed in bewilderment.

"Yeah. Don't worry. I'll be in touch."

"Where are you going?"

"I don't know. I got me a few dollars and soon as spring comes I'll pick up some cash working the fields."

"You can't leave. Your hearing's the day after tomorrow."

"That's why I'm going. I know they're gonna indict me."

She gripped his wrists and pushed his hands from her shoulders. "No, Luke, I won't let you do this. If you run they'll send you to prison forever. They'll throw away the key!"

He picked up a gray duffel bag; it could have been the one he'd carried in the war. "You can't stop me, Beth. Nobody can. I got it figured. There won't be no trial if I just take off and disappear. It'll save everybody a heap of trouble."

"What about Knowl? You were released to his custody. He took you in, knowing he was risking his own reputation."

Luke flashed a crooked smile. "I don't figure our brother's

reputation will suffer that much. Tell him he was right all along. There's always a bad apple in the bunch, and I'm it."

Tears beaded in Beth's eyes. "If you run they'll think you're guilty for sure."

"That's a chance I gotta take."

"They'll catch you, Luke, and put you in jail."

"They gotta find me first."

She seized the front of his plaid flannel shirt. "Don't go, Luke! You're all I've got left of Mama!"

"Nah! You got Knowl and Cath and all the rest. They took you under their wing. They're your kin now."

"I need you, Luke!"

"I'll never fit in here. I'm a wild card, a rebel, a maverick."

"But you're not a murderer, Luke. If you run, you'll never clear your name."

"Don't you see, Beth? It could go either way. It's a toss of the dice. Win or lose. I can't take that chance. I'd die in prison. Shrivel up like a little worm and die. Better I spend my life running."

"I won't let you go. They won't imprison an innocent man!"

He pulled her into his arms and squeezed her tight. "Be happy, little sister. Marry your preacher, if that's what you want. You got my blessing. Love each other and have lots of little babies. Name one of them Luke, for me, okay?"

She held on to him. "Please don't go."

He freed himself and held her wrists at arm's length. "You're a strong girl, Beth. You'll get by just fine. Don't ever lose that spunk, okay?" He tossed the duffel over his shoulder. "Tell Knowl thanks for taking me in. He's a real fine man." With a little farewell salute he opened the door and strode out into the hallway and down the carpeted stairs.

She followed after him, taking the stairs two at a time. "I'll call Knowl. He'll stop you!"

He glanced back at her as he crossed the marble foyer to the door. "Knowl's at work. Who else you gonna call? Annie's over at Cath's. There's nobody to stop me. Anna's too old, Maggie's too young, and you're too weak."

"I am not!" She lunged forward, tackling him from behind, and wrapped her arms around his neck. He teetered momentarily, then shook her off with ease. He grinned down at her where she sat sprawled on the floor. "Tell them you did all you could to stop me. You're a good girl, Beth. Tops in my book."

He grabbed his leather jacket off the hat rack, put it on, and fished a wool cap and leather gloves out of the pockets.

She scrambled to her feet, breathless. "Your truck's in Fort Wayne. You don't have a car—"

"Don't worry. I'll hitchhike home, get my pickup, and be across the state line by nightfall, long before anyone knows I'm gone." He paused in the doorway. "You won't call the cops on me, will you, Beth? You wouldn't turn in your own brother?"

"I will! If you walk out that door, I'll call them right now!"

"No, you won't." He gave her a knowing smile, blew her a kiss, and was out the door, sprinting off toward the street.

She stood in the doorway sobbing. "Don't go, Luke! Please! Don't make me tell on you! Don't make me tell!"

He was already out of sight. She knew he wouldn't be back. Swallowing her tears, she shut the door just as Anna appeared from the kitchen, drying her hands on a dish towel. "Is someone here?"

"No," said Beth, sniffing. "Nobody's here."

Anna lingered a moment, giving Beth an appraising glance, then with a little shrug returned to the kitchen.

Beth sat down on the tufted sofa in the living room and pressed her palms against her temples. She rocked back and forth, murmuring Luke's name over and over. At last she took a deep breath, stood up, and walked to the telephone. With trembling fingers, she dialed

Herrick House Publishers. "I need to speak to Knowl Herrick," she told the receptionist who answered in a professional voice. When Knowl came on the line, she said in a grim monotone, "Luke's gone. Run off to Fort Wayne. Do whatever you've got to do to bring him back."

"Call the Witherspoon house," said Knowl. "Tell your friend Jake to keep Luke there until I arrive, even if he has to hogtie him to the fence post. Tell Jake I'm on my way."

Knowl brought Luke home that evening fit to be tied. Both men were livid with rage—Luke at being caught, and Knowl at Luke's stupidity. "You ever pull a stunt like that again and I wash my hands of you," Knowl warned, clutching Luke's collar in his fist.

"Hey, tough guy, I'm shaking in my boots!"

"Listen, little brother, you want tough? See what happens when you don't show up at that hearing!"

"What's it to you?" Luke shot back. "Let me go and you can forget you ever had a brother."

"Fine. Go! Throw your life away!"

"Why shouldn't I? It won't be worth two cents in prison!"

"You think it'll be any better on the run?"

"I'll take my chances." Luke strode to the front door, opened it, paused for a long moment, head lowered, then slammed the door hard and bolted across the room and up the stairs without a backward glance.

On Friday, January 20th, Knowl took the day off and drove Luke and Bethany to the courthouse in Fort Wayne. Outside the courtroom they met Joseph Kimbrough, the renowned Indianapolis defense attorney that Arnold Kraslow had recommended—a big, barrel-chested man with slick black hair that looked like it might be a toupee. He carried a thick leather briefcase and wore galoshes and a tan trench coat over his brown pinstripe suit. He shook Luke's hand vigorously and looked him straight in the eye. "I'll do the best I can for you, Mr. Henry. We'll enter a not guilty plea and insist on bail, but I can't tell you much more until I see what the district attorney has up his sleeve. But I'll be frank. If this goes to trial, as I expect it to, you've got to tell me everything. So far, you've refused to talk. I can't represent you effectively if I don't have all the facts."

"He doesn't know anything," said Beth. "We were asleep when someone killed Mama and started the fire."

"I know that's Luke's story. But I've done my homework and I know the police have an eye witness who saw Luke in the house with your mother less than an hour before her death."

"That's the cabbie's story," sneered Luke.

"Exactly." Kimbrough drummed his fingers on his briefcase. "And what I'll need to hear, Luke, is your story."

Ten minutes before court was to convene, Joseph Kimbrough escorted Knowl and Beth into the large, high-ceilinged courtroom. Passing half a dozen rows of spectators' benches, he showed them to several plain pinewood chairs directly behind the defense table. To the left was the jury box, looking as innocent as a choir loft. But if Luke went to trial, a choir wouldn't be filling those seats; a group of strangers would sit there and decide Luke's fate.

Bethany shivered. The room was cold and smelled stale and musty, like the pages of old books. A large flag stood beside the judge's immense, oak-paneled desk. On the wall behind the desk were portraits of George Washington and Thomas Jefferson, separated by a large, framed map of Indiana. The map looked old, like it might have been used a hundred years ago. Even the name of the state was printed in scrolled letters that were hard to read. Faded, brown pull-shades hung from the high oak-trimmed windows lining two sides of the room. Bethany could see snow flurries swirling against the frosty panes.

Suddenly a door near the huge desk opened and two men emerged. The first, a thin, balding man with prominent teeth, stepped forward and declared, "Hear ye, hear ye, the court of Judge Louis McPherson is now in session." The judge, a gray-haired, thick-jowled man in a flowing black robe, walked over to his desk and sat down. His dark riveting eyes took in the entire room in a single glance.

For Bethany, the next hour was a nightmare. She sat numb and in shock as the district attorney methodically presented his evidence against Luke. Speaking in a deep, compelling voice, he made Luke sound guilty beyond a doubt. Even when Joseph Kimbrough stood up and called Luke a war hero and spoke eloquently of his innocence, Bethany knew the judge would order Luke to stand trial. Then, when the judge did just that—when he declared that Luke was charged with one count of arson and one count of first degree murder—her mind railed in disbelief. She clutched Luke's clammy, trembling hand and choked back a sob.

Judge McPherson minced no words. "How does the defendant plead?"

"Not guilty," Luke declared hotly.

Kimbrough was quick to request bail, but the judge came back even more swiftly with, "Bail denied. The defendant will be taken into custody immediately after this hearing."

Kimbrough protested, but Judge McPherson snapped, "The charge is murder one. I said, no bail!" He looked solemnly at Luke. "Mr. Henry, your trial is scheduled for six weeks from today, March 3rd, 1950. Ten A.M. You will be tried before a jury of your peers. Do you understand the charges that have been brought against you?"

Luke nodded. "But you're making a mistake, your honor. I swear it! It's all a big mistake!"

"You'll have your say in court, Mr. Henry. Next case!"

Bethany ran to Luke and offered an embrace, but he stood with his arms limp at his sides and stared down at her with eyes dark with desolation. "Man alive, first degree murder, Beth! I could get life! I could get the chair! Why didn't you just let me run?"

In the weeks that followed Bethany went through the motions and routines of daily living; on weekdays she attended her classes at Willowbrook Junior College; on Sundays she went to church and sang in the choir. Occasionally she had a dinner date with Reverend Marshall.

But while her existence was outwardly serene, her emotions roiled just beneath the surface, threatening to erupt at the slightest provocation. Her nerves were frayed to the breaking point; she walked a tightrope between hope and despair. Her thoughts were constantly with Luke—her roguish, devoted, fun-loving brother who languished day after day in a dreary cell. As long as Luke remained in jail, her own life would hang in limbo.

When March 3rd finally arrived, Bethany felt as if she herself were about to stand trial. She was relieved to have Knowl drive her to Fort Wayne and sit beside her in the gloomy, suffocating courtroom. She couldn't have faced this day alone—or this horrible place. The air in the antiquated building was heavy with the sharp, musky smell of old wood, varnished floors, and aged leather. Sounds and voices echoed eerily and were swallowed up in the cavernous, high-ceilinged room. The heavy sleet pelting the windows reflected the icy dread thundering in her heart.

Joseph Kimbrough was already seated at the defense table. Seeing Bethany and Knowl, he leaned over, greeted them, and told them what to expect in the days ahead. "Jury selection will occupy the first couple of days," he said in his smooth, bell-clear voice. "It'll be a bit tedious at times, but it's all part of the process. I'll do my best to get a sympathetic jury."

Moments after the judge entered the courtroom and took his seat, Luke, in drab, green prison garb, was escorted in by two officers, one on each side. He walked with shoulders back and chin high, his expression stoic, as if he were marching to war.

Don't give up hope, Luke, Beth wanted to shout to him. *The battle's just begun, but we're going to win the war!*

As the judge pounded his gavel on his desk, the bailiff stepped forward and announced, "The court of Judge Louis McPherson is now in session. Presenting the people of the state of Indiana versus Lucas Henry."

Bethany shuddered, fighting misgivings. It sounded so ominous—all the people of Indiana against her poor brother Luke! What chance did he have?

By the following Tuesday, March 7th, the jury had been selected—four men and eight women—all plain, down-to-earth, neighborly looking folk. A grocer, a bank teller, a salesman, two clerks, and several farmers and housewives. They looked like people Bethany could have passed on the street, or sipped lemonade with on the front porch, or chatted with in Hubbell's General Store a mile down the road from the Witherspoon farm—people she wouldn't mind calling her friends and neighbors. Would they see the truth—that Luke had nothing to do with Mama's death or the fire?

On Wednesday the prosecutor and defense attorney delivered their opening arguments. Strutting around in his fine wool suit like a peacock on parade and sounding like an actor reciting lines on a stage, the prosecutor declared, "The state will prove beyond a reasonable doubt that Lucas Henry deliberately, maliciously, and with premeditation murdered his mother, Laura Henry, and, to cover his crime, set fire to his own house while his sister slept innocently in another room. We will show that Lucas Henry is an impulsive, hot-headed young man whose mind has been affected by the ravages of war and the taste of death on the battlefield, an unstable man who could erupt at any time and commit another deed as heinous as murdering his own mother!"

When Joseph Kimbrough stood to present his opening argument, Bethany knew he had a tough act to follow. What could he say that would deflect the prosecutor's deadly blows? For nearly a minute Kimbrough paced back and forth before the jury box, rubbing his chin. Finally he planted his hands squarely on the rail and leaned in toward the jury, his eyes moving intently from face to face. "Ladies and gentlemen, the state would have you believe that Lucas Henry is a vile murderer, a monster who would in cold blood take the life of a woman he devoted his life to. Nothing could be further from the truth. The defense will show that this young man is a son any mother would be proud of. Because his father traveled constantly and was later in failing health, Luke took upon himself the emotional and financial support of his mother. He spent his life working the family farm, giving up any chance of college or a personal career. When our country needed him, he eagerly enlisted and bravely fought at the battle of Normandy to ensure our nation's freedom. He asked nothing of his country, nothing of his family, except to be allowed to work and to serve. Does this sound like a man who would destroy the mother he adored and the home he sacrificed his life for? I submit to you, ladies and gentlemen, not only has the prosecution made a terrible mistake in accusing Luke Henry of his mother's death; by proceeding with this trial the state is cruelly promoting a tragic miscarriage of justice. The man standing trial before you today is no murderer; he's a war hero victimized by a system that insists on finding someone—anyone—to blame, even at the expense of the truth and the appalling cost of a young man's future."

From Friday, March 10th, through Friday, March 17th, the prosecution presented their case against Luke. The prosecuting attorney questioned the officers and firemen who had responded to the fire alarm that fateful night and the arson investigators who had sifted through the debris at the site.

One investigator testified how the fire had started. "Someone piled up old rags—what looked like torn bed sheets and towels—in the middle of the living room, not far from the body, doused them in kerosene, and set them on fire. Whoever did it obviously didn't want anything left afterward."

Another officer reported that a shotgun had been found by the front door of the house, partially burned but still containing the fingerprints of both Laura and Luke Henry. When asked what significance he attached to the gun, the officer replied, "I figured the man and woman must have fought over the gun. When the defendant couldn't wrestle the weapon away from her he went into a rage and threw her against the trunk."

"Objection! Pure conjecture!" stormed Kimbrough.

"Overruled," declared the judge.

The coroner and medical examiner both confirmed that Laura Henry died instantly when her temple struck the corner of the metal trunk. They agreed that it wasn't an accident; brute force had caused her to careen against the trunk. The coroner placed the time of death around eleven P.M.—the time the taxicab was at the Henry house, give or take a half hour. As he repeated the results of the autopsy, Bethany slipped out into the hallway. She didn't want to hear grisly details about her mama's death. It was bad enough knowing someone had shoved her and made her hit her head against that old trunk.

It was a fluke that they even had the trunk. Luke had found it in a second-hand shop in France and had it shipped home after the war; it was filled with stuff he'd collected over the years—clothes, mementos, papers, pictures. Mama thought it made a nice table. She kept a basket of fresh flowers on it in the summertime and a bouquet of dried flowers and leaves in the winter. She never would have guessed a silly old trunk would end up causing her death.

Because Knowl had to return to work, Catherine and Todd were taking turns now accompanying Bethany to the trial. The days had fallen into a routine just as Joseph Kimbrough had predicted—hours of tedium, monotonous arguments, endless discussion, and mountains of seemingly inconsequential details. The effect was numbing on the mind.

Bethany didn't want to hear one more attorney say, *Objection!* or *Argumentative, your honor*. She was tired of hearing Judge McPherson reply in his deep, droning voice, *Overruled, Counsel* or *Sustained!* She didn't want to hear about inadmissible evidence and hearsay, about provocation and mitigating circumstances. Why couldn't people just come right out and say what they meant in simple, everyday language?

If Luke's future weren't at stake, Bethany would stay home and wait for it all to be over. As it was she was missing her college classes and might have to take the semester over. But she knew Luke needed someone in his corner rooting for him. She would be there, whatever the cost.

On Sunday morning, March 19th, Beth welcomed the chance to go to Willowbrook Christian Church instead of the dreary courthouse. It felt good to be in the choir singing about the love of Jesus instead of listening to lawyers yammering about criminal intent, cross-examinations, and corroborative evidence. It felt even better, after singing, to settle into the first pew and fix her eyes on handsome Todd Marshall as he delivered his sermon in his usual polished, genteel manner.

He was in top form today, speaking fervently about God's love for a lost world and mankind's love for one another. In his most eloquent voice he read from I Corinthians 13: "Though I speak with the tongues of men and of angels, and have not charity, I am become as sounding brass, or a tinkling cymbal . . . and though I have all faith, so that I could remove mountains, and have not charity, I am nothing.

"Charity never faileth," he continued, turning his earnest blue eyes on Beth. "Charity beareth all things, believeth all things, hopeth all things, endureth all things."

As his gaze locked with hers, his voice broke for an instant. She thought he had lost track of his sermon notes and was going to stop right there. But after a moment's pause his gaze swept over the entire congregation and his voice rang out stronger than ever. "My friends, five years ago we won a world war because we were united in purpose and dedicated to the concept of freedom for all. We were willing to sacrifice our comfort, our security, our very lives to win the battle against oppression. Now we have embarked on a new decade of freedom and tranquility, of calm and prosperity.

"But let us not take our good fortune for granted," he warned, his forehead bright with perspiration and his eyes glinting with a devout intensity. "Let us not grow lazy and indifferent, for we are in a war far greater than the two world wars that have scarred this century. We are in the war for men's souls. We are in Christ's army, battling the wickedness of the Evil One. We can win this battle only with unsullied devotion to our Savior and unconditional love for one another. I challenge you to show Christ's love wherever He may lead you today. As Scripture reminds us, we have faith, hope, and love—these three. But the greatest of these is love!"

Expressions of approval rippled through the congregation, and several old men murmured, "Amen!" Todd wiped his forehead with his handkerchief. He was beaming.

Bethany lowered her gaze and smiled inwardly. Nothing made Todd happier than to stand in his pulpit and preach from his heart. If only she could feel such consuming, single-minded commitment to something. Perhaps she did—to *someone*. Todd Marshall.

Todd was praying now, entreating God to bless His church and touch and change lives in this very congregation. After his prayer, he gave his usual invitation. Most of the folk at Willowbrook Christian Church had been Christians for years, so only an occasional soul ventured up to the mourner's bench. When no one responded, Todd extended his invitation to anyone who needed special prayer.

This time there was a rustling in the back pew. Bethany looked around as a woman shuffled forward with a young boy. Odd that Beth hadn't noticed these strangers before.

Thin as a rail, the woman moved as if the very act of walking were an effort. She was darker than most of the folk in Willowbrook, with a mass of curly black hair tumbling around her shoulders. She had an exotic look—as if she were Greek or Italian. Her features were striking—large, dark, almond-shaped eyes, full lips, and a long, graceful neck. And yet there was something in her face that marred her beauty—a pallor to her skin, a darkness around the eyes, a twisting of the mouth.

The boy with her looked about eight, with straight brown hair, large, expressionless blue eyes, thin, unsmiling lips, and a determined chin. He stayed close by her side, like a shadow, quietly watchful.

The woman stopped at the altar, her head bowed, the boy beside her, waiting.

What happened next startled Bethany; no doubt startled the whole congregation. As Todd leaned forward to speak to the woman, he stopped suddenly and his face blanched a ghostly white. He gripped the pulpit with both hands until his knuckles whitened. Beth heard him murmur *no!* under his breath.

For almost a minute a strange hush held the people spellbound as Reverend Marshall and the woman stood gazing at each other. Finally he said gently, "How can I pray for you?"

The woman looked up at him and said, "I . . . I'm ill. I need a home for my son. A good, Christian home. I pray to God a family in this church will take my boy in and raise him as their own."

A murmur of sympathy rose from the congregation.

Todd bent forward and asked, "Why did you come to Willowbrook?"

She met his gaze and said softly, "God sent me."

From the far side of the second pew came a loud gasp and a rustling of clothing as Todd's mother stood up, made a groaning sound, and fanned herself—in late-winter!—with the morning's bulletin. The woman at the altar turned and stared at Mrs. Marshall, opened her mouth as if to speak, then sank to the floor.

Todd sprang into action, darting from the platform to the altar and gathering the crumpled form in his arms. "Is Dr. Galway here?" he shouted. "Someone get Dr. Galway! Quick!"

Bethany watched in astonishment as Todd carried the unconscious woman to the choir room and shut the door. Dr. Galway shambled up from the last pew, his stout frame straining the seams of his tweed suit as he barked, "Someone get my medical bag out of my car!" A deacon jumped up and ran out as Dr. Galway followed Todd into the choir room. Again, the door shut soundly.

Mr. Spencer, the choir director, stood up, shrugged, and said, "I think we're dismissed, folks. Say a prayer for that young lady and her son here. We'll see you tonight at the evening service."

A cacophony of whispers stirred the air as people made their way outside and headed home. While the rest of the congregation dispersed, Beth remained in her place, wondering whether to go to Todd and offer her help. Strange, but she sensed he would consider her presence intrusive.

Beth noticed that Todd's mother remained in her place as well, shaking her head and blowing into her hanky. Beth considered going over to her and making conversation, but she knew she would only be rebuffed. If Todd wanted his privacy right now, his mother would certainly insist on it even more so.

Then Bethany noticed the young boy. He was still standing by the altar looking frightened and alone. He was a handsome child—

pensive, solemn. She slipped out of her seat and went to him, putting a gentle hand on his shoulder. "Don't be scared," she whispered. "Your mama will be just fine. Dr. Galway's the best doctor in these parts."

The boy looked up at her with dark blue, soulful eyes. "Mama's been to all the doctors. None of them can help."

Bethany felt taken aback. The boy spoke with such finality and maturity. "What's your name?" she asked.

"Daniel. Daniel DiCaprio. They call me Danny."

"What a nice name. It sounds like music."

The boy sat down on the pew and swung his legs under the seat. He was humming something to himself, a tune Beth didn't recognize. "Where are you from?" she asked.

The boy stopped humming and looked at her. "New York."

"New York? You've come a long way."

"We took the train."

"The train? Really? I bet that was fun."

"Except when we walked between the cars. It was noisy and everything shook."

"Goodness, I bet that was—"

"Bethany?" It was Annie's voice. Beth turned around. Annie was looking at the boy, then at Beth. "Everyone's in the car. Knowl wants to know if you are coming with us."

"Yes, I am," said Beth, flustered. She didn't want to go; she wanted to stay and wait for Todd, but who knew how long he would be or whether he would want her to stay? She looked back at the young boy. "I'm sure no one would mind if you went in the room with your mother. She's probably looking for you right now."

"Really?" he asked, his face brightening.

"I'm sure of it," she said and watched as he darted across the sanctuary and disappeared into the choir room.

Bethany turned to go, but not before she cast a lingering glance at the closed door. Who was this strange woman? Why had she prompted such an unsettling response from Todd Marshall? And why did her presence stir such a dark sense of foreboding in Bethany's heart as well?

16

After dinner on that blustery Sunday afternoon, the Herrick family sat in the parlor listening to their favorite Andrews Sisters album and discussing the strange incident at church. Anna served steaming hot chocolate with marshmallows, a welcome contrast to the blinding snow flurries pummeling the frosty windowpanes. With a crackling fire in the fireplace, the parlor was the warmest room in the house—and the most peaceful, until the phone rang, its jarring noise shattering the tranquillity.

Everyone looked at one another to see who would do the honors. Hardly anyone called on Sunday afternoon. Finally, with a groan, Knowl put his newspaper aside and went to answer it.

Bethany, sitting cross-legged on the braided rug by the fireplace, turned her attention back to little Maggie. The two were playing blocks, making a tower of alphabet cubes which Maggie would swat, then laugh with glee as they toppled.

When Beth heard Knowl mention Todd's name, her ears perked up and she waited, listening, expecting Knowl to call her to the phone. Instead, Knowl spoke briefly in low, serious tones and then hung up the receiver.

"Didn't Todd want to talk to me?" she asked as Knowl sat down on the Queen Anne chair and picked up his newspaper.

"No, he didn't, Beth. But he said he'd call you tomorrow."

"Why did he call you, then?"

"He asked me to lead the evening service."

"Tonight?"

"Yes, tonight."

Annie, sitting in the rocker by the bay window, set down her pen and leather journal. "Reverend Marshall wants you to preach?"

Knowl sounded a trifle perturbed. "Yes, I suppose that's exactly what he wants."

"But you're not a preacher," said Beth.

Knowl rattled his paper. "No, but I'm head of the deacon board, and I preached my share of sermons when we were between pastors."

"And you did a wonderful job," said Annie.

"But why won't Todd be there?" persisted Beth.

Knowl cleared his throat uneasily. "He said he has some urgent business to attend to."

"He didn't say what it was?"

"No, Bethany, he didn't. I could tell he didn't want to get into it."

"What's wrong, Knowl?" asked Annie.

"I don't know, dear. Frankly, he did sound shaken."

"Maybe I should call him back," said Beth.

"No. I wouldn't. He said he'll be in touch with you."

Beth made another tower of blocks, which Maggie promptly demolished. "Did he mention what happened with that woman and her little boy? Did they have a place to go, someone to help them?"

Knowl was behind his newspaper now. "No, but I have a feeling that's the urgent business he mentioned."

"They appeared destitute," noted Annie. "I feel so sorry for them."

Beth nodded, not quite convinced. "Todd's too busy to help them. There are plenty of other people in the church."

"I'll do whatever I can," said Annie, her pen still poised over her journal.

Why would Todd miss the evening service for them? Beth wondered as she placed another block on the precarious tower.

Predictably Maggie knocked them over again with a delighted chortle. "Again, Aunt Benny! Again!"

Beth gathered the scattered blocks and began stacking them for the umpteenth time, but her thoughts remained on Todd. Church wouldn't be the same tonight without Todd Marshall there. What had happened to cause him to shirk his responsibility? Something was wrong. She felt it in her bones. Even when Todd was ill he was reluctant to have another man fill his pulpit.

On Monday morning, March 20th, Bethany's concern mounted when Todd telephoned and told her he wasn't free to drive her to Fort Wayne, as they had planned. "You'd better see if Knowl or Catherine can drive you the rest of the week," he suggested, his voice clearly not his own.

"What's wrong, Todd?" she asked.

"I'll tell you when we have time to sit down and talk."

"When will that be?"

"Maybe tonight or tomorrow night, if you get back from Fort Wayne in time."

"Will you call me?"

"Yes, Bethany. I'm sorry to be so mysterious. It's just—it's a very long story. I can't get into it now."

Since Knowl's work was piling up at the publishing house, Catherine drove Beth to Fort Wayne. Beth thanked her more than once, knowing how much Cath disliked making the trip and seeing Luke. "One of these days I'm going to learn how to drive a car," Beth promised, "and I won't need to beg for rides."

Cath deflected Beth's gratitude with her typical bemused, offhanded attitude. "I don't mind doing my sisterly duty," she quipped. "Besides, you help me out with Jenny often enough. She's devoted to you. The least I can do is stand by you through this mess of a trial."

Beth was more than thankful to have Catherine beside her in the chilly, sunless courthouse. She knew it was going to be a grueling day when the prosecuting attorney concluded his case by calling the taxi driver to the stand. The stubby little man walked with a loose-jointed gait, his knees and elbows too large for his gangly arms and legs. His knobby chin showed the shadow of a beard and his eyes were like shiny black ball bearings in a narrow face with too many angles. At the attorney's prompting the cabbie related his story, the gist of his testimony disturbingly clear. "That woman, Laura Henry, was alive when Mrs. Herrick left the Henry farmhouse that night. The last person to see Mrs. Henry alive had to be her son, Luke Henry. I seen him with my own two eyes, standing in the doorway with her."

"Objection!" roared Kimbrough. "Mere speculation! No one knows the last person who saw Laura Henry alive!"

"Objection overruled," intoned Judge McPherson.

Catherine stole a glance at Beth, as if to say, *See? I warned you what your brother was like all along!*

The two were silent as they drove back to Willowbrook that afternoon. Hearing the cabdriver speak firsthand had jolted Beth. He sounded so convincing, so sincere, so honest. He apparently had no ax to grind and felt no malice against Luke; he simply told his story, and it rang with truth.

Beth started to wonder, *Was it possible Luke was guilty? Could he have deceived his own sister?* If she had been wrong all along—if the brother she adored could commit such madness, who could she ever trust again?

"It must be awfully upsetting sitting in that courtroom day after day," Catherine sympathized as she turned off the highway and drove down Willowbrook's Main Street.

"Every night I tell myself I'm not going back, but every morning I get up and go."

"I hope Luke realizes what a loyal sister he has."

"Right now I don't feel loyal. I feel sick."

"Are you doubting Luke?"

Beth closed her eyes. "I can't doubt him. That would mean I believe he could hurt Mama, and I'll never believe that."

Gently Cath said, "You believed my mother could do it."

"I was wrong. I'm sorry. But I'm not wrong about Luke."

"I hope you're right, Beth. For everybody's sake, I hope you're right."

Minutes later Catherine dropped Bethany off at the Herrick house on Honeysuckle Lane. "I'm not coming in," she said as Beth stepped gingerly out of the automobile into the slush beside the curb. "Robert and Jenny will be waiting for me and reminding me I need to get my rest for the baby."

"They're right," said Beth, clutching her fur collar tight around her neck. "I almost forgot about the baby. You can't keep driving me to Fort Wayne. You'll be too tired. I'll just stay over in a hotel—"

"No, Beth. I'm good for a few more days on the road. When I'm too tired I'll let you know."

Beth gripped the door handle and leaned inside the car. "I'm glad you were with me, Cath. It was hard today, but you made it easier."

Cath tucked several stray red curls back under her scarf. "Thanks, Beth. I'll see you in the morning. Pray for clear weather."

Bethany waved as the car pulled away, then turned, lowered her head into the wind, and stomped through drifting snow up to the house. She welcomed the warm draft of air that met her as she stepped inside the foyer. She hung up her coat and scarf and pulled off her rubber boots, then headed straight for the kitchen and the tantalizing aroma of beef stew.

Anna was at the stove, adding celery, carrots, and onions to the huge, steaming kettle. Wisps of gray hair had worked loose from the bun at the nape of her neck, and her cheeks were ruddy and bright from hours of cooking. Impulsively Bethany leaned over and kissed her warm forehead.

"Goodness, child, what was that for?"

Beth turned to the stew, suddenly tongue-tied. "Smells good," she managed.

"I hope you're hungry."

"Starved. Can I help?"

"Set the table, if you like. Everything else is done. Just waiting for my brood to get home."

"Where's Annie?"

"Had an interview at the radio station downtown about her new book. She's eager for all the publicity she can get."

"Where's Maggie?"

"Napping. I tired her out building snowmen in the backyard. We made a whole family. Mama, Papa, and little snowbaby. The stew's missing a few carrots—they made fine noses—and my button bag's a little lighter now, but our snow family has the biggest, brightest eyes. We had a grand time!"

Beth pushed up the sleeves on her fleecy white sweater and tied a frilly apron around her corduroy jumper. "It sounds like so much fun. I wish I'd been here."

Anna patted Beth's arm. "So do I, dear. I know how hard it is for you going to that trial every day."

"At least I get to come home to you and this house." Beth opened the pantry door and removed four folded linen napkins and four polished teakwood napkin rings. She looked over at Anna as she stirred the simmering kettle with a long-handled wooden spoon. "Don't you ever get tired of taking care of us, Mother Reed? Don't you ever wish someone would wait on you for a change?"

Anna bustled over and clasped Beth's slim cold hands between her thick warm ones. "Let me tell you a secret, child," she said, her eyes twinkling. "When my husband, Jon, died during the war and I sold this house to strangers, I felt as if I had died too. I moved to Chicago and took care of my sister, Martha, until she died. But my life was empty as a broken teacup. Then, when Knowl bought this house for my daughter Annie and invited me to come live with them, I was in my glory. I had my home back, and my family, and I was needed again. I wouldn't trade a minute of my life for all the tea in China."

Bethany gave Anna a hug. "I wouldn't trade *you* for all the tea in the world!"

Anna's face clouded. "I just remembered. You got a phone call."

"From Todd?"

"No, from Isabel Clarenton."

"Isabel? Why would she call me?"

"I don't know. At first she asked for Knowl, and when he wasn't available, she asked for you. I promised her you'd call. The number's by the phone."

I will never like that woman! Beth thought as she trudged out to the hallway. She dialed the number and waited.

Isabel answered on the second ring and, recognizing Beth's voice, came right to the point. "I just thought you should know, Bethany. My parents visited Reverend Marshall today and found that strange woman and her son living in his house. All settled in like they were relatives or something. Now maybe it's none of our business, but we don't think it's proper, him being a single man and all. There are places for poor people to go for help, but certainly not the parsonage."

Bethany listened, stunned but glad that Isabel rattled on without expecting a reply.

"We're not trying to be busybodies, but we think your brother Knowl should look into this right away," Isabel rushed on in her shrill, grating voice. "After all, he's head of the deacon board and appearances are at stake. If anyone can make Todd—um, Reverend

Marshall—see reason, it's Knowl. You will speak to him about this, won't you, Bethany?"

At last she found her voice. "Why don't you speak to Knowl yourself, Isabel?"

"I would, but I really think it might be better coming from you. I wouldn't want him thinking I'm poking my nose where it doesn't belong."

Your nose is big enough to poke just about anywhere! Beth thought. But aloud she said, "Thank you for calling, Isabel. Your concern is downright touching, but I'm sure Reverend Marshall can take care of himself. Besides, he's got his mama there in his house, and she's very good at playing chaperone."

Beth hung up the phone with more force than necessary, but remained standing in the shadows of the hallway, trying to comprehend the significance of Isabel's words. Her bravado was gone now; she was left alone with questions and doubts. Why would Todd take that woman and her son into his house? What terrible secret was he keeping?

As she turned back to the kitchen, the phone rang again. She picked up the receiver and declared, "Now what, Isabel?"

From the other end of the line came the deep, resonant voice of Todd Marshall. "Hello, Bethany. Were you expecting someone else?"

"No," she said, flustered. "You're the only one I want to hear from."

"Good. Can we get together tonight, to talk and have a bite to eat?"

"Anna's got dinner ready here. Do you want to come over?"

"No, we need to talk away from our families. I know a modest little restaurant out on the highway. The Dew Drop Inn. Plain furnishings, home cooking, and lots of peace and quiet. I go there and drink hot black coffee and gaze out at the pine trees. Sometimes I even work on my sermons."

"It sounds nice."

"Then I'll pick you up in half an hour, okay?"

"I'll be ready." But would she be ready to hear what Todd had to tell her? Was she ready to face losing him, maybe forever?

The unsettling questions still swirled in her mind as she and Todd headed out of town along the dark, snow-encrusted highway.It took forever to reach the rustic little bungalow nestled beside the road, its unvarnished sign askew and rosy light seeping through its narrow bottle-glass windows.

"It doesn't look like much, but I think you'll like it," Todd told her as they crunched through deep snow to the door. Inside, the restaurant looked like an early American cabin with its split-pine walls, rough-hewn ceiling beams, and wide-board floor. The room's scant light came from milk glass oil lamps on round pedestal tables. A scrubbed pine sideboard stood beside a plain pine counter. On the wall behind the counter hung a pair of antlers, a stuffed pheasant with wings spread, and a photograph of Will Rogers framed in birch bark. On a side wall a black bearskin hung between the bottle-glass windows.

"I like it here," said Beth. "I bet my papa came here during his traveling days."

"If he did, Rosa would remember him," said Todd as a squat, gray-haired woman bustled toward them.

"Hello, Reverend. Nice to see you on such a chilly night. I see you brought a friend this time." Rosa's round face beamed.

"I want her to try a bowl of your special chili, Rosa."

"Fine. Come! I'll give you a nice back corner table."

They followed her to the back of the room and sat down in spindle chairs, facing each other across the table. Todd pushed the oil lamp to one side and reached for Beth's hand. "You look beautiful in the lamp light," he said softly. "I just wish we were here under different circumstances."

"Why are we here, Todd?"

He massaged the back of her hand with his thumb. "It's a long story, Beth."

"You said that before."

"I know. I'm still trying to comprehend it all myself."

"What? I don't understand."

Rosa came back with menus. "You two need some time?"

"Yes, Rosa. Just bring us some coffee right now. That okay, Beth? Two coffees."

"Black?"

"Cream and sugar for me," said Beth.

Todd waited until Rosa was back behind the counter before meeting Beth's gaze again. Something in his expression sent a little alarm through her. His face had changed somehow, grown older and younger at the same time. His eyes looked weary, the lids heavy, and yet they possessed a childlike vulnerability she had never seen before.

"Are you okay, Todd?"

"No, Bethany, I'm not."

"Are you ill?"

"No. Just sick at heart." He held up her hand and pressed his palm against hers, then locked fingers so hard she winced. "I wish I never had to give you up."

"You don't have to," she said quickly.

"If it were my choice, I wouldn't, Beth, but it's beyond my control. I'm losing everything I've ever dreamed of."

"You're scaring me, Todd. Don't talk in riddles. Say what you mean."

Rosa came back with two heavy ceramic mugs and set them on the table. Todd released Beth's hand and they both picked up their mugs. She swallowed too quickly and the scalding coffee seared her throat.

"Careful," he warned. "Let it cool first."

She cupped her hands around the warm mug and drilled Todd with her gaze. "Tell me what's wrong."

He cleared his throat, but his voice still came out gravelly. "Remember me telling you about a girl I courted back in New York during my college days?"

Beth nodded. "The girl who stopped writing, the girl you couldn't find."

"Yes. Her name was Claire DiCaprio."

She froze. "DiCaprio? That's the name of that little boy—the one with that woman in church yesterday."

He looked at her, flinching slightly. "What do you know about her?"

"Nothing. I saw her in church. I saw her faint. I saw you pick her up."

"That's all?"

Beth turned her mug between her palms. "I heard she's staying at your house. Is she?"

"Yes."

"Who is she, Todd?"

He waited, glanced around, waited some more. He finally said the words he'd been leading up to. "Claire is the woman I loved and lost."

Bethany ran her fingertips over her lips. They felt dry, chapped. It was this cold, windy weather. It dried the skin, turned it to parchment. Sometimes her lips got so dry they bled. Her heart felt that way now—dry as crepe paper.

"Did you hear me, Beth?"

She sucked on her lower lip, feeling where it was cracked, tasting the blood. "I heard you."

"Do you want to hear the whole story?"

Her throat burned from the hot coffee, but another ache was taking its place. She nodded. "Yes. Tell me."

"Her parents owned a little restaurant in my hometown. Antonio's. Good Italian food. Pasta, pizza, spaghetti. After her father died, Claire and her mother ran the restaurant. That's where I met her the summer I came home after my first year at Columbia.

"We started dating, dated all summer. I admit it got pretty serious. Then summer ended and I headed back to Columbia. Claire and I promised to write each other, and we did for a while. Then, after a few weeks, her letters stopped coming. I didn't worry about it at first. I was busy with school, and I figured she was busy too.

"But when I went home for Christmas, she was gone. The restaurant had been sold, and another family was living in her old corner brownstone on Richmond. She had left no forwarding address; no one knew where she had gone; it was as if she'd vanished from the face of the earth."

"What did you do?" asked Beth.

"I tried to find her, of course. Then it dawned on me that she didn't want to be found, and I realized how much I must have hurt her."

"Hurt her? How?"

Todd stared down into his steaming mug. "By stealing her innocence. I had pushed her into a relationship she wasn't ready for. At the time I had no knowledge of God, and yet I knew I was taking something from her I had no right to. For years I was convinced that was why she fled; my unbridled passions had wounded her. I lived with that guilt until I received Christ's forgiveness. But even though He forgave me, I never quite forgave myself. I never felt I could fully trust myself with a woman again."

Beth gazed at him in astonishment. Now she understood. "Is that why you've held back from me all this time?"

The blue in his eyes deepened as his voice grew fervent. "Don't you see, Beth? I didn't want to make the same mistake with you. I'm a minister of the Gospel now. A single man! To be honest, I'm ashamed I've shown such a lack of restraint with you."

"But you haven't!" she protested.

He looked down at the table. "In my heart I have."

She sat forward, every muscle tense. "You have? I'm glad, Todd! Don't you see? I was afraid you were above such passions. I thought I could never be good enough for you."

He smiled grimly. "You wouldn't say that if you knew—"

She leaned across the table and whispered, "I do know. I'm glad you want me. I want you too. I love you, Todd. If we love each other, there's nothing wrong with what we feel."

He sat back, straightening his shoulders. "It's not that simple, Beth."

"Yes, it is. To me it is."

"Maybe last week I would have agreed. Even two days ago. But not now. Not since—"

"Since . . . since what? Since Claire came to town?"

"Since Claire came to town with her son."

Beth waited. A nerve under her eye felt jumpy, but she hoped Todd didn't notice it. "Her son?" she repeated, letting the question hang in the air. "What does he have to do with you, Todd?"

Todd inhaled sharply. "He's *my* son."

"No!" Bethany covered her face with her hands.

"I'm sorry, Beth. I swear I didn't know about Danny until yesterday."

Beth's hands were trembling. "He looks eight, nine years old. Where's he been all this time?"

Todd's brow furrowed. "That's what I'm trying to tell you."

"Maybe she's deceiving you, Todd. He could be someone else's child."

"She wouldn't do that, Beth. Besides, look at him. He's got my eyes, my chin. He's the spitting image of me."

Rosa sidled back over with a notepad and pen in hand. "You two ready to order? We got a special on corned beef hash, or top of the menu is smoked ham with a fine honey glaze. Or, like the Reverend said before, the chili's good as long as you like it hot and spicy."

"I'm not hungry," Beth said in a small, tight voice.

"We'll wait awhile," said Todd. "Just a refill on the coffee, Rosa, if you don't mind."

"Suit yourself, Reverend." She left and was back moments later with an aluminum coffeepot. Humming a little melody, she filled their mugs to the brim. "Maybe on a cold night you two would like a bowl of homemade chicken noodle soup. It's good for what ails you."

Todd nodded. "That sounds swell, Rosa."

"Okay. Two soups it is."

When they were alone again, Todd sat forward, both elbows on the table. "Listen, Beth, I never meant to hurt you."

She blinked back tears. "Just tell me the truth."

"I'm trying." He sipped his coffee. "I didn't know the whole story myself until yesterday when Claire filled in the missing pieces. She told me what happened that autumn when she stopped writing. She had just found out she was going to have a baby. My baby."

Rosa reappeared with two steaming bowls of chicken noodle soup. As she set them down, a little broth sloshed over the rims. "Saltines?" she asked brightly. Without waiting for a reply she put a plate of crackers between them. "We got plenty of crackers. Let me know if you want more."

"Thanks, Rosa," said Todd evenly, his gaze still on Beth. "This'll do it for us."

As Rosa lumbered off, Beth asked, "Why would Claire stop writing you at a time like that?"

"She was frightened. Didn't know where to turn. So she went to see my mother. Told her about the baby. Wanted to know what to do."

"Your mother knew?"

"Yes. She's known all this time." The lines along Todd's mouth were taut. He dipped his spoon into his soup and stirred absently. Veins along his temples throbbed. "My mother told her I was never to know about the baby. She said it would ruin my life." His voice hardened. "She told Claire how my father died—committing suicide because he couldn't deal with the harsh realities of life. She told Claire the same thing could happen to me if I learned about the baby."

"And Claire believed her?"

Todd pushed his soup away. "Oh, yes, she believed her. My mother can be very convincing. She persuaded Claire to disappear. My mother even gave her money to start a new life somewhere else."

"Claire took money from your mother?"

"She felt she had no choice. The restaurant was losing money after her father's death, and her mother's health was failing. So they sold the restaurant and moved out of state. Claire kept her word. She never told me about my son. She raised him all these years without a father."

A lump tightened in Beth's throat. "I know how hard that is. My papa was gone more than he was home."

"But it didn't have to be that way with Claire. If only I'd known!"

Bethany took a mouthful of soup. It felt warm and soothing going down. "Why did she tell you now, after all this time?"

Todd pinched his nostrils and blinked back the wetness from his eyes. His words erupted in a spasm of anguish. "She's dying, Beth."

"What?"

"Claire. She's dying of tuberculosis."

"TB? Oh, Todd, I'm sorry!"

"Her mother's gone. She has no one else. She spent months tracking me down. She had to find a home for her son before she dies."

"A home with you."

"That's what she hoped for, but she insists she didn't come here to tell the world about my past. She wanted me to know about the boy, but she's willing to let me place him with a family without acknowledging he's my flesh and blood. Can you imagine, Beth? She's still trying to protect me."

Bethany raised another spoonful of soup to her lips. "She still loves you."

"I suppose so. We didn't talk about love."

"Do you . . . still love her?" The words were hushed, hardly audible.

Todd's eyes closed momentarily, and the lines along his nose and mouth sagged; he seemed to be aging before her eyes. "It's not a question of love, Beth. Frankly, I'm numb. But my heart goes out to Claire. She's ready to go off to a sanatorium to live out her days while someone else raises her son. She's willing to give him up for his own good. And I can't let her do that, Beth. I've got to do the right thing—finally."

Beth hardly dared ask. "What are you going to do?"

Todd reached across the table for her hand. "Beth, I was up all night praying, pleading for God's guidance. Now I've got to do the only thing I know to do."

Beth shook her head. "Don't say it."

"I've got to, my darling. I can't let Claire go off to a sanatorium. I can't let some other family raise my own son."

"No! I don't want to hear it!" Tears rolled down Beth's cheeks. She blotted them with her napkin.

Todd pressed her fingers against his lips. "I'm sorry, Beth. I've made my decision. I'm going to marry Claire, and take care of her, and give my son a name."

Beth let out a little sob. "What about . . . the church?"

A tendon along Todd's jaw tightened. "I'm meeting with the deacon board tomorrow night. I'll confess everything and offer my resignation."

"You can't! You're the one who taught me about God! Now you're just walking away?"

"It's out of my hands, Beth. Please, tell me you understand. Tell me you don't hate me."

She stared open-mouthed at him. Raw, hot emotion rose in her veins like lava. "Hate you? Yes, I hate you, Todd Marshall!" She sprang to her feet and shoved her bowl of soup across the table into his lap, then ran out of the restaurant into the frosty, biting wind, the heavy pine door clattering noisily behind her.

17

On Tuesday morning, March 21st, Catherine arrived at seven to drive Bethany to Fort Wayne. As Beth settled into the front seat beside her, Cath said, "You don't look well. Are you up to making the trip?"

"Yes. I just didn't get much sleep last night."

"I understand. You're worried about Luke."

Beth didn't reply. No sense in telling Cath about Todd's plan to marry his lost love. She would find out soon enough.

On the way out of Willowbrook Cath said, "It's such a beautiful day, Beth. Would you like to stop by the cemetery on our way home?"

Beth stared at her in surprise. "Go see Mama's grave?"

"And our Papa's too. Maybe even plant some flowers."

"I'd like that," said Beth, marveling. Was Cath softening in her resentment toward Papa? She rarely talked about him and never mentioned how she felt about him leaving her mama to take up with Beth's mama.

But all too soon, as Bethany entered the courthouse she became preoccupied once again with Luke and his future. The defense attorney was presenting his case now, taking the prosecution's evidence and attempting to discredit it, piece by piece. In his most eloquent voice Kimbrough argued, "Every shred of evidence the prosecution has presented is circumstantial; there's nothing concrete. Every argument they've presented is a wild assumption from which they've made vastly incorrect conclusions. With a young man's life hanging in the balance, we can't in good conscience assume anything. We must know! But not one tiny fact has been offered that ties Luke Henry to the murder of his mother. Without solid evidence, ladies and gentlemen, he cannot be found guilty beyond a reasonable doubt."

But Beth sensed that the jury wasn't convinced. They sat with stony faces, watching, listening, but rarely revealing the slightest emotion. Beth noted, too, that when the jurors entered and left the jury box, they never looked Luke in the eye. Surely he was already guilty in their eyes.

Court recessed early because Judge McPherson had other business to tend to. Bethany was relieved. Now she and Cath would have time to visit the cemetery and still arrive home before dark. Cath stopped by a small nursery several blocks from the courthouse and purchased two potted plants. They drove on to the cemetery and stopped by the guardhouse to borrow a shovel. The sun was a pale orange ball in the sky by the time Catherine parked her car on the gravel road near the gravestones. Without a word she and Beth stepped from the car, each with a plant, and walked over to the grassy knoll containing two modest grave markers. Knowl himself had purchased the stone for Beth's mother, selecting one that matched Papa's headstone.

For several moments, they stood and gazed in silence at the markers, as if some new truth or insight could be gleaned from simply observing them. Finally Beth stooped down and ran her fingertips over the letters on each marker. Cath remained at a distance, watching.

"Hello, Mama. Hello, Papa," Beth said softly. "I miss you. Luke does too. He sends his love. Cath is with me. She's right here, Papa."

Beth stood up and stepped back beside Cath. "I know Papa's glad you're here."

Catherine shrugged. "I never knew what to say to Papa when he was alive. I don't know what to say now either."

"Just say . . . you love him."

Cath dabbed at her eyes. "Yes, well, Papa and I had a rather stormy relationship. We made our peace at the end, but I never knew how to talk to him."

"When I was little he read me the funny papers sometimes," said Beth. "Jiggs and Maggie, Mutt and Jeff. Dick Tracy. Dagwood and Blondie."

Cath nodded. "On the Sundays Papa was home he'd read the funnies to me too. Sometimes he'd get out construction paper and show me how to draw cartoons. He was quite good. I tried my best to draw like he did. The first time I knew I had artistic talent was when I looked at a comic strip and drew it, and Papa said, 'Hey, my little girl's a regular Walt Disney!'"

Beth looked at Catherine with tear-glazed eyes. "That's how I started drawing too. Papa was always so pleased when I showed him my sketches. Sometimes he'd even get tears in his eyes. I bet he was remembering the drawings you made for him."

Cath's voice caught with emotion. "I didn't even think he remembered."

"He did. I'm sure he did." Bethany pulled a handkerchief from her coat pocket and blew her nose. "Did he surprise you with little gifts from his salesman's valise?"

Catherine's brows arched with recollection. "Yes! I'd forgotten. When he came home from his travels he'd reach into his big black Fuller Brush satchel and pull out little prizes for Knowl and me. Little black combs, scrub brushes, wire whisks, and bottle openers. When we were younger we thought he was a magician who could pull anything from his bag of tricks. Later we figured he was just trying to appease us for missing so much of our lives."

A light breeze rippled Bethany's hair. She brushed a stray wisp back from her forehead. "Papa was the loser too, not just us."

"But he had a choice, Beth. We didn't."

"We do now. We can be angry—or we can forgive him."

"Now you're starting to sound like Reverend Marshall."

"Heaven forbid!"

Cath stepped forward and plunged the shovel into the hard earth beside her father's grave. She dug a small hole, set the plant in, and packed the dirt tightly around it. She handed Beth the shovel and said, "Go ahead."

Beth shoveled out the dirt near the head of Mama's marker and put in the remaining plant, covering the earth around it. She gazed at Cath. "Should we say a prayer or something?"

"A silent prayer maybe? Only God knows what two sisters could say to parents like ours."

They stood, shoulder to shoulder, heads bowed, the biting March wind rising, rustling around them, whistling through tree limbs, whispering secrets over the dead brown earth.

In the silence Bethany stole a glance at Catherine and felt a surprising wrench of emotion. Cath. Her sister. Bone of her bone. In their own ways they both loved Papa, needed his love, still carried that need in a crevice of their hearts. Sisters, ten years apart in age, they'd grown up strangers, worlds apart. But Papa was the cord that tied them to each other in a way they could never put into words.

Beth blinked back tears the wind had started in her eyes. She wanted Papa back like he was when she was small, sitting her up on his knee, reading her the funnies. She wished she and Cath hadn't been born into two families, separate, never knowing the other existed. Why couldn't they have been one family like other people, normal and happy?

Cath broke the silence. "Shall we head home? It'll be dark soon and Anna will have dinner on the table."

Beth nodded. Tonight she would learn whether the deacon board had accepted Todd's resignation.

Cath smiled. "This has been a special time, hasn't it?"

"Yes, it has," said Beth, returning the smile. Without thinking she and Cath linked hands as they turned and headed back to the car.

That evening, Knowl arrived home from the deacons' meeting looking weary and drained. He sat down at the kitchen table and Annie brought him coffee. "What happened, sweetheart?"

Bethany sat sipping hot chocolate, pretending not to be interested.

"Todd told us the whole story about that mysterious woman and boy in church Sunday," said Knowl, reaching for the cream. Knowl proceeded to tell Annie everything Todd had confessed at the deacons' meeting. "He offered his resignation. But we refused to accept it."

"I'm glad," said Annie. "Decisions like that shouldn't be made impulsively."

"I agree. We need time to thoroughly investigate Todd's situation, consider the details of his confession, and pray for God's direction. It may take weeks or months, but we're not going to make a rush to judgment."

Anna set a plate of cookies on the table. "Will Todd continue to preach at services?"

"No. Not until the board presents its findings to the church body. At that time the members of Willowbrook Christian Church will vote to keep Reverend Marshall or to accept his resignation."

Annie took a cookie. "What will happen to that woman, Claire?"

Knowl cast an uneasy glance at Bethany. "Todd plans to marry her. I imagine the wedding will be in a week or two."

Anna's brows raised sharply. "That will certainly have tongues in Willowbrook wagging."

With a jarring motion Bethany pushed away her hot chocolate and stood up from the table. "Excuse me. It's been a long day, and I . . . I've got to get up early for the trial." She covered her mouth to stifle a sob and dashed from the room.

* * *

On Wednesday morning Luke's attorney stopped Beth in the hallway outside the courtroom and said, "Miss Henry, I'd like to talk with you a moment."

She met his solemn gaze. "What's wrong, Mr. Kimbrough?"

"Nothing's wrong. I'd just like you to know what I have planned for your brother's defense. And I'd like to ask a favor of you."

"Sure. I'll do anything to help Luke."

"Fine. That's what I like to hear." He touched her arm and said confidentially, "Today I'll be calling several character witnesses in your brother's behalf—Jake Witherspoon and his parents, among others. Tomorrow I expect you, your brother Knowl, and your sister Catherine to take the stand and tell the jury what a fine, upstanding man Luke Henry is."

Beth slung her purse strap over the shoulder of her gray wool gabardine coat. "You can count on me, Mr. Kimbrough, but I wouldn't ask Catherine to testify."

"Why not?"

"It's a long story. Just take my word, don't ask her."

Kimbrough shifted his briefcase from one hand to the other. His wide forehead was lined with annoyance; his well-oiled hair gleamed like black patent leather. "I hope you realize, Miss Henry," he said, his deep baritone vibrating with authority, "the defense will be resting its case this week."

"So soon?"

He lowered his voice perceptibly. "Perhaps you've noticed that we have very little to work with in this case. Frankly, I don't think the jury's buying Luke's story that he was asleep when your mother died."

"But it's true."

Kimbrough took Beth's elbow and steered her over to an isolated corner. "Miss Henry, let me be brutally honest with you. I've represented many clients over the years, and I've developed an amazing sixth sense. I can tell when a client's lying. Believe me, Luke knows more than he's admitting. I've confronted him over and over, and I get nothing. We have a few days left to make our argument stand. Would you talk to Luke? Tell him I need to know everything, and he'd better talk fast."

"I've tried. He says there's nothing more to tell."

"Try again, Miss Henry. It's imperative—if your brother's freedom is important to you."

"But what if he won't talk to me?"

"Try anyway. Tell Luke this is his last chance."

Beth clutched her purse strap between her clammy fingers. "I'll ask Catherine if we can stop by the jail on our way home."

Later that afternoon Bethany was ushered into the jail's drab visiting room where faded sunlight hardly penetrated the grimy barred windows. She sat down at the screened partition and waited for Luke, nervously twisting the gold clasp on her purse, snapping it open, then shut, open, shut.

When Luke was finally escorted over to his side of the partition, he sat down with a swagger and gave Beth an insolent glance. "What's the special occasion, Sis?"

She leaned forward, her mouth just inches from the screen. "We need to talk."

"Sure. How's the weather? How's the family? How's my future?"

"That's what Mr. Kimbrough is worried about. He thinks you're holding back, Luke."

"Does he?"

"Are you?"

"Nothing he needs to know."

"Luke, he can't defend you if he doesn't have all the facts. What haven't you told him?"

Luke shook his head. "Nothing. He's doing his job A-okay."

Bethany drew closer to the net. "Luke, I've got to ask. Did you have anything to do with Mama's death?"

Luke pushed a strand of umber-brown hair back from his forehead. "I told you a million times, Beth—"

"No, Luke, listen to me. Will you swear on Mama's grave you had nothing to do with her dying? Just swear it so I'll never have to ask again."

Luke sat with his elbows on the table, massaging his knuckles. His lips were closed tight but he moved them as if he were chewing something that wouldn't go away.

"Answer me, Luke!"

He lowered his head, his face etched in shadows. "Go home, Beth."

"No, not till you tell me."

He rubbed his eyes with his sturdy fingertips, pressing so hard the orbs seemed to recede into their sockets.

"Luke!"

"You don't want to know, Beth."

She pressed her palms against the rusty wire mesh. "Luke, no, you didn't!"

His large hands nearly covered his angular face. "Go home, Bethany Rose."

Hot tears stung her eyes. "Don't do this, Luke. Don't make me doubt you!"

Luke turned and signaled the guard, then glanced back at her as he unraveled his rangy, six-foot frame. "See you in court, Sis."

As he shuffled away, she pressed her face and hands hard against the screen. "Don't go, Luke!"

He went out without a backward glance, disappearing behind a gray door. She sank back against the rail-back chair and stared at the place where he'd been. He had as much as admitted he was guilty. The implications pierced her mind like shards of glass.

Dazed, Beth made her way through a maze of bleak hallways and met Catherine in the visitors' waiting area. Together they stepped out of the gray-walled facility into the dusky evening and walked half a block to the car.

Cath tied a silk scarf around her red hair. "Are you okay, Beth?"

"Yes."

"You look upset."

"I'm fine." Beth climbed in on her side and slammed the door. Too late, she realized she'd shut the door on the hem of her gabardine coat. She tugged but it held fast. She yanked harder. With a ripping sound, the coat was free. Beth fingered the torn material. "I've ruined it!"

"It's okay," said Cath. "You can buy another one."

"How could I be so stupid?"

"It's just a coat, Beth. I'll take you shopping and we'll find one just like it."

Beth examined the frayed gabardine. "Stupid, stupid!"

Cath reached over and took her hand. "What's wrong, Beth? What did Luke tell you?"

"Nothing!" Tears rolled down her cheeks and made dark spots on her coat. "I want to go home."

Cath turned the key in the ignition. "Did you and Luke have a fight?"

"Sort of."

Cath pulled out into the street and accelerated. "That brother of ours is as high-strung and excitable as they come. Has he always been that way?"

Beth nodded. "Especially since the war."

Cath turned onto the highway and merged with traffic. "Well, his impulsive streak will always get him into trouble. The way he rides the edge emotionally, he'll be the death of us yet!"

"If he doesn't destroy himself first." Bethany shivered and stared out the side window as they took the familiar route home. Night crept over them in hushed shadows, sinister as a stalking animal. The two-lane highway was like a washboard and the lights of oncoming cars seemed like glaring eyes, reading Bethany's soul.

The truth had lodged in her throat like a cold, hard egg. It could be digested only in very small pieces. Luke had done the unthinkable. Her Luke! The images blazed behind her eyes, monstrous, incomprehensible.

That night Beth lay awake for hours, staring into the darkness and struggling to make sense of things. It all came back to Luke. Her worst nightmare was true. He was guilty.

The hurt swelled inside her like a sponge soaking up water, growing bigger, heavier, compressing her ribs. She didn't want to face another day of trial. If Luke was guilty, he was no longer her brother. She would despise him for the rest of her life. But without Luke she had no security; she was a ship adrift, stripped of her moorings.

Beth drew up her knees and hugged her pillow. *Help me! Please help me!*

Was she praying? She wasn't sure; knew only a deep, aching neediness vast as a moonless night. No one could change things; no one could bring Luke, or Todd, or Mama, or Papa back again.

She was alone.

Or was she?

"Jesus," she whispered into her pillow. "Jesus." The name comforted her. She imagined Jesus holding her in His arms, imagined herself an innocent child against His breast. Over and over she whispered His name in the darkness until slumber ebbed over her like a slow, soothing wave.

When she awoke the next morning, she felt better. She had rested well. She didn't feel alone. "Thank you," she whispered like a shy child. Was God easing her pain? Was He there for her even though she had doubted Him?

At breakfast Knowl was already nursing a cup of black coffee and reading his newspaper. "Would you believe, wages are up 130 percent from 1939. Says right here in a Labor Department report. Trouble is, buying power increased only 35 percent."

Beth sat down and reached for her glass of orange juice. "Good morning," she said softly.

"You look rested," said Annie as she passed the toast.

Beth took a slice and passed it to Knowl. "I feel better than I did last night."

"Good. We were worried about you. You came in looking so exhausted. I think this trial is too much for you."

"No, really, I'm okay, Annie."

"Well, Catherine's a little under the weather this morning. She called and said she won't be able to drive you to Fort Wayne. I imagine it's morning sickness."

Beth looked over urgently at Knowl. "I need to be there."

He folded his newspaper. "Don't worry, I'll drive you. Kimbrough called, asked me to be there today and testify in Luke's behalf. Just let me make a call to the office. Then we'll be on our way."

When they arrived at the Fort Wayne courthouse, Joseph Kimbrough was pacing the hallway and looking agitated. Seeing Beth, he strode over with an air of determination, shook hands civilly with Knowl, then turned and placed a paternal hand on her shoulder. "We need to talk, Miss Henry."

Again? She tried to keep her voice casual. "What's wrong?"

Kimbrough's jowls swelled with consternation. "Luke asked to meet with me this morning. He wants to take the stand and tell his story."

Knowl scowled. "What on earth does he plan to say?"

"That's just it, Mr. Herrick. He won't reveal a word until he's on the witness stand. Do you realize how dangerous this can be for him? A lot's at stake here. The wrong word and he seals his fate. It's over."

Alarm knotted Beth's stomach. "Tell him he can't do it."

"I make recommendations to my clients, Miss Henry, but I can't dictate. I've already told Luke I don't want him taking the stand. It's risky. He could be throwing his life and his freedom right out the window. But the final decision is his."

Bethany clasped the attorney's arm. "Make him listen to you, please!"

"I'll do what I can." He pushed back the sleeve of his houndstooth jacket and looked at his watch. "It's time to go in. Court starts in five minutes. I'll be calling you and Knowl to the stand first thing. Then we'll see what Luke decides to do."

When court convened, Knowl was first to take the stand. His manner was formal and reserved, but he spoke well of Luke, and his voice was compelling as he confirmed that, from what he had seen, Luke was a devoted son and brother.

When it was Beth's turn, her heart pounded and her knees were shaking as she swore on the Bible to tell the truth, the whole truth, and nothing but the truth. Of course she would tell the truth! But what if she said something that made the jury aware of her own doubts about Luke?

Kimbrough asked her first about the night of the fire. She repeated what she had already told the prosecution. She had seen nothing out of the ordinary that night except a woman's shadow on the wall and had heard nothing except two women arguing—her mother and the woman she knew now to be Betty Herrick.

"And you never heard any kind of argument between your mother and the defendant, Luke Henry?"

"No. Nothing."

"What was the nature of Luke's relationship with his mother?"

"It was good. He would do anything for Mama. He loved her."

During cross-examination, the prosecutor challenged Bethany's statement. "Surely there were times when your mother and brother didn't see eye to eye. How often did they argue?"

"Hardly ever," she insisted.

"But they did fight occasionally."

"Sometimes."

"Perhaps the night of the fire?"

"No!"

"But you don't know for sure, do you, Miss Henry? You were asleep."

"Yes, but—"

"Anything could have happened that night. You testified earlier that you took sleeping pills, and you were in a drugged sleep. Isn't it true that Luke Henry could have killed your mother and set fire to the house and you wouldn't have known?"

"I . . . I don't know!"

"No further questions, Miss Henry."

Bethany sat down, trembling, as Mr. Kimbrough stood up and announced, "The defense calls to the stand Mr. Lucas Henry."

She watched, numb with dread, as Luke marched forward, was sworn in, and took his seat on the stand. He gazed directly at Beth and seemed to be telling her something with his eyes; but she couldn't quite read them, or perhaps she was afraid of glimpsing a truth she couldn't face.

Mr. Kimbrough circled the floor in front of Luke, his hands behind his back, his head down. "Mr. Henry, is it true you're testifying today against the advice of your attorney?"

Luke sat hunched over, looking ill at ease in his pea green jail coveralls, his hands clasped between his knees. A thatch of wheat-brown hair hung over his forehead; his heavy, arched brows drooped over his dark, glowering eyes. "Yes, sir."

"All right, Mr. Henry, there's been a lot of conjecture and speculation in this courtroom about what happened the night your mother died. Would you like to tell us now in your own words what happened on the night of August 17, 1949?"

"Yes, sir." Luke shifted in his seat and cracked his knuckles. For a moment Bethany thought he had changed his mind and would bolt out of his chair and scramble back to the defense table. But no. He heaved a sigh, shifted in his chair, and seemed to settle in.

She could see his mind working, pulling together the words to tell his story. She felt a sudden urge to run up and grab his hand and lead him from the courtroom before he said something stupid. But at the same time she sat mesmerized, her heart racing, impatient to hear the truth that had eluded everyone for over half a year.

His voice came out in a slow drawl. "It was hot that night—the night my mama died—even with the sun down. Hot and humid. The kinda night you can't sleep because the air is dead still and you're drenching wet with sweat. Even the flies were listless, droning slow around the room like it took all their effort to stay airborne."

"Please get to the point, Mr. Henry," urged Kimbrough.

Luke nodded. "I had just dozed off when I heard someone at the door. I turned over and went back to sleep, figuring it was probably Jake Witherspoon come to see my sister again. But pretty soon I hear people arguing. Women's voices. Mama and someone I don't know. I get up and stand by my door, listening. They stop talking a minute and I look out through a crack in my door."

"What did you see, Mr. Henry?"

"I see this woman done up fancy in a silk dress and a hat with a big feather sticking out. I watch her go to Bethany's room and just stand there in the doorway, looking. For the longest time she just stands there staring in at Beth by the light of the hall. I begin to think she's crazy or something, maybe even dangerous.

"I'm about ready to go see what's up with this dame, but I'm in my skivvies, so I go pull on my trousers. When I come back to the door she's gone and I hear her and Mama at it again in the living room. I go down the hall and stand there listening, out of sight. What I hear freezes my blood. This dame is blaming Mama for stealing her husband!"

"Did you know who this woman was, Mr. Henry?"

"Yeah. It dawns on me this is Betty Herrick, Knowl and Cath's mama from Willowbrook. Papa's other wife. She's ranting and raving about Mama stealing her man and ruining her life. I can smell liquor on her all the way into the hallway, so I know she's stewed."

"Mr. Henry, do you recall any of the conversation between your mother and Mrs. Herrick?"

"Some of it. For a while my mama tries to calm her down, saying she didn't mean no harm by marrying Tom Henry; she didn't know beans about his other family. She says, 'Don't blame me. Tom lied to both of us.' But nothing helps, and finally Mama gets just as riled as the Herrick woman and starts shouting back at her, telling her Papa wouldn't of strayed if she'd been half a woman to him."

"Where were you at the time?"

"I'm standing in the hallway, listening, and I figure these two women are gonna kill each other. So I step out and try to break them up, but it don't work. Pretty soon we're all shouting and shoving each other around. Finally, the Herrick dame marches to the screen door and says, 'I was Tom's real wife; you were just his mistress, a cheap trollop. He never loved you. He loved me!'"

Luke's gaze drifted across the courtroom. "She goes stomping out the door, and for the first time I see a taxi waiting in the driveway, its lights on like it's waiting for a fast getaway. Mama follows the Herrick dame to the door, shouting, 'Tom loved me, not you!' The woman's already climbing in her taxi when Mama grabs Papa's shotgun by the door and aims it, shouting, 'I'll kill that woman! I'll kill her!'"

The courtroom was hushed. "On instinct I lunged for the gun and jerked it hard from Mama's arms, flinging her backward. I heard her head hit hard on the sharp metal corner of the trunk, and she just slumped to the floor like she was asleep. I swear I was just trying to keep her from shooting that gun and having a murder on her conscience. But next thing I know she was dead."

A loud sob broke the stunned silence. Bethany looked around, startled, then realized the wrenching sound came from her own throat. Knowl handed her his handkerchief. She covered her mouth, the convulsive sobs wracking her frame. Knowl moved close and drew her into his arms, pressing her head against his chest, her tear-stained cheek resting against the textured fabric of his jacquard suit.

Kimbrough spoke up, his own voice uneven. "Do you wish to continue, Mr. Henry?"

Luke bowed his head, blinked rapidly, and pinched his nostrils. "Yeah, I gotta get it all out once and for all." His voice wavered, heavy with emotion. "That old trunk, I brought it home from France. Carried all my stuff in it. I loved that trunk. But when I saw what it did to Mama, I wanted to take a hatchet to it.

"At first I thought Mama couldn't be dead. I bent down and called her name. I said, 'Mama, get up. That woman's gone. It's okay, Mama.' But she didn't move. Then I saw the blood oozing out by her ear. I sat down on the floor and held her in my arms, cradling her head and smoothing back her hair, pleading with her to wake up and be okay. But she was still as a gravestone, limp as an old rag doll. I kept saying, 'I'm sorry, Mama. I didn't mean to hurt you. Come back, Mama!'

"But I knew all along she was dead. In the war I saw my buddies die. I walked over their bodies on the beach at Normandy. I know how a body looks when the spirit's gone out of it and there's nothing left but the shell. That's how Mama looked. She was long gone."

Bethany heard someone in the jury box weeping. Luke cracked his knuckles, one hand, then the other. He lowered his head, cupped his fingers at the back of his neck, and rocked back and forth, slowly, rhythmically, as if putting himself in a trance.

"Son, you don't have to go on," said Judge McPherson.

Luke shrugged. "Don't much matter now, your honor," he said in a slow, hollow drawl. "I just sat rocking Mama in my arms like a baby, but in my head I was back at Normandy, scaling that bloody beach, heading for the cliffs, climbing over my comrades lying twisted and broken around me. I could smell death, taste it in my mouth, hear the sound of it shrieking in my ears. I was back running up that hill, stumbling over glassy-eyed corpses, racing pell-mell into a ragged dawn splintered with screams and artillery fire."

Luke sat back and raked both hands through his thick umber hair. He inhaled deeply and released the air slowly through pursed lips. His eyes were closed; his Adam's apple moved as he swallowed.

Judge McPherson cleared his throat. "Do you wish to continue, Mr. Henry?"

Luke looked up as if surprised to see someone else in the room. "Yeah, Judge, I'm okay." He sat forward again and stared down at his hands. He ran his thumb over each large knuckle. "It was ten, maybe twenty minutes I sat there with Mama. After a while I knew I had to do something. I couldn't have Bethany waking up and finding Mama like that. So I laid her down gently on the floor. I went to my room and pulled the sheet off my bed and gathered towels from the hamper. I put them in a pile beside Mama. Then I went to the barn, got some kerosene, and doused the heap real good. Don't ask me what I was thinking. I *wasn't* thinking. I just knew I didn't want Bethany thinking I hurt Mama. I'd never hurt Mama."

Another sob broke from the jury. Bethany could hear several weeping now, just as she was.

"What did you do then, Mr. Henry?" asked Kimbrough.

"I grabbed the matches and lit the rags," said Luke. "They exploded into flames so fast I had to jump back. It scared me, seeing how the fire raced off in every direction, like it had a mind of its own. I grabbed up my jacket and started swatting the flames. I tried to put it out, but it was too late. It just took over."

"What did you do then?"

"I panicked. I screamed for Bethany, but the room was turning black with smoke. I was getting disoriented. I tried to find her but I went down the wrong hall and lost my bearings. Thank God, she woke up and crawled into the living room. I found her there and carried her outside to safety. She thought I was a hero. Isn't that a hoot? Luke Henry, a hero!"

After a long silence, Judge McPherson turned to the prosecutor. "Do you wish to cross-examine the defendant?"

"Under the circumstances, your honor, the prosecution requests a recess until tomorrow to review this new information."

Judge McPherson looked at Luke. "Thank you, Mr. Henry. You may step down now." Rapping his gavel on the desk, the judge intoned, "Court is dismissed until nine o'clock tomorrow morning."

18

On Friday, March 24th, both the prosecution and the defense delivered their closing arguments, and the trial was over. On Monday the jury would begin its deliberations, and soon Bethany would know her brother's fate.

When Catherine dropped her off at Herrick House on Friday evening Beth felt emotionally drained and physically exhausted. She didn't want to see or talk with anyone. These were her darkest days since her mother's death. Piece by piece her life was crumbling before her eyes. She wanted nothing more than to soak in a hot tub, get in bed early, and forget that her brother's life hung in the balance and the man she loved was about to marry another woman.

But when Bethany stepped inside the foyer and smelled Anna's pot roast, she decided to head for the dining room for just a bite to eat before going upstairs to her room.

The rest of the family was already at the table, chatting amid the clink and clatter of silverware. Bethany paused in the doorway, welcoming a little pleasant banter. Instead she heard an alarming snatch of conversation.

"Who knows? Maybe this wedding will silence the gossipmills," Anna was saying.

"What disturbs me," said Annie, "is that members of our own

church have chosen sides like players in an athletic event. Some condemn Reverend Marshall with such smugness, it sets my teeth on edge."

"Don't forget, Annie, many others have rallied around him and insisted he be forgiven."

"But until we're of one mind, this thing could tear our church apart," said Knowl. "I've never seen people so convinced their view is the only one. Only God can bring us through this as one body."

"Willowbrook Christian Church has survived the trials and upheavals of half a century," noted Anna. "We'll survive this too."

Bethany stood listening in the doorway until Annie looked up, startled, and saw her. "Beth, we didn't hear you come in. Come, sit down. We just started dinner."

Bethany took her place next to Annie and spread her napkin in her lap. "What were you talking about?"

"Nothing that can't keep," Annie replied.

"Tell me. I want to know."

"All right." Knowl sopped up the gravy on his plate with a crust of bread. "We were talking about Todd. We were saying maybe tongues will stop wagging after he and Claire are married."

Beth reached for the mashed potatoes. "No one's told me, have they set a date?"

"Yes," said Annie quietly. "It's tomorrow."

"So soon?" Bethany felt as if she had been slapped.

"Todd thinks it's best not to delay it," said Knowl. "Old Reverend Henry will be doing the honors."

"Reverend Henry?" echoed Anna. "He's so frail these days—and rather forgetful."

Knowl smiled. "They're bringing him out of mothballs for the occasion."

Annie shook her head. "Knowl, what would the deacons say if they heard you speaking so disrespectfully of Reverend Henry?"

"I got it from old Henry himself. He complains about being put out to pasture, but he's good-natured about it. He'll enjoy having a wedding to perform, even if it is Willowbrook's most controversial."

Annie glanced over at Beth, then back at Knowl. "Dear, I'm sure Bethany doesn't want to hear about Reverend Marshall's wedding."

Knowl looked at her, his brow furrowing. "I'm sorry, Beth. I'm sure this isn't an easy time for you. I know how you feel about Todd."

Bethany twisted her linen napkin. "No, you don't know how I feel. I don't care what Reverend Marshall does. I don't care if he . . . if he . . ." Her throat closed up, cutting off her words. Dropping her napkin on her plate, she pushed back her chair, jumped up, and ran upstairs to her room. She shut her door and threw herself on her bed.

Yes, of course she cared! She cared more than she could ever admit. She couldn't imagine Todd exchanging wedding vows with another woman.

Why was God playing such cruel tricks on her, letting her love a man who seemed a saint, then revealing his feet of clay and snatching him away?

An old, familiar question ricocheted in her mind—the niggling doubt she had tucked away in recent months. Had she committed her life to God just to please Todd Marshall? And now that Todd had been torn from her life, was God gone as well? Did He still love her? Did she even want His love anymore?

At noon on Saturday, March 25th, Knowl and Annie left to attend Reverend Marshall's wedding. Only a handful of people had been invited; Bethany wasn't one of them. Not that she would have gone anyway. She wasn't fool enough to punish herself that way. No, as far as she was concerned, she would just as soon never lay eyes on Todd Marshall again.

She couldn't bear to sit around the house doing nothing while Todd was saying wedding vows to his first love, so she bundled up in her nubby wool coat and went out for a walk in the crisp, rain-washed air.

She walked along Honeysuckle Lane, breathing in the heady scents of spring—green buds emerging on bare tree limbs, sprigs of tender grass breaking through the thawing earth, blue skies and billowy clouds replacing the gray haze of winter. Amazing how suddenly the snow was gone, leaving the earth free to rouse itself and come alive again.

But it was still winter in Bethany's heart; a turgid chill had settled over her spirits, so frigid even a warming world couldn't thaw it.

She walked several blocks to a small park with varnished redwood benches nestled among weeping willows, twisted oaks, and hearty maples. She recognized the park from several of Catherine's paintings; it was here Cath first met Luke several years ago. If Luke hadn't introduced Beth to Papa's other family, she never would have come to Willowbrook; she'd probably still be in Fort Wayne, maybe married to Jake Witherspoon.

The thought of Jake made her shiver. Once she might have been satisfied with Jake, but not now—not after she had tasted what real love could be.

Beth sat down on a bench under a gnarled oak and unbuttoned her coat. She shook her long, burnished curls loose and stretched out her bare legs. She was wearing a mohair sweaterdress and saddle shoes with rolled white socks. After the suffocating warmth of the house, the cold air felt invigorating. It wouldn't be long before summer came and she could wear her gauzy spring dresses.

But she dreaded facing spring and summer without Todd; she dreaded facing the rest of her life without the man she loved. Would she ever love anyone so wholeheartedly again?

Aloud she said, "Why did you do this to me, God? I promised to love You and serve You; I promised to be a good Christian. I thought I could trust You, but You keep taking things away from me. You took

Papa and Mama and Luke—I don't know how long he'll be in jail, maybe the rest of his life—and now you're taking Todd. What do I have left?"

She had her new family, of course, and a glimpse of how wonderful life could be when two people in love served God together. So God had given her much and taken away much. How could she figure it all out? How could she ever understand God's mysterious ways?

"Why should I keep trusting You, God?" she whispered, her voice sounding hollow in the rain-scented air. "Is there anything You can tell me to make this hurt go away, to show me things will be all right again?"

From her memory came the words from Romans, *He that spared not his own Son, but delivered him up for us all, how shall he not with him also freely give us all things?* Bethany wasn't sure what the words meant, but in a way it made sense. If God gave His Son to die for people's sins, He wouldn't turn around and play tricks on them. If God had already given the most precious part of Himself, why wouldn't He freely give other good things as well?

Bethany sat forward and put her head in her hands. "I thought it was going to be the three of us, God—You, me, and Todd. Now it's just the two of us. I didn't bargain on that. I don't know if I can do it."

She sat on the park bench thinking things through until she was sure the wedding would be over. Then she walked back home, at once dreading, yet desperate to hear how the wedding had gone.

Knowl and Annie were already home, sitting in the parlor, chatting with Anna. Beth slipped in and sat down in the rocker by the bay window. The house felt stifling after the clean, cold air outside; her heart was pounding and she couldn't quite catch her breath.

Anna gave Beth an expansive smile. "Well, dear, the wind has put some red in your cheeks. Did you have a nice walk?"

Beth nodded. "I went to the park. The trees are budding."

"Yes, I love this time of year. It'll only get better."

Bethany turned her gaze to Knowl and Annie. "The wedding?"

"Do you really want to hear about it, Beth?" asked Annie.

She lifted her chin. "Yes. Tell me."

"It was at the parsonage," said Knowl. "Only a few people were there. It was very brief. Reverend Henry had them recite their vows and that was about it."

"Was she pretty—Todd's bride?"

"She wore an old-fashioned lace dress," said Annie, "and she was in a wheelchair. She looked very pale."

"How did Todd's mama like him getting married?"

"She didn't approve, Beth. In fact, she moved out of the house two days ago. Packed her bags and went back to New York."

Beth sighed. "I guess that's one way to get rid of the old battle-ax."

Annie covered her mouth, stifling a smile. "Goodness, Bethany, such language!"

They all laughed.

"I'm sure the woman means well," said Knowl, composing himself.

"I'm not," said Anna. "That woman's a troublemaker. Todd and his bride will be better off without her."

"I'm not so sure," said Annie. "Todd was counting on his mother to help him care for Claire and the boy. He's made some inquiries for help, but people are afraid of catching TB—even though doctors have assured Claire she's unlikely to be contagious at this stage of her illness."

"I'd help, but I have my hands full around here," said Anna.

Annie nodded. "I'd like to help, too, but I have Maggie—and Jenny, some days."

Knowl removed his tie. "There must be someone at church who could help out. I'll check into it myself."

For a moment Beth thought, *I'd help if I didn't have Luke to visit and worry about*. But she quickly swallowed her words. There was no way she would go help Todd with his new family. No thanks! No way on earth!

On Sunday morning Bethany stayed in bed while the rest of the family had breakfast and dressed for church. When Annie peeked in and inquired about her health, Beth groaned, "I'm feeling plumb poorly. You go on without me."

"All right, dear, you just rest, and I'll bring you up some hot tea and toast."

Beth rolled over and pulled her pillow over her head. Tea and sympathy wouldn't cure her misery; nothing would heal the ache of seeing Reverend Marshall walk into church with his new bride on his arm. Beth stayed in bed all day, until hunger drove her to the kitchen, where Anna fixed her a sandwich, plied her with Jell-0, and checked her forehead for fever.

On Monday morning, as Bethany's thoughts turned to Luke, heartache gave way to anxiety. Today the jury would meet and decide Luke's fate. At any moment he could become a free man—or a condemned man. All day Beth listened for the phone, convinced Mr. Kimbrough would call and tell her the verdict was in. But the phone remained maddeningly silent.

On Tuesday and Wednesday Beth's concern grew. Why was it taking the jury so long? Wasn't it obvious that Luke was innocent? Why hadn't they reached a decision?

Early Thursday morning, as Anna was serving breakfast, Kimbrough called at last. Bethany jumped up from the table and ran to the phone, but the news was disappointing. "Two jurors have taken ill—the flu, I suppose—so they won't meet again till the first of the week."

"It's taking forever," Beth complained. "How long will we have to wait?"

"No one knows," said Kimbrough, "but I suspect we'll have a verdict before the week is out."

"Do you have any idea—?"

"How it'll go? No, Miss Henry. It could go either way. Trying to second-guess juries is a waste of my time—and yours. Don't sit around moping. Get out in the fresh air and sunshine. Do something to keep your mind off things."

"I will. But how is Luke?" she asked, ashamed to admit she hadn't seen him since the trial. What would she say to him? She was still sorting out a torrent of mixed emotions.

"Luke's on edge, impatient, but he's holding on. Go see him. You two need each other. He could use a friendly face."

"I'll try," said Beth halfheartedly. *But don't you understand? I don't want to go back to Fort Wayne until I can bring Luke home!*

She returned to the table and helped herself to the scrambled eggs, but she wasn't hungry anymore.

"Any news?" asked Knowl.

She shook her head.

"I know it's trite," said Annie, "but maybe no news is good news."

Beth poked at the fluffy mound on her plate. "I'll go crazy if I don't hear some news soon."

Anna, wisps of hair flying loose around her face, scooted in from the kitchen with a platter of bacon and set it on the table. "If anyone wants more coffee, it's on the stove."

"Goodness, Mama, you're buzzing around here like a little bumblebee."

"I know, daughter. After breakfast I'm going to the A&P for some vegetables and beef stock. I promised Reverend Marshall I'd bring over some homemade soup this afternoon."

Beth looked up, suddenly alert. "Reverend Marshall?"

Anna nodded. "That poor man is wearing himself out caring for that new little family of his. He doesn't know the first thing about cooking, and his bride is too ill to get out of bed."

"I thought the ladies' auxiliary was taking food in," said Knowl, sipping his coffee.

"Oh, they've brought plenty of cakes and casseroles, but most folks don't want to go in and scrub a floor, change a bed sheet, or scour a sink. Like I said, the reverend has his hands full."

"What about the boy?" asked Knowl. "Is he adjusting?"

"He's enrolled in school now. Third grade at Willowbrook Elementary. Isabel Clarenton's class. The bus picks him up just down the street from the parsonage. It's good he gets away from the house. He's so worried about his mother."

Bethany traced the water ring from her juice glass. "You don't suppose—Todd won't catch tuberculosis, will he?"

"He doesn't seem worried about it," said Anna. "He says he's taking proper precautions. The doctors tell him she's not that contagious now anyway, even with prolonged contact."

"They could be wrong," said Beth. "He might be risking his life for that woman."

"It's his choice," said Annie gently.

The wrong choice! Beth chewed her last bite of toast, but it was dry and hard to swallow.

A lot like life! she mused glumly.

19

On Saturday morning, April 1st, as the sun shone down with a golden, healing warmth, Bethany took little Maggie out to the backyard gazebo to play. Dressed in a seersucker pinafore and white sandals, Maggie carried a drawstring bag of wooden clothespins. Beth carried her paint box, scissors, glue, and scraps of fabric. She planned to create an entire clothespin family for Maggie before lunchtime.

After spending so much time in a stuffy courtroom, Beth welcomed the fresh air and sunshine. It was unseasonably warm for April—a promise perhaps of an early summer. The craggy oaks and sturdy maples were coming alive with the green confetti of budding leaves, their twisted limbs stretching to form a canopy over a garden giving birth to yellow, purple, and white crocuses. Beth welcomed the feeling of rebirth in the fragrant air; how her own heart needed healing and reviving.

As a brave sparrow twittered on the gazebo's latticework, Bethany opened her paint box on the little whitewashed bench and removed several small brushes. Maggie opened the cloth bag and produced a handful of clothespins which she thrust at Beth. "Paint me! Paint Maggie!"

"I will," said Beth. "I'll paint a big red smile, two big blue eyes, and a little button nose." As she opened a jar of poster paint, she noticed someone walking through the garden toward the gazebo. It was Todd Marshall.

"Hello, Bethany." In a casual long-sleeve shirt and khaki slacks, he ambled over, planted one foot on the pinewood platform, and leaned against a whitened post. It had been only a week or more since she had seen him, but he looked thinner somehow, his eyes shadowed, his cheekbones leaner and without color. "Anna told me you were out here with Maggie. Just thought I'd come out and say hello." He smiled, not the smile she remembered, but a pale imitation. "I brought back the kettle from the soup Anna made us."

"Oh. Did you like it?"

"I've never tasted better."

Beth picked up a clothespin and twirled it between her fingers. "Anna loves cooking for people. She'll probably make you some more soup. Or maybe a casserole."

"I hope she does. My culinary skills are woefully limited." Bethany turned her attention to the clothespin in her hand. She dipped a brush in the red and painted a half-moon smile.

Todd stepped closer. "What are you making?"

"Clothespin people for Maggie."

"Really? Clothespins?" He took the one she was painting and examined it. "I wouldn't have imagined."

"She loves them."

"Mine!" Maggie grabbed the pin from his hand.

"Wait, Maggie. Be nice. Besides, it's not done yet." Beth took the pin and finished with a few quick strokes of red, blue, and brown, and handed it to Maggie. "Now you sit right here on the floor and play, okay?"

Todd moved the paint box and sat down beside her. He drummed his fingers on his knees as if he were waiting for something. Then he glanced around the garden as if he hadn't seen trees before.

Bethany patiently screwed the lids on her paint jars.

"You look quite well," he said finally. "I heard you were under the weather last Sunday."

She nodded. "I'm better now."

"Good. I'm glad. Knowl told me the trial's over, and he mentioned your brother's testimony. I imagine you must have been devastated by it all."

She nodded again. "At least now I know the truth. Luke didn't try to hurt Mama. It was all a terrible accident."

"And the fire?"

"Luke was crazy to burn down the house. He gets crazy sometimes. Does crazy things. But he didn't do it to be mean."

"So you've been able to forgive Luke?"

She wanted to say, *I've forgiven him, Todd, but not you!* But she held her tongue and said only, "He's my brother. I love him."

Todd smiled wanly. "I admire your loyalty. It's very rare these days."

"Is it?" she asked coolly.

He ignored the question and asked instead, "Do you have any idea when the jury will reach a verdict?"

"No one knows. We just have to wait."

"That must be very hard."

Beth nodded.

"Are you still taking your college classes?"

"I won't go back to school till I know about Luke. I've missed so much, I'll probably have to take the semester over."

Todd moved his hand toward hers, then withdrew it, as if thinking better of the idea. "I've missed you, Beth," he said in a voice edged with pain. "I never dreamed my life would take this turn—that I would find myself a married man with a young son. It's quite an adjustment."

She picked up another clothespin and began painting its face.

Black eyes, a jagged mouth, uneven nose. Her hand shook. She didn't want to hear about Todd's marital adjustments.

He must have sensed her sudden coolness, for he said quickly, "I'm sorry. You're the last person I should burden with my troubles."

The dismay in his voice softened her and prompted her to ask, "What troubles?"

"Nothing, Beth. I spoke out of turn."

She handed the painted clothespin to Maggie; the child had surrounded herself with pins and was pushing them one by one through the latticework. Beth looked back at Todd. "I mean it. I want to know."

He looked at her, his eyes a vivid blue. "Are you sure?"

"I asked, didn't I?" She wanted to know and didn't want to know in equal portions.

He shifted his torso, facing her on the narrow bench. "The truth is, I'm not sure how long I can manage. God knows I don't want to do it, but I may have to commit Claire to a sanatorium. And the boy! I'm at my wit's end. I don't know the first thing about raising a child!"

"Can't you get help? Hire someone—a nurse?"

"I've looked into it, but I can't afford much on a minister's salary. And, of course, if the people vote me out . . . but that's a bridge I don't have to cross quite yet."

They both lapsed into silence. Bethany looked down at Maggie. She had curled up and fallen asleep on the hard floorboards, using the clothespin bag for a pillow.

Todd noticed too, and smiled, a faint, bittersweet smile. "Precious little life. So innocent and trusting."

Beth nodded. "She doesn't know yet how hard life can be."

"I guess none of us realize it, until it's too late."

"What about the people at church? Aren't they helping?"

"Oh, they've been very kind—most of them. There are a few who have made it clear they think Claire's tuberculosis is the result of our

. . . our sin. But most folks have expressed sympathy and concern. Some even stop by and bring flowers and pies and pot roasts and visit a moment; but then they're gone."

"Your mama—maybe she'll come back."

Todd's brows arched sharply. "No, Bethany, my mother is gone for good. Back to New York where she belongs."

"But if she knew you needed help?"

He made a sound in his throat, like laughter, only hard and bitter. "My mother has controlled my entire life, Beth. Did you know that? I didn't. Not until Claire arrived and revealed the truth. My mother sent Claire away, knowing she was carrying my child. Paid her off, swore her to secrecy. Never said a word to me in all these years."

"Maybe she was just trying to protect you."

"Yes, that's what she said, but I won't accept it. I've been a fool long enough. Now I see it so clearly—her endless manipulations, the frowning little looks, her peevish tone of voice. How I shuddered inside, how I died a little, when I sensed her disfavor. I dreaded her disapproval more than the wrath of God. God shows mercy. But not my mother."

Todd stood up, absorbed in his own private reverie; he took several circling paces, then sat back down. "Who knows? Perhaps she controlled my father as well. Perhaps it wasn't the stock market crash that caused him to fire the shot that sent him to his grave. Perhaps it was my mother with her hateful, wheedling ways."

"Todd, don't do this to yourself." Beth hadn't intended this reaction, but her heart went out to him; she felt his pain to her very marrow. This man she had idolized had never seemed so needy, so broken.

She placed her hand on his shoulder, a gesture meant to be comforting; but touching him was electric and made her yearn for more—the warmth of his arms, the sweetness of his kiss. She saw the same yearning in his eyes.

He moved toward her, his face just inches from hers; then he shrank back and swiveled away from her. "I'm sorry, Bethany. I've surrendered my right to express my feelings for you."

Again, there was a long, uncomfortable silence. Beth was about to suggest it was time for her to take Maggie inside, but she resisted, not wanting to end these few fleeting moments together.

Todd looked at her as if he wanted to say something, then folded his hands, pressed them against his chin, and gazed off into the distance. At last he cleared his throat and said, "It's been a rude awakening for me, Beth. I've always seen myself as a capable man, a godly man, an honorable man. Now, all of that is ashes in the wind. I'm not capable, I'm hardly honorable, and lately I doubt even that I'm a godly man.

"Since my reputation has been sullied, I realize that much of my righteousness was self-righteousness; much of my moral uprightness was simply pride. You see, Beth, even if the church chooses to keep me as their pastor, I'm not sure I can remain. I sincerely doubt I'm equipped to shepherd them."

"Don't talk that way, Todd, please. You're the one who taught me all I know about God. You're the one who made me want to love Him like you do."

Todd put his face in his hands. "And I do love Him, Beth. Perhaps now more than ever before. But since I learned about Claire and the child, I've had to reexamine all my old assumptions about who I am and what God has called me to do. Everything I believed about myself, my life, has been turned inside-out, upside-down."

He looked at her, his eyes moist, desolate. "I'm not capable. It was my mother. She was always there taking care of me, fixing my meals, washing my clothes, running the household. Now that she's gone I'm a bumbling idiot. Claire had to show me how to poach an egg, iron a shirt, put clothes through the wringer. I'm helpless when it comes to coping with everyday life."

"You'll learn, Todd. It just takes time."

He chuckled to himself. "It's irony at its most exquisite. I can read the Bible in Greek and Hebrew; I can quote hundreds of passages of Scripture from memory; I can prepare a perfect three-point outline. And yet I feel as if nothing in all my years of seminary training prepared me to navigate through real life."

Beth picked up a clothespin figure and tucked it in Todd's shirt pocket. "I don't know anything about seminary or Greek or Hebrew, but you taught me the most important thing."

He patted the wooden figure in his pocket. "Really? What's that, Beth?"

She pushed a silky ringlet behind her ear. "Jesus loves me. The Bible says so."

He nodded. "And that's what I have to hold on to right now." He heaved a sigh, stood up, and stretched. "I've overstayed my welcome. I'd better head home. Danny's watching his mom."

She stood up too, desiring to engage Todd in conversation for as long as possible. The terms of their relationship no longer mattered; she needed to see him, be with him, hear his voice, share his thoughts. "Do you have to go?"

He gazed at her for a long moment, a look so penetrating she felt it to her very toes. She wanted to say, *How do I forget you? How do I tear you from my heart now that you're part of me*? Instead, she said, "Tell me what to do . . . to help you."

"Help me? You want to help?"

She hadn't thought of it before, but there it was, suddenly as clear as the April sunshine warming their faces. "Yes, I want to help."

"You mean, help me at the parsonage? With Claire? With Danny?"

She nodded. *No! Was she mad? She couldn't possibly enter the house he shared with that woman and their son!*

Todd scratched his head, his eyes brightening. "Well, if you're serious, you could come over sometime and fix a meal, or maybe help Claire with her bath, or read Danny a bedtime story. Or maybe he's too old for stories, I don't know. Is that what you mean? You really want to lend a hand?"

She swallowed over a lump in her throat. She tried to speak, but her mouth was dry. She stammered, "I . . . I don't know when—"

"How about Monday? I'll drive over and pick you up."

She shaded her eyes with her hand to block the sun's glare. "All right. Unless the jury comes back with their decision."

"Fair enough. I'll see you Monday."

"What about Sunday? Will I see you at church?"

His brow furrowed. "If I can find someone to spell me, I'll be there. But, of course, I won't be preaching."

"I know. My brother Knowl's been preaching."

"And doing a fine job. But it's hard to be there and not be in the pulpit. Pride, I suppose. But I'd better learn to subdue it before it crushes me."

"Don't, Todd. You're too hard on yourself."

He shrugged. "Or maybe not hard enough."

Beth glanced back toward the gazebo. "I'd better go get Maggie before she wakes up and finds me gone. I don't want her crying."

"Sure. I'll see myself out." Todd gave a little self-conscious salute. "It was good talking with you, Beth. You don't know how good. I feel better about things, thanks to you."

She watched him turn and stride back to the house, her gaze lingering until he was out of sight. Even then she resisted turning away, lest she lose the sweet sensation of his presence. When she heard his car pull out of the driveway, she stirred and turned back to the gazebo. Inhaling sharply and rolling her eyes toward heaven, she wondered what on earth she had gotten herself into, promising to help Todd Marshall with his new family!

20

As he had promised, Todd picked Bethany up on Monday morning and drove her to the rambling two-story parsonage on the east side of Willowbrook. Beth had little to say on the ride over; her mind was whirling with questions and doubts. What had possessed her to help the man she loved care for his ailing wife? Was she so desperate that she would do anything to be with him? Would his wife and child resent her presence or consider her an intruder? Was Bethany risking her own health by exposing herself to someone with tuberculosis?

She pushed the questions to the back of her mind when Todd pulled into the driveway of the old gothic residence he called home. Beth sensed an aura of gloom as he helped her out of the car and escorted her up the uneven steps to the gabled porch. She wasn't coming here for his birthday dinner or a Christmas party, as she had before. She had no future with Todd.

At the paneled front door, he told her, "I must warn you, Beth, the house is a bit mussed. Since Mother left I haven't had time to keep it up, what with caring for Claire and Danny."

"It's okay. I'll straighten things up."

"Another thing." He touched her elbow; she was wearing her fleecy cardigan and denim jumper. "Claire didn't want you to come."

"Why? Did you tell her about . . . us?"

"I told her we're good friends. She just doesn't want to impose on you. All along she's wanted me to commit her to a sanatorium so she wouldn't be a burden."

Beth wanted to sav, *Then why didn't you?*

Todd unlocked the door and opened it a crack. "I'd just like vou to reassure her that it's best for her to be here where I can care for her. I owe her that much."

Beth resisted a curt reply, *What about what you owe me?* But anger and indignation wouldn't do at a time like this. Silentlv she prayed, *Help me, God, not to hate this woman. Help me to be kind no matter how hurt I feel.*

With Todd just behind her, Beth stepped inside the carpeted fover and crossed the hallwav to the living room. The air smelled heavv—of foods not quite fresh and bathrooms not quite clean; and medicinal—of emollient, Vaseline, camphor, or something equally pungent; and acrid—a hint of bacon grease with a slightlv rancid smell, and other foods overcooked or scorched.

The room itself seemed ajar, with a bov's shirt tossed over the flowered settee, a tweed jacket thrown over the Queen Anne chair, a toy metal truck on the floor, and stacks of vellowed newspapers and unopened mail on the mahoganv tables. The red velvet drapes were closed, giving the dark paneled woodwork an even drearier cast.

Beth let out a little exclamation of surprise. Todd, apparentlv seeing the room as she saw it, said, "I told vou, Beth. I'm sorrv. I've bungled everything I've touched latelv."

"It's okav," she assured him. "Mavbe I'd better see what I can do in the kitchen."

"It's not a pretty sight," he warned as thev crossed the dining room where more papers and toys, medicine bottles and dishes were stacked on the walnut table and rosewood hutch.

In the kitchen Bethany stifled a groan. Dirtv dishes were piled high in the deep enamel sink and on the whitewashed counters, along with stale, half-eaten cakes and pies left by well-wishers days ago Gingerly Beth inspected the icebox, which bulged with crusted casseroles, wilted salads, half-empty bottles of milk, and more medicine jars.

"I know it's gotten out of hand," said Todd, putting a cereal box in the cupboard as if it would make a difference in the clutter.

Beth rolled her eyes. "Your mama would curl up like a little snail and die if she saw this place."

"I know. I need help, Beth. I'm beside myself."

"You weren't kidding, were you!"

"About what?"

"About being better at writing sermons than housekeeping."

He smiled haplessly. "I've disillusioned you, haven't I?"

"No, just reminded me that you're not perfect."

"On that note, I should take you in to meet Claire."

"How is she feeling?"

"She has her good days and bad days."

Todd led Beth down the hall to the guest room and knocked gently on the closed door. "Claire? It's me. I'm back with Bethany Rose. Are you up to having a visitor?"

Bethany heard a muffled, "Come in."

Todd held his hand on the doorknob. "Beth, if you're worried about Claire being contagious—what I mean is, would you feel more comfortable wearing a mask over your mouth when you're around her?"

"Do you?"

"No. She's my wife; I don't want her feeling isolated. I think as long as we exercise proper hygiene—"

"Then I won't wear one either."

He opened the door and went in; she followed just behind him, her gaze taking in the flowered wallpaper, dark woodwork, and heavily draped windows. Claire lay propped on pillows in a four-poster bed, her long black hair framing a pale face with two immense dark eyes—eyes that would be striking were they not so shadowed and sunken. Her skin was the color of bleached bones, with just the slightest hint of pink in her full lips. She looked childlike in a flannel gown with ruffles around the neck and sleeves, her frail hands resting on the comforter like small porcelain doves.

"Claire, this is Bethany Rose Henry. Bethany, this is Claire DiCaprio—I mean, I'm sorry—Claire Marshall."

Bethany nodded; Claire managed a faint smile. Beside the bed stood a large green oxygen tank on a wheeled rack, and next to it a wheelchair. On the other side a rosewood nightstand held a ceramic water pitcher, medicine bottles, Claire's rosary beads, and a crucifix.

"Thank you for coming," said Claire in a soft breathy voice. "Sit down, please."

Bethany walked over and sat down stiffly in a flowered overstuffed chair near the bed. She remained on the edge of the cushion, as if at attention, her hands folded in her lap, her eyes moving restlessly around the room. She scoured her mind for something to say, anything to make conversation, but the harder she tried the more tongue-tied she felt. What was she doing here? This had been a bad idea, and now she was trapped in this dark, depressing house with Todd and this sick woman. Perhaps she could make some excuse to leave; perhaps Luke's lawyer would call with the verdict and she would have to go immediately to Fort Wayne; or perhaps she had left something urgent undone at Herrick House and Anna would phone and tell her to come right home. But she could think of nothing that required her attention and the phone remained silent.

"What a kind, generous heart you must have to come here like this," Claire was saying. "I've very grateful."

Beth's conscience nudged her. "I . . . um . . . I'm glad to help. Can I get you something—tea, or toast, or juice, or something?"

"I'm fine for now." She nodded toward a tray on the dresser. "Todd already brought me breakfast."

Beth stood up, clenching and unclenching her fingers. "Then maybe I'll go clean up a little in the kitchen." She glanced around at the darkened room. "Would you like some fresh air and sunshine? It's spring and everything's ready to blossom. On the farm it's the prettiest time of year. You can smell the earth coming alive and turning green."

Claire smiled wanly. "It sounds wonderful. At the sanatorium we lived on fresh air and sunshine, even in the middle of winter."

"You're absolutely right, both of you." Todd strode across the room, spread the drapes, and opened the windows. Bright, golden light swept in on a clean, tangy breeze, chasing away lingering shadows

"You won't catch a draft now, will you?" asked Todd, drawing the downy coverlet up around Claire's shoulders

"Don't worry. I'll call if I get chilled."

Todd touched Claire's hair with his fingertips. "Then I'll go help Bethany. Maybe we can whip up something special for lunch."

"Better leave the cooking to her," said Claire. She coughed, pulled a handkerchief from the sleeve of her gown, covered her mouth, and coughed again, a dry, hacking cough. Her forehead glistened with a feverish sheen.

Todd bent over the bed. "Do you need some oxygen?"

She waved him away with a little flutter of her hand. "No. Go help Bethany. Scoot!"

The two returned to the kitchen where Bethany removed the dirty dishes and filled the sink with scalding soapy water. "Bring me all the fresh vegetables you can find," she told Todd as she put the soiled china and glasses to soak.

"What are you making?"

"Soup." She browsed through the icebox, examining the contents of several containers before throwing them away, then held up a plate of roast beef wrapped in wax paper. "Is this still good?"

"I think so. We had it two nights ago."

"It'll do." She forked the beef into a kettle and poured in several cups of water. "My mama used to make the best vegetable beef soup in Fort Wayne. We'd eat soup for days and never get tired of it. Luke would crumble saltines in his, so many he could eat it with a fork." She handed Todd a paring knife and nodded at the potatoes on the table. "Make yourself useful."

He sat down and awkwardly began peeling potatoes while she sat across from him and cut up carrots and onions. "Claire looks awful bad," she ventured.

Todd nodded, his lips set in a firm line.

"She's pretty though," said Beth. "Real pretty. Even with the sickness you can see it."

"Yes, she is pretty. But you should have known her before. She was beautiful, so vital and alive, always laughing. You couldn't miss her laugh." His tone became brooding. "Now it takes all her strength just to smile."

"What do the doctors say?"

Todd stabbed a potato with the point of his knife. "She won't get better, only worse."

"It's just a thought, but maybe she should go back to the sanatorium where they know how to take care of her."

Todd's brows lowered in a scowl. "She's been there, Beth. In several hospitals, in fact. It isn't what she wants. She keeps telling me to send her back, but she's told me horror stories about those places. Some hospitals are fine, of course. They're like upscale boarding houses where patients are treated like vacation guests. But others are nightmares. Patients are crowded together in long rows, bed against bed."

"You could make sure she went to a good one."

He ignored her, caught up in his own reverie. "Claire told me about waking in the night at one place and hearing a death rattle in the next bed. She saw the shadows of nurses rushing around, removing the corpse so they could have the bed made fresh by morning. She doesn't want to die that way—alone and anonymous in some decrepit asylum."

"I wouldn't want that for her either."

Todd met her gaze with an unnerving directness. "I know I've hurt you, Bethany. I never meant to. I never dreamed my past would come back to haunt me. That's a poor choice of words, but I don't know how else to explain it."

She took a potato and began cutting it into jagged pieces. "You don't have to explain anything."

"Yes, I do. And there's something else you should know. Claire didn't come looking for me to marry her. She was against it at first; she came to Willowbrook hoping I'd take the boy so she could go to a hospital somewhere and die in peace. But I knew the moment I saw her walk up the aisle with that boy. I looked at him and saw myself when I was his age. I knew he was mine. And I knew before she said a word I would do the right thing, the only thing I could do. Marry her. I know it was sudden. I know people were shocked. But there wasn't time to prepare people or worry about appearances. Do you understand?"

"It doesn't matter what I think."

"It does, Beth. To me. It'll always matter."

She took the vegetables over to the sink, rinsed them, and emptied them into the kettle of beef stock. "Does Claire have any other family?"

Todd joined her at the sink, turned on the tap, and rinsed his hands. "No one I know of. Her mother died several months ago. For years she followed Claire from sanatorium to sanatorium, renting a room nearby to care for the boy while Claire was receiving treatment.

After she died Claire had no one to take care of Danny. If she hadn't found me, the boy would have gone to an orphanage. Thank God, she found me before the authorities took him away from her."

"Are you . . . going to legally adopt him?"

"Yes. I've filed the papers. It's just a matter of time."

She forced a smile. "How does Danny like having a daddy?"

"I'm not much of a dad, Beth." Todd gathered the vegetable peelings into a paper sack. "Sometimes I think Danny likes it here; other times he seems remote, even angry. Maybe he resents me or considers me an intruder in his mother's life. So far he won't talk to me, except as one stranger speaks to another. I'm hoping you can get him to open up."

"Me? I don't know anything about little boys."

"Maybe not, but I think he'll like you." Todd smiled, almost winked. "You have a special way with the boys, you know." His smile vanished, as if he sensed he had overstepped his bounds. He turned away abruptly, tossed the remaining vegetable scraps into the trash, and headed toward the hallway. "I'm going to go check on Claire," he called back, his voice strained.

Bethany stood at the stove, stirring the soup. A warmth flushed her face that had nothing to do with the flames under the kettle. How dare Todd prattle on about his wife and son as if she were just a concerned friend! How dare he assume she was perfectly happy to help out like some scullery maid! How dare he dismiss the love they felt for each other for some cockamamie sense of duty!

At noon Beth took a lunch tray in to Claire—a steaming bowl of soup, saltines, applesauce, and a glass of milk. Claire sat up in bed, her eyes showing a hint of vitality. "Thank you, Bethany," she murmured as Beth set the tray on her lap.

Beth managed a tight smile. "I hope you're hungry."

A look of dismay flickered in Claire's eyes. "I'm sorry, Beth. I'm never hungry. I wish I were. I don't remember what it feels like to desire food."

"Well, try anyway."

"I will. It looks delicious, much better than Todd's burnt offerings."

They both chuckled. The merriment revived Claire and sparked a brightness in her eyes. "At one sanatorium," she confided, still smiling wanly, "I don't recall whether it was Stonywold or the Trudeau Clinic, or maybe another—after awhile they all blend together in my memory. Anyway, they fed me a diet of milk, butter, and raw eggs. Actually, it wasn't milk; it was a quart of heavy cream a day. Sometimes they flavored it with vanilla or chocolate, but it was still nauseating. I gagged every time."

Bethany made a face. "Ugh!"

"Exactly!"

"Todd says you didn't like the hospitals."

"No. The physicians call their clinics 'fresh air schools.' It sounds so pleasant, doesn't it? But to me they're camps of death. Patients come chasing the cure. Some get better; most don't."

Claire dipped her spoon in her soup and lifted it to her lips, sipping slowly. "Life hands us such ironies, doesn't it, Bethany? At one clinic I remember feeling overwhelmed by the beauty of the scenery and the hopelessness of my condition; such pure joy and pure sorrow lumped together in one great swell of emotion. The earth was snow-covered that February, so clean and white it nearly blinded the eye. There was a railroad station one hundred yards away and a lovely white church. We could hear the trains coming and going and see patients who were well enough going home. The sound of trains still stirs something in me, that haunting, faraway sound of a train in the night."

Claire coughed, nearly spilling her soup. Bethany quickly steadied the tray while Claire clasped her hanky over her mouth, coughing and sucking for air.

"You're talking too much," said Beth. "I'd better go so you can eat."

Claire lifted her hand. "No, don't go, please. It's been so long since I've had someone to talk to—a woman who understands a woman's feelings. I've bottled up so much. I need to talk while I still have the energy. Some days aren't this good."

"All right, I'll stay." Bethany sat down in the overstuffed chair and folded her hands in her lap, watching as Claire took another swallow of soup.

"This is good, Bethany. Your mother's recipe. The best I've ever had." Claire brushed a tangle of black hair back from her forehead and flashed a sad, helpless smile. "I must look a sight. I've lost the strength to primp and do my hair, but I'm afraid I haven't lost my vanity."

"I'll do your hair for you—brush it and wash it and trim it if you like. It won't be hard. It's healthy hair, thick and long and very pretty."

"At least something about me is healthy." Claire shivered. "The air's a bit chilly."

Beth closed the windows halfway. "Is that better?"

"Yes. I like the air, but too much dries my throat. At the sanatorium fresh air was everything. Even in forty-degree weather they put us outside on the porch facing the mountains. They wrapped us in blankets and rugs so tight we couldn't move, and put us on lounge chairs with our feet elevated. There we were, a whole row of us like bundled eskimos, with only our faces showing. I'm sure we made a comical sight."

Beth chuckled politely, but she saw little humor in the life Claire described. Perhaps what Todd offered her here *was* better, or would be once Beth helped him get the house in order. "You'll have to tell me your schedule, Claire, your usual routine—when you like your morning bath and your linens changed—so I'll know what to do and when to do it."

"Does that mean you're coming back?"

"If you and Todd want me to."

"We do, Bethany."

"All right. Now about your schedule—"

Claire grimaced, her breathing labored. "I hate schedules. The sanatorium kept such a strict schedule. I had to lie flat in bed. Every hour a nurse would come and turn me, from side to side to back. I felt trapped, isolated, less than human."

Beth approached the bed. "You're getting too tired, Claire. Don't talk. Just finish your lunch and take a nap."

Claire pushed the tray away and laid her head back on the pillow. "Yes, I need to sleep. But Danny will be home soon."

"You'll see him when you wake up. Oh, but, Claire, you didn't finish your soup."

"No more." She closed her eyes, her breathing still ragged.

Beth stared at the oxygen tank and wondered if Claire should be using it and, if so, how it worked. She would have to ask Todd. She picked up the tray and slipped from the room, aware of a tension moving through her muscles, forging an ache behind her eyes.

Todd was in the kitchen scrubbing the counters with Lysol. "I don't know how I let this place get so out of hand, but with you around, Beth, I should get the hang of this domesticity thing."

She laid the tray beside the sink and sat down at the kitchen table. "I don't know if I can do this, Todd."

He sat down across from her, concern etched in his face. "She's so sick, Todd. And she still loves you. I see it in her eyes when she watches you. But she needs a nurse—someone who knows what to do—not me."

Todd massaged his jaw, a desolate expression in his eyes. "I've felt that way too, Beth. I feel it every day. I ask what I got myself into. Why did I have to be the white knight rushing in to rescue the damsel in distress? I don't know why. I just know God brought her back into my life for a reason. I don't have any answers, just a lot of questions, and all the questions bring me back to the same fact. Claire and the boy are my responsibility." He reached out and put his hand over hers. "But they're not your responsibility, Beth."

Her throat tightened with emotion. "She worries about not being pretty. I . . . I told her I'd do her hair."

"Oh? Her hair? That's kind of you. It's something I couldn't do. I'd be all thumbs. I'd—"

Beth sat forward, urgency in her voice. "How did she get it, Todd—this horrible wasting disease?"

"Tuberculosis? I don't know. I think her father died of it. They say the disease can incubate as long as fifty years."

"I don't know much about TB, except what I've read in the newspapers."

Todd wearily shook his head. "TB—consumption—is the greatest killer known to mankind. They call it the white plague. Since Claire arrived I've done a lot of reading about it. The germs ride on dust particles in the air. When they invade the lungs, the body builds up a wall of cells and fibers to confine them. This becomes a small hard lump or tubercle. As long as the capsule remains unbroken, the bacteria cause no harm. People with this primary infection may never even know they have the TB germ."

"Then what made Claire get sick?"

"Medically? The germs broke out of the tubercles and consumed healthy tissue. What happened to Claire emotionally is my fault. But it's the TB germs that have left empty pockets or cavities in her lungs."

"She has holes in her lungs?"

Todd's voice deepened. "Claire has only one lung. The other was so diseased the doctors removed it surgically. That's why it's so hard for her to breathe."

"Can't the doctors do something—a specialist somewhere?"

"Claire tells me she's seen them all."

"But there are new medicines, aren't there? Miracle drugs? I remember reading about them in the newspaper not long ago. They say tuberculosis could be wiped out in a single generation."

Todd lowered his head and rubbed his eyes. He looked older than she'd ever seen him. "The truth is, Bethany, it's too late for Claire. When streptomycin came out a few years ago, she took the drug with high hopes of a cure. The side effects were horrible but her health improved for a while. Then the germs became resistant and the disease flared up again."

"But there are new drugs!"

"I know. Scientists speculate that patients will respond best to a combination of several new drugs, but, as I said, it's too late for Claire."

"It's not fair."

"I know, but we must trust God to work even this for good."

"How can Claire's sickness be God's will?"

"I don't know, Beth. The better I know God the more I realize I don't know, and the more I know I have to trust Him."

Beth pushed back her chair and stood up.

"Where are you going?"

She reached for the Lysol. "I've got a house to clean before your son gets home."

21

Danny arrived home from school just as Bethany was placing the clean china in the rosewood hutch. She heard the front door open and bang shut, sending a reverberation through the entire house. A moment later the boy trooped into the dining room, his umber-brown hair windblown, his denim jacket rumpled, and a book bag slung over his shoulder. He took one look at Bethany and stopped dead in his tracks, his eyes widening like saucers. "Hi. You're the lady I met at church."

She smiled. "Yes, I'm Bethany Rose. I talked to you that day you and your mama came to Willowbrook Christian Church. I haven't seen you since."

"I know. We go to St. Michael's back home." He eyed her curiously. "What are you doing here?"

"Helping your mama."

"Is she okay?"

"Yes. She's resting."

"Then I can't go see her now?"

"Maybe in a few minutes. I'll see if she's awake."

Danny tossed his bag on a chair. "Where's the reverend?"

"Your dad? He's with your mama."

He looked at her, his eyes narrowing, his lips settling into a pout. "He's not my dad."

Bethany's mind raced. Hadn't Todd told the boy he was his father? Surely he had. Or maybe not. "Uh, well, let's see. Reverend Marshall married your mama, so doesn't that make him your—?"

"If he's my dad, how come I just met him? Dads are supposed to be there when you're born and when you're growing up."

"But they can't always be. My papa was gone most of the time when I was a little girl."

Danny's right brow arched with interest. "Where was he?"

"It's a long story, but I'll tell you sometime. Right now I bet you're hungry as a bear. Come to the kitchen and I'll get you some cookies and milk."

On the way to the kitchen Danny glanced around. "Where's all the stuff?"

"We cleaned house. If you're missing something, it's probably in your closet." She put a hand on his shoulder as he pulled back a chair. "Wash your hands first." She set a plate of gingersnaps on the table and poured a tall glass of milk as he ran tap water over grimy fingers. When he finished she handed him a towel, which he grabbed, scrunched up, and tossed aside, his hands still dripping.

"Danny, hang the towel up, please."

She sat down across from him and wondered if this was the routine mothers followed when their children came home from school. It seemed right. Wash up. Eat a snack. But what next? Danny swallowed several gulps of milk and looked at her, a white mustache beading his upper lip. "You gonna live here too?"

Her face warmed. "No, I'm just here to help."

He stuffed an entire gingersnap into his mouth but still managed to ask, "Are you coming back?"

Beth thought a moment. "Do you want me to?"

"Will you make more cookies?"

"If you want me to."

"Sure. Can I go watch television?"

"Do you have homework?"

"Nah. That's for older grades. I'm in third."

"What are your favorite television shows?"

He reached for two more cookies and held one in each hand. "Hopalong Cassidy, Milton Berle, and Kukla, Fran, and Ollie."

"Me too! I especially like the one-toothed dragon Ollie."

Danny chewed slowly. "I like the pretty lady, the way she laughs. That's how my mom used to be before she got sick."

A sound came from the other room and a moment later Todd appeared in the doorway, a smile flickering on his lips. "Hello, Danny. I didn't hear you come in. How was school?"

The boy hunched over his plate and blew bubbles in his glass of milk. Todd sat down at the table, watching, his jaw tightening. "Come on, Danny. How was school?"

Danny's gaze remained focused inside his milk glass. "Fine," he mumbled, making more bubbles.

Todd's temple pulsed. "You're supposed to look at someone when he asks you a question, son."

Danny cast him a reproachful glance. "I'm not your son."

Todd looked over at Beth, as if to say, *What am I supposed to do with him?*

"Danny was telling me about the television shows he likes to watch," said Beth brightly. "We like the same shows."

"Really? Sounds like you two were having quite a conversation."

"Just a friendly little talk," said Beth.

"Well, that's more than Danny and I seem to manage. Right, son?"

Danny's eyes narrowed with obvious hostility. "I'm Danny. Danny DiCaprio. Nobody's son."

"All right, Danny." Todd stood up abruptly, barely suppressing his exasperation. "I'll let you two talk while I take Claire some hot tea."

Beth gave Todd a look. *Thanks a lot!* When he had gone out, she gazed appraisingly at Danny. "Don't you like living here?"

He shrugged. "It's better than the other places."

"How so?"

"I have my own room. I don't have to sleep on a cot in the kitchen or hallway anymore. And I don't have to work."

"Work?"

He wiped the back of his hand across his mouth. "Yeah. In the old places I peddled newspapers. And I helped street vendors sell apples and vegetables and stuff."

"Didn't you go to school?"

"Yeah. Most days. Except when my grandma took me to visit Mama in the hospital."

"That was nice of her. I bet your grandma took good care of you."

He nodded. "She did until . . . until . . ." His shoulders sagged and his chin puckered. "My grandma died."

Beth sat forward, both elbows on the table. "That's very hard. But you have your mama home with you now."

He lowered his gaze. "Mama's going away too."

Beth felt a chill sweep over her. "What do you mean?"

Danny cupped his glass and moved it around the table, making deep, guttural noises, pretending it was a vehicle of some sort. Just as she was about to repeat her question, he stopped the noises and said, "My mama's gonna die just like Grandma."

Beth sat back, startled. For a moment her mind was blank. "You don't know that, Danny. Nobody knows when someone's going to die."

He picked up another cookie and crumbled it in his hand. "She's gonna go away just like my grandma did."

Bethany reached across the table and touched his hand. "Does that make you feel scared inside?"

He looked down at the table and let the cookie fragments drop from his fingers onto the linen tablecloth.

"Danny, my mama died last summer," she said softly. "I felt sad for a long time."

He looked at her. His face was smooth and round, a child's face, but his stark, shadowed eyes belonged to someone far beyond his years. "Did you cry?" he asked.

"Yes. It's okay to cry when you're sad."

He stuck out his lower lip. "I won't cry. Not ever."

"But I stopped crying after awhile," she went on gently. "I found out there were people who cared about me. Even God cared. I wasn't alone. You're not alone either, Danny."

He brushed the crumbs from his hands. "Can I go watch television now?"

"Yes. Go ahead."

He scooted out of the chair and bolted for the door. In the doorway he stopped short and looked back at Beth. "Will you be here tomorrow?"

"If you want me to."

He grinned sheepishly. "Okay. See ya!"

Beth was clearing the table when Todd returned with the tea tray. He made a little humming sound and smiled. "I see our boy's in the parlor watching television."

"Is that okay? I said he could."

Todd squeezed her shoulder approvingly. "You have a way with him. He likes you. But I'm afraid he's not ready for a father, especially one who's been absent all his life."

"I know how he feels. My papa was absent too. But I got over it." Beth filled the kettle and put it on the burner. She was in the mood for a cup of tea. "Danny will come around. I can tell. He's lonely and scared inside. Just give him time."

"What else can I do? I've got all I can manage right now taking care of his mother." Todd sat down, elbows on the table, chin resting on folded hands.

Beth watched him, saw the slackness in his jaw, the redness rimming his eyes. He looked like a man at the end of his rope. He met Beth's gaze with a wordless plea. She waited, holding her breath, desperate to read beyond the clear fathomless blue of his eyes. The moment hung between them like a bubble in the air, fragile as a dream, gone the moment it's grasped. "Bethany."

She waited.

"Would you mind pouring me a cup too, Beth?"

She closed her eyes, savoring the moment even as it slipped away. She brought over two cups of tea and sat down; they relaxed in companionable silence, with only the wall clock ticking and the television droning in another room. The sun's last faded rays seeped into a mauve darkness, making the house feel safe and closed in, barricaded from the world.

Where had the day gone? How could night have stolen in without a warning? She steeled herself, refusing to let go of these fleeting moments. It was so little to ask for—a handful of seconds with the man she loved. God had required so much of them lately; surely He wouldn't begrudge them this little time alone.

"More tea?" she asked.

"No. This is just right."

She watched him, tracing his features in her mind—the solid planes of his cheekbones, nose, and jaw; the sensitive, generous mouth, so solemn with honor and duty; and the sky blue eyes, piercing as glass.

She imagined the two of them married, sitting in this kitchen sipping tea, knowing they would always be part of each other, knowing without speaking what the other was thinking.

"In case you haven't noticed, you're good medicine around here, Bethany."

His voice startled her. "What?"

"You're good for this entire household. Claire likes you. So does Danny—obviously. And you know how I feel. I hope you'll come over often. We need you—not just to scrub a floor or cook a meal. We need *you*. Say you'll come back."

Absently she ran her index finger around the narrow rim of her teacup. The china was so dainty, so lovely, so easily broken.

"Well, Bethany?" he said, his voice almost a whisper. "How about it?"

Her words were barely audible. "How can I say no? Besides, I promised Danny I'd come back."

22

After dinner that evening Todd drove Bethany home, walked her up the porch steps, and waited while she searched her purse for her key. She was about to unlock the door when it swung open and Annie stood in the doorway, excitement animating her face. "I was waiting for you to get home, Beth."

She felt a wave of alarm. "Is something wrong?"

"No, Bethany. It's what you've been waiting for. Your brother's lawyer called. The jury has reached a verdict. They'll announce it in court tomorrow."

A mixture of jubilation and terror struck her at once. "Oh, Annie, it's taken so long, but now that it's here I'm scared to death." She looked up at Todd. "I wish you could be with me."

He glanced at Annie. "Maybe I can—if I had someone to stay with Claire and Danny."

"I'll be glad to go over," said Annie. "Anna can take care of Maggie." She touched Beth's arm. "You should phone Catherine. She may want to go too. I know Knowl plans to go."

"Really? I'm glad."

Annie smiled. "I think Luke will be pleased to see his family there supporting him."

His family! Beth felt a ripple of satisfaction. Annie was right. The

Herricks were Luke's family, just as they were hers. It occurred to her suddenly—they would all be Herricks if Papa hadn't taken on the name *Henry* to hide his secret life.

Todd clasped her hand between his palms. "It's settled then. I'll pick you up in the morning. If Knowl and Catherine are willing, we can all ride over together."

She beamed. "I'd like that."

The next morning, as everyone filed into the courtroom Beth noted that the place was drearier than she remembered. The walls, the furnishings, the people all seemed painted in mauve tones, subdued, edged with gloom. Voices murmuring across the room seemed indistinct. Beth sat in the first row of seats behind the defense table, between Todd and Knowl, her hands folded so tightly her knuckles ached.

When the guards brought Luke in, he looked her way and smiled faintly, but she could see worry etched in his face. He looked thinner, his long face almost gaunt and dark circles shadowing his eyes. *Prison is doing this to him,* she thought ruefully. *Please, God, let him go free!*

As Judge McPherson pounded his gavel on the desk, Beth studied the faces of the jury, trying to read the decision in their expressions, but they all sat solemn-faced, their eyes turned away from Luke toward the judge's bench. These simple, ordinary-looking people held her brother's fate in their hands. If only she could speak to them herself and convince them her brother hadn't meant to hurt Mama. If she could just make them see that punishing Luke wouldn't bring Mama back.

As the judge ordered Lucas to stand, Knowl leaned over and whispered, "Keep your spirits up, Bethany. We'll see Luke through this, whatever happens."

"Mr. Foreman," intoned the judge, "has the jury reached a verdict in the case of the people versus Lucas Henry?"

"Yes, we have, your honor."

Todd slipped his hand over Beth's clasped fingers. They exchanged a brief glance, then she turned her attention to the jury foreman.

Judge McPherson instructed, "Will the foreman read the verdict, please."

The balding, middle-aged man announced in a slightly accented voice, "We, the jury, find the defendant, Lucas Henry, guilty of one count of arson."

A murmur of voices rippled across the courtroom. Luke hung his head; his attorney, Joseph Kimbrough, put his hand on Luke's shoulder. Bethany felt a sinking sensation in the pit of her stomach, verging on nausea.

The jury foreman continued, "We, the jury, find the defendant, Lucas Henry, not guilty of murder in the first degree."

A titter of exclamations swept the room. Kimbrough gave Luke a hearty pat on the back. Todd gave Beth an impulsive hug. She collapsed against him, her legs weak as butter. "That's great news, Beth!"

She looked from the jury to the judge who was pounding his mallet vigorously, demanding that the court come to order. When the room was quiet again, Judge McPherson declared sonorously, "The defendant will appear in this courtroom one week from today for sentencing. Court is recessed for today."

As people streamed from the room, their voices melding in an indistinguishable buzz, Bethany ran to Luke and held him tight. He gave her an enormous bear hug and kissed the top of her head. "We did it, little sister! I'm almost home free!"

Kimbrough vigorously shook Luke's hand, then Beth's. "It's a wonderful victory, Luke. The jury believed you. They're saying your mother's death was indeed an accident. You won them over."

Kimbrough turned to shake Knowl's hand and Todd's. "Now the arson charge—we couldn't get Luke out of that one. He admitted he set the fire deliberately, so the jury had to find him guilty. Let's just hope the judge shows leniency and gives him a short sentence."

"Then Luke will still have to stay in jail?" asked Beth in alarm.

Kimbrough picked up his briefcase. "Looks that way, Miss Henry, but I don't anticipate a long sentence."

Luke shook his head and slammed his fist against his palm. "Any more time in that jail and I'll go bonkers."

"Hold on for another week, Luke," said Kimbrough. "Maybe the judge will have good news."

Bethany stepped back as Todd and Knowl greeted Luke, shook his hand, and wished him well. Knowl gripped Luke's hand an extra few moments. "When this is all over, Luke, if you want to come to Willowbrook, I'll put you to work at the publishing house. The shipping department again, if that's what you want. We want you to know, Luke, that Bethany's become an important member of the family, and we want you to feel welcome too."

Luke nodded and mumbled something nobody quite heard. Bethany had a feeling he was saying, *Thanks, but no thanks*. Before anyone could question his words, the guards stepped forward and escorted him out of the courtroom.

On the way home to Willowbrook, Bethany felt immensely relieved that Luke wasn't going to spend the rest of his life in prison, and yet a shadow lingered. Her brother could still go to prison for months, even years. There was nothing to do now but wait and pray—again! She had to believe that in one more week her brother might be free!

On Wednesday, April 11th, Knowl drove Bethany to Fort Wayne for Luke's penalty hearing. There was no question but that she would go; Luke needed her and his attorney wanted her to testify again in Luke's behalf. Still, her heart and loyalties were divided between Willowbrook and Fort Wayne, between Todd and Claire on one hand and her brother Luke on the other. Throughout the drive she fretted about how Todd would manage without her.

"I should be there," she told Knowl. "Todd can't get Claire to eat like I can. He doesn't have the patience. When she refuses food, he just accepts it. And there's Danny. He and Danny don't always see eye to eye. They talk but don't hear each other. I interpret. I should be there."

Knowl glanced over at her from the driver's seat, his hands square on the wheel. "Listen to yourself, Beth. One week and look how involved you're getting in Todd's family. It's not good for you. You're sacrificing your own life. You should be back in school. You should tell Todd to hire a nurse for Claire."

"No!" She said the word so forcefully Knowl flinched. "Please don't say anything. I help Todd because I want to. God wants me to do this, Knowl." Even as she said the words, the idea startled her. She hadn't articulated it before, but it was true. She believed it with all her heart. God had called her to be there for Todd and Claire and Danny.

She looked at Knowl. "Can I tell you a secret, something I've never told anybody else, ever?"

He smiled at her. "Sure, I'd be honored if you'd tell me."

Her voice came out soft and breathy, with a hint of wonder. "All my life, Knowl, I've felt like there was something I was supposed to do, someone I was supposed to be, something grander than anything I could imagine. I used to dream of being a movie star, someone glamorous that everybody admired. I thought that's what this hunger inside me was. But it wasn't that at all. Now I know that finding my dream means doing something that God calls me to do. It's like He's the rainbow I was chasing all along."

Knowl reached around the seat and squeezed the back of her neck, a casual, brotherly gesture. "I can't argue with an answer like that, Beth. Just be careful. Don't get hurt, okay?"

"You sound like . . . what is it, Knowl? Is there something you're not telling me?"

He kept his eyes on the highway, his hands white-knuckled,

gripping the wheel. "I didn't want to say anything, but a few people at church are clucking their tongues about you spending so much time at the parsonage with Reverend Marshall. They have nasty little minds, Beth. They may use your visits as ammunition to further discredit Todd when the congregation votes."

"But we're not doing anything wrong! I swear we're not!"

"I believe you, Beth. I just thought you should know."

They lapsed into silence until they reached the courthouse. Having people see evil in her charitable deeds galled her, but she couldn't allow herself the luxury of sulking. She had to concentrate now on Luke. His future was at stake. She had to be there for him—wholeheartedly.

Judge McPherson opened the hearing by instructing both the prosecution and the defense to present any final arguments that would have a bearing on the sentence he imposed. The prosecutor delivered a rehash of his previous arguments—Luke was an impulsive, unpredictable, hot-headed young man who had caused his mother's death, accidental or not, and who had deliberately burned down his own house and endangered the life of his sister; he deserved to be sentenced to the full extent of the law.

Luke's attorney countered with a reminder that Luke had been a law-abiding citizen with no criminal record, that he had fought for his country in the war, and that he had been a devoted son and brother. Kimbrough called Knowl, Jake Witherspoon, and Jake's parents to the stand once again to testify of Luke's war service and devotion to his family. They all spoke well of Luke, vouching for his character and assuring the court he was an upstanding member of the community.

Then Bethany took the stand. She wasn't shaking this time; she knew what she had to say. She folded her hands in her lap and met Judge McPherson's steady gaze. "Judge, when I was a little girl and got scared in the night, I didn't run to my papa, because he wasn't there. I ran to my brother Luke. I knew he'd comfort me and make me feel better. When my mama needed a man with a strong back to work the farm, she looked to Luke too. He was always there for us. He never complained about having to take Papa's place and be the man of the family."

Beth's voice wavered as she brushed away tears. "The only time Luke left us was when our country needed him more. But as soon as he got done fighting he was right back on the farm, plowing the fields and looking out for Mama and me. I know if Mama was here today she'd beg you to let Luke go free, just like I'm begging you. He's a good man, Judge, and he has a family who loves him and wants him to come home." She looked at Knowl and saw him nod, then fixed her gaze on Luke. He was sitting tall, his eyes glistening, a trace of a smile on his lips.

When she returned to her seat, Kimbrough clasped her hand and whispered, "Good girl. You had the whole room in tears."

"That's not why I said those things," she retorted. "I said them because they're true!"

Judge McPherson gazed solemnly around the room and inquired, "Is there any further testimony?" When both attorneys answered, "No, your honor," he cleared his throat and peered down at Luke. "Lucas Henry, will you please stand for sentencing." Eyeing Luke directly, he said, "For one count of arson you are hereby sentenced to three years in prison."

Bethany gasped. Luke groaned and hung his head.

"However, because this is your first offense, I'm reducing your sentence to six months in prison and two years of probation. Since you've already served nearly four months, I am remanding you to the county jail to finish the remaining two months of your sentence." He pounded his gavel again. "Case closed."

With a cry of relief, Bethany rushed into Luke's arms. They

embraced for a long while. "Looks like it won't be long and I'll be home, Sis," he murmured, his voice heavy with emotion.

"Not long at all, Luke. Just hold on a little while longer and you'll be home where you belong."

Joseph Kimbrough gripped Luke's hand. "You're a fortunate young man, Luke Henry."

"How's that?"

Kimbrough leaned close and confided, "With the charges you faced, they could have locked you up and thrown away the key. Thank your lucky stars you'll only be doing time for a couple more months."

"It's not lucky stars we should thank," said Bethany with a knowing smile.

Kimbrough grinned, his jowls expanding with pride. "Right! I did pull our boy out of the fire, didn't I?—excuse the pun."

"Oh, you worked hard, Mr. Kimbrough, and we're mighty appreciative of your efforts, but I was talking about *God*."

Kimbrough belched out a blustery protest. "Well, yes, naturally. We do have the Almighty to thank, and I was most happy to help Him along!"

Knowl gave Beth a bemused wink, as if to say, *Save it, Beth. You can't argue with an ego as big as Kimbrough's!*

Outside the courtroom Bethany encountered Jake Witherspoon, looking handsome in his church going brown suit, string tie, and cowboy boots. His blond hair was slicked back behind his ears and his pale blue eyes crinkled with merriment. He looked taller, ruddier, and heartier than she remembered, his physical presence as riveting as an embrace. His spicy, earthy smell filled her nostrils, reminding her of the farm, the plowed fields, the golden alfalfa, the tangy-sweet country air. "Sure good to see you again, Bethany Rose," he declared, clasping her shoulders in his rugged hands. "You're a sight for sore eyes."

"So are you, Jake." She felt her cheeks grow pink under his

approving gaze. "Thanks for speaking out for Luke. You're a good friend."

He pulled a handkerchief from his breast pocket and rubbed it across his bright, bronzed forehead. Then he took her hands in his and pressed them to his heart. She could feel his muscled chest under his starched white shirt. "I'm still looking to be more than a friend, Bethany Rose. I haven't forgotten you for a minute. If you're ever fixing to come back to Fort Wayne, my mama and papa and I got a place all ready for you. It's time I take me a wife and have a family of my own."

She looked at him and wondered fleetingly, would it be better for Todd and Claire—for all of them—for her to return to Fort Wayne and marry Jake? Jake had always been part of her past. Was he part of her future as well?

After a long moment she gently pulled her hands away. "I'm sorry, Jake. I care about you, I do. I always have and always will. But my life is in Willowbrook now. That's where I belong."

23

As the blossoming, rain-washed days of April slipped away, Bethany's routine was set. Every morning Todd picked her up and drove her to the parsonage; every evening he drove her home to Honeysuckle Lane. She spent her days caring for Claire, fixing meals, doing chores, playing games with Danny, and sharing an occasional cup of tea with Todd. In an odd twist of irony, Beth had become an accepted member of the Marshall household. Stranger still, she sensed that she had become the hub that kept the spokes turning.

Even more startling, the reverse was true. Beth had come to cherish her role in Todd's family. The deep emotional ties lacking with her sister, Catherine, were already growing strong between Claire and herself. They spent long, quiet afternoons together, reading, listening to the radio, sketching—Beth sketched, Claire watched—and chatting on Claire's good days.

As the spring weather grew balmier, Bethany took Claire outside in her wheelchair. Often Todd came and sat with them on the little backyard patio, the Bible or a theology book open on his lap, his forehead crinkled in a studious frown as he pored over ponderous texts. He said little, leaving it to the women to engage in casual conversation. But Beth savored his presence, stealing private glances at his stalwart profile, pleased to be an integral part of his life, however unlikely her role.

She knew Todd missed being actively involved in ministry—preaching, counseling, shepherding his flock. He was a vital, energetic man forced to grow stagnant while his church bickered among themselves over whether to keep him as their pastor. Most of the time he endured his crucible in stoic silence, but occasionally he made reference to the ecclesiastical deadlock that kept him in limbo.

"I've become such a hot potato the deacon board keeps putting off the vote," he told her one morning over coffee. They were sitting at their favorite place, the kitchen table, with the late April sun streaming in the windows, bathing the room in a golden glow.

It was too lovely a morning for dark thoughts, so she tried neutralizing his frustration with humor. "You don't look like a hot potato."

He ignored her feeble joke. "I think they're afraid that forcing the issue, calling for a vote, will split the church in half," he said, his voice heavy with futility. "I just can't let that happen. These are my people, Beth."

"But they can't let it drag on forever," she told him. "It's not fair to you or the church."

"People forget what's fair when their emotions are riding high and they're convinced their way is the only way." With a raw nervous energy he pinged his china cup with thumb and forefinger. "I keep telling Knowl to accept my resignation and look for someone else, but he considers that a cowardly way out—for me and for the church. He thinks all of us will be stronger if we can resolve this with—what were his exact words?—'harmony, unity, and a sense of God's purpose and direction.'"

"Knowl's a smart man. I think he's right."

"But how can the church know God's will in this issue when I don't even know? Everything seminary taught me to be—all the preconceived notions about ministry—has been shattered. I'm starting from scratch, Beth. My hands are empty; my faith is shaken. Not my faith in Christ, but my faith in myself, in what I thought I could be."

Bethany sipped her coffee and listened, weighing Todd's words. "I don't know anything about theology," she admitted, "but maybe it's okay *not* to have faith in yourself as long as you have faith in God."

Todd's eyes crinkled in a smile. "I once agonized with God for your soul; now you turn me from despair by your simple faith."

He said it pleasantly, with even a hint of whimsy, but she retreated a little, not wanting to be reminded that he was mortal, that at times she might be stronger than he. She didn't feel strong; at least not in the way he was, or the way she perceived he was.

She was strong on a certain inborn, elemental level. She could, when she had to, confront life and people head-on, could rise up out of her own ashes if she had to. Hadn't she died a little with each new loss—Papa, Mama, Luke, Todd—and found herself again, forced strength back into her body, forged a strong will, a renewed spirit when hers had been trampled? She was strong within certain limits.

But when Todd entered her life she was a fledgling sparrow, still grounded, afraid to try her wings. He had shown her the world of the spirit, the power of prayer, an abundance of joy in a Savior named Jesus. He had opened the heavens to her. How could she possibly see him as a fallen wayfarer struggling back to faith?

He was watching her, a smile lingering in his eyes. More than a smile. Tenderness. Affection. "I thank God for you, Beth. I hope you know, Claire, Danny, and I couldn't have survived these days without you."

She returned his smile, but the praise felt hollow. She knew in her heart of hearts what Todd would never imagine—how uncharitable her motives were and how often she acted out of her own deep, unconfessed needs.

At times guilt plagued her; she pretended to be Claire's friend, *was* Claire's friend, yet envy pierced her as she watched Todd hover over his frail, bedridden wife. He was always so attentive, so consoling, often holding Claire's hand, stroking her brow, lifting her in his strong arms and tenderly carrying her to the lounge chair in the backyard.

If only Beth could be selfless and giving, the way Christ commanded, instead of consumed with her own desires. *Love one another as I have loved you; love your neighbor as yourself*. She wasn't there yet. She couldn't be sure she wasn't waiting for Claire to die so she could have Todd for herself. If she loved Claire the way Christ did, she wouldn't agonize over the fact that Todd had chosen Claire, not her, chosen her for the best of reasons, with an altruism most admirable. But even Todd's purest of motives didn't diminish Bethany's heartache.

On the last Friday evening of April, as Todd drove Beth home, he said in a voice not his own, "Maybe I have no right to tell you this, Bethany, but it's important to me that you know. I have a marriage in name only. With Claire so ill, there is no physical intimacy in our union."

She stared ahead at the darkened street, startled. "Don't, Todd. Don't tell me. We shouldn't talk about such things."

He sighed with resignation. "You're probably right, but I just wanted you to know."

On Monday morning, May 1st, when Bethany returned to the Marshall house, she thought about how reassuringly familiar it was. She belonged here; she had found her place here. The first thing she did was take Claire her breakfast—tea, toast, a poached egg, and orange juice. As she set the tray on the four-poster bed, she was startled by Claire's appearance, by how much thinner and weaker she seemed. Her eyes shone darker and larger than ever in her lean, ashen face. She wore the nasal prongs and was breathing with the aid of her oxygen tank. And she seemed hardly able to lift her hand off the coverlet.

Still, she smiled feebly as Beth fluffed her pillow and spread a linen napkin over her lap. "Not my . . . good day," she managed. "I missed you. Do better . . . when you're here."

"Don't try to talk," Beth told her, hoping her concern didn't show in her expression. Had Todd noticed that Claire had weakened significantly in just a few short days?

"Would you like me to feed you?" Beth volunteered when Claire made no effort to touch her food.

She closed her eyes. "Not hungry."

"You've got to eat. You need to keep up your strength."

Claire shook her head, her colorless lips firmly set.

"Then at least sip some tea. I put sugar and cream in it. It's the English way. It'll give you a little nourishment."

Beth held the cup for Claire as she drank.

"That's a good girl. Now I'm going to give you a few bites of egg, just a little at a time, and we'll wash it down with a swallow of juice. It's freshly squeezed and so sweet. Come on, Claire. Just a bite. That's it. Good!"

When Beth returned the tray to the kitchen, Todd was there, pouring himself a cup of coffee. "How'd it go? Did she eat?"

Beth nodded. "I managed to get a little food into her."

"Wonderful! She wouldn't touch a thing for me all weekend."

"I can't get over it, how much she's failed since I last saw her."

Todd sipped his coffee. "She's been coughing more, and I know she's in pain, but she won't complain. She needs the oxygen more often now too. I don't know what to do for her, Beth."

"What do her doctors say?"

"Nothing. They say there's nothing more anyone can do for her but keep her comfortable. It's in God's hands now."

"Are you saying . . . she's dying?"

He gazed out the window. "She's been dying for a long time."

"Does Danny know?"

"I think he knew before any of us. That's why he goes around here so sullen and angry all the time. He's lived with this disease for a lot longer than we have."

Bethany picked up a dish towel and absently twisted it in her hands. "I watched my papa die little by little, but I held on to him until his last breath. I made him fight back. I wouldn't let him go until there was nothing left. I . . . I'm going to make Claire fight too."

"How? She's so weary. She has nothing left to fight with. Maybe she just wants us to let her go."

Beth twisted the terry-cloth towel until her palms stung. "No. I'll figure out something. I won't let her give up."

The next day Claire was feeling better—smiling more, talking more—but she still seemed painfully fragile and weak. Beth was determined to do something. Maybe she couldn't keep Claire's body from wasting away, but she refused to let her spirits languish. She went around and opened the windows wide, letting the fragrant breeze fill the stale, airless room. Then she pushed the wheelchair over by the bed. "It's May, Claire. A fine May day. The flowers are starting to bloom. You should see the lilacs, lush and full as grapes."

"I wish I could see them," Claire said softly.

"You will. I'm taking you out to the garden."

"I can't. It takes all my effort . . . just to breathe."

"Don't worry. Todd will lift you out of bed, and I'll wheel you outside. He'll bring your oxygen. You can just relax and soak up some sun." Bethany picked up a brush and ran it gently through Claire's ebony hair. "You have such beautiful hair."

"No, not anymore." Tears formed on Claire's lids. "Before the illness . . . I used to be . . . pretty."

"You still are." Bethany slipped over to the bureau, picked up several items, and returned to the bedside. She dabbed a hint of rouge on Claire's cheeks and red lipstick on her chapped lips. "There, that's all you needed."

Claire smiled wanly. "You're so good to me, Bethany. How can I thank you?"

Beth turned away, biting back a sudden swell of emotion. "Listen, I'll go get Todd, okay? I'll just be a minute."

Claire lifted her head. "No, wait. Let me tell you . . ."

Beth drew close, searching Claire's eyes. "What's wrong? Are you in pain?"

"Yes, but it's not that. I want to ask a favor."

"A favor? Yes. Anything. Tell me."

She raised her hand toward Beth's face. "Danny likes you."

"I like him too. He's a good boy."

"Take care of him . . . for me."

"I am. I'm doing everything I can."

"I mean later. When I'm gone."

Beth glanced toward the window and back again. Her throat felt tight. "Don't talk about such things, Claire. You're going to be here for a long time."

"No. Let me say this." Her fingertips brushed Beth's cheek. "Todd . . . loves you."

Bethany clasped Claire's hand and pressed it against her cheek. "No, he married you. He's your husband."

"Take care of him, Bethany. And take care of Danny. They need you. Promise me."

Tears welled in Beth's eyes. "I . . . I promise. But only if you promise not to leave us yet."

"I . . . I can't leave until I tell my son . . . good-bye."

They spent the rest of the day—and every day that week—in the garden. Beth sketched the blossoming flowers and trees and brought Claire little bouquets to smell, and touch, and hold in her lap. When Beth had drawn all the flowers in the garden, she amused Claire with caricatures of everyone they knew—people in Willowbrook as well as movie and television personalities.

Even Danny was captivated by Beth's renderings. "Draw Hopalong Cassidy. Draw his horse," he would tease. Soon his requests expanded. "Can you draw my favorite baseball stars?"

"Who? Joe DiMaggio?"

"Sure! And Ted Williams, and Stan Musial!"

Bethany drew whatever he asked, eager to win his approval. She knew she had succeeded when Danny clasped the drawings in his hand and begged, "Can I take these to school to show the kids?"

When Claire was too weak or dispirited to talk, Bethany read her the comic strips, stories from *Good Housekeeping*, and articles from her own dog-eared television and movie magazines. Claire would nod slightly or manage an amused smile while Beth carried on a non-stop conversation. "Did you hear what George and Gracie did now? . . . Listen to this, Claire. Did you know Perry Como was once a barber? . . . Look at this swell picture of Laurence Olivier, Claire. . . . Imagine Rita Hayworth being married to that wealthy Prince Aga Khan!"

One afternoon, while Claire dozed, Todd asked Bethany, "Why do you read her all those stories about movie stars? You can see she's not interested."

"To keep her here," Beth said simply. "To keep her thinking about people and places and events in our world. To keep her from slipping away where we can't reach her anymore. To keep her here so she can tell Danny one more time she loves him."

Todd rubbed his chin, the glimmer of a smile on his lips. "Who knows? Maybe someday I'll be as wise as you are, Beth."

After supper in the evenings, a ritual of sorts developed. Todd gathered Beth and Danny in Claire's room and read from the Scriptures. Sometimes they sang hymns from an old songbook, Todd's deep baritone blending with Beth's clear soprano. "In the Garden," "Amazing Grace," "Rock of Ages." When Claire began to tire, the four of them would join hands around the bed while Todd prayed. He always closed with a heartfelt petition for Claire's healing, to which everyone whispered "Amen." He concluded their devotional time by reading Claire's favorite verses from John 14. *Let not your heart be troubled. . . . In my Father's house are many mansions. . . . I go to prepare a place for you . . . I will not leave you comfortless . . . because I live, ye shall live also.*

24

Claire's condition worsened through May and June. Feverish, verging at times on delirium, she coughed herself into exhaustion and woke in the mornings drenched from night sweats. In every sense she was wasting away, growing weaker, thinner, her arms and legs frail as straws, her face so gaunt her dark, sunken eyes seemed enormous. One evening late in June, as Bethany sat softly crooning a hymn, Claire broke into a sharp, hacking cough that convulsed her chest with wracking pain. When the coughing subsided and she removed her hanky from her parched lips, the white linen was stained with bright red drops. She stared up at Bethany with desperate, haunted eyes, her skin leaden, her raven hair tangled as she gasped for air.

Bethany moved quickly, inserting the nasal prongs in Claire's flaring nostrils and adjusting the oxygen, but Claire flailed her arms and turned her head away, as if rejecting anything that would prolong her life.

She wants to die, Bethany realized with a shudder. *And I don't blame her. I'd want to die too!*

"I'm not going home tonight," Beth told Todd later as they put away the last of the supper dishes.

He finished wiping a china plate and put it in the cupboard. "You're spending the night here?"

"Yes. I can't leave Claire. She's worse." She rinsed out the deep enamel sink, sweeping soap suds and grease-speckled water down the drain.

Todd wiped the countertop with his towel. "I know how you feel, Beth, but it's not necessary to stay."

"Yes, it is," she shot back. "As long as Claire's alive, I'm not leaving this house."

Huskily he said, "You sense it too, don't you? We won't have her much longer."

Beth stared at the desolation in Todd's eyes. "No, we won't." All that consumed them these days was Claire. Claire getting through the night without pain, Claire gaining sustenance from a cupful of broth, Claire surviving another day.

"She shouldn't be alone anymore," said Beth, touching Todd's arm. "One of us should be with her all the time, so when the time comes we can get Danny and all be together at her bedside."

Todd shook his head. "She won't want Danny there."

"Did she tell you that?"

"I just know."

Beth forced out the words. "What . . . what will it be like?"

He drew her over to the table and they sat down. His face looked haggard, his eyes shadowed. "It's a hideous way to die, Beth, and a horrible thing to see."

"I've seen death on the farm. Watched my papa die."

"The doctor says patients like Claire usually burst a vessel in their lung and drown in their own blood." He shook his head despairingly. "By now her remaining lung is mush. She'll hemorrhage to death, and there's nothing we can do to stop it."

Bethany reached across the table and clutched Todd's hand. "We'll be there for her. She won't be alone."

For three days Todd and Bethany took turns sitting at Claire's bedside. On the third evening, during devotions, she rallied enough to utter a few words to Danny, who lay beside her, cradled in her arms. Lifting her fingers off the comforter to his forehead, she whispered, "I love you, son. Your father . . . loves you. Love him . . . for me."

The boy wrapped his arms around her neck and began to weep, his round, innocent, unblemished face contorted in grief. "Don't die, Mama. I'll be a good boy. I'll do my chores. I won't fight with the boys at school. I'll even love the reverend—just don't die!"

She summoned a weary smile as Todd lifted the boy gently into his arms; then she coughed, a harsh, rib-cracking cough, until the familiar crimson soaked her handkerchief. She looked intently at Beth. "My rosary."

Beth handed her the beads. Claire wrapped bony fingers around them and with effort crossed herself. "Jesus . . . loves me," she said, so softly Beth had to strain to hear her.

Todd, still holding Danny, leaned over the bed and covered Claire's hand with his. "Yes, He loves you, Claire, and we know you'll be with Him soon and all the pain will be gone. He'll wipe the tears from your eyes and give you a body that'll never be ill again."

She smiled feebly, looking from Todd and her son to Bethany. "Sing. Read me your stories. Bring me . . . flowers . . . from the garden."

That night, just before midnight, as Bethany sat by Claire's bed, drowsy-eyed, slipping in and out of slumber, she heard a rasping sound that jolted her awake. Heart pounding, she groped in the shadows for the table lamp and nearly overturned a glass of tepid water on the nightstand. As the sallow light spilled across Claire's pillow, Beth looked into dark, exquisite eyes fierce with alarm. Claire opened her mouth to speak, but only a gurgling sound emerged. Bethany sprang to the bed and cradled Claire's head against her breast as blood spurted from Claire's lips and soaked their nightclothes with the deep, bright red of garden roses.

Three days later, on June 30th, as radios blared with news of President Truman sending ground forces to Korea, a small group of mourners gathered in the solitude of Willowbrook Cemetery to bid farewell to Claire DiCaprio Marshall. Bethany, Knowl, Catherine, and their families joined the handful of parishioners attending the brief service. Todd, officiating his first funeral as an ordained minister, read Psalm 23, offered a simple prayer, and spoke eloquently of the woman he had loved and lost twice in his lifetime.

It was the sort of day Claire would have loved. Golden sunshine streamed through towering oaks, warming grass strewn with dandelions and clover. Robins and blue jays twittered overhead, blending with the choir of solemn voices singing "Rock of Ages."

Danny, in his new blue suit and bow tie, stepped forward and placed a long-stem red rose on his mother's polished mahogany casket. "I love you, Mommy," he said, rubbing a tear-streaked cheek. The breeze ruffled his slicked-back, umber-brown hair. He toed the grass with one shiny patent leather shoe and wrinkled his nose in a forlorn frown, then turned away, head lowered, chin grazing his chest.

Todd leaned down and held out his hand to the boy. For a long moment Danny stood motionless, his lower lip quivering; then with a sob he flung himself into his father's arms for a long, consoling embrace.

For over a week after the funeral Todd and his son remained sequestered in the parsonage; no one saw them or heard from them except briefly at church on Sunday morning. When folks asked how he was doing, Todd said, "I just need some time alone to think things through." Even when Bethany offered to come over and help him sort Claire's things, he told her, "Not yet. I need time. I'll call you."

But he didn't call.

With the funeral over, Knowl rallied the congregation and urged them to support Reverend Marshall by voting unanimously to keep him as their pastor. "This man needs to know he still has a flock to shepherd. We put off voting so we could pray and seek God's direction; we waited nearly three months so he could care for his wife. Now it's time to welcome him wholeheartedly or let him go."

Ten days after the funeral Knowl and Bethany drove over to the parsonage to deliver the results of the vote. "Let me go in first," she urged, nervously fingering the gold buttons on the bodice of her silk dress. "I need to be the one to tell him."

Knowl nodded. "I think it's best coming from you."

"You don't mind?"

"No. I'll drop you off, run a few errands, and pick you up at noon."

"I wonder how he'll react. He hasn't called. He's avoiding everyone."

"He's been remote since the funeral," Knowl acknowledged, his knuckles white on the steering wheel. "I worry about his frame of mind. He doesn't even answer his phone."

Bethany lifted a determined chin. "I'm getting inside if I have to break the door down."

But minutes later, as she walked up the porch steps to the parsonage door, her bravado gave way to trepidation. Would Todd let her step back into his life? Perhaps now that he no longer needed her to care for Claire he wanted nothing more to do with her. But no, Todd wasn't that sort of man.

Still, why did he refuse to let anyone share his grief?

It wasn't as if Beth didn't understand his anguish. Grief was a thankless, consuming labor; a ruthless tyrant, unpredictable and unrelenting; a cunning animal striking savagely the moment you let down your guard. Some days her pain over losing Mama washed back over her like a huge wave, knocking her under, leaving her stunned, as if Mama had died all over again. Death couldn't be accepted once and for all and be done with. Your mind fought it, so that you had to endure countless little deaths over and over again until it became real.

Beth had respected Todd's need for privacy, knowing that mourning required a certain amount of solitude. But now it was time for him to return to the land of the living—for Danny's sake, if not his own. Besides, it was urgent that she see him.

She knocked soundly on the paneled door—once, twice, three times. When no one answered, she tried to see through the door's small stained-glass window, but it was too opaque. Finally she tried the knob. To her surprise the door opened. A sense of foreboding passed over her.

"Todd?" she called as she stepped inside the silent house. The air was still and muggy, heavy with summer's heat. The room smelled familiar, of scents too indefinable to name, stirring feelings and memories fragile and fleeting as confetti. "Todd, are you here?"

The closed red velvet drapes and dark paneled woodwork shaded the living room with mauve and brown tones. As her eyes grew accustomed to the shadows, Beth felt a ripple of shock. Furniture was draped with sheets and the massive mahogany tables were shorn of personal effects. Gone were all the knickknacks, books, paintings, photographs, and toys. Stacked by the door were cardboard boxes and wooden shipping crates marked in large black letters with a New York address.

Fighting alarm, Beth called Todd's name again, but the room had a hollow sound, as if the walls already recognized that people no longer lived here. She remembered Todd saying, "It's better that I leave than have the church split over me. The people need peace and harmony; if I can't inspire unity, God must have someone else for them."

"Todd!" she called again, more urgently now.

She heard a rustling sound in the next room, and suddenly

Eleanor Marshall swept in, looking as forbidding as ever in a gray tailored dress and a small brimless hat with lace veil. She eyed Beth coldly and asked, "What are you doing in this house?"

Bethany held her ground. "I came to see Todd. What are *you* doing here?"

Eleanor's gray brows arched sharply. "If it's any of your concern, I came to take my son and grandson home with me. Back to New York. To the life Todd knows, where he'll be happy and content—and appreciated."

Beth strode across the carpet and peered into the dining room. "Where is Todd?" she demanded.

"He's gone."

"Gone? To New York?"

Eleanor pulled on a pair of white gloves, carefully working each finger. "No. He drove over to the school to pick up the boy. We'll be leaving on the train this evening." She gestured toward the ghostly, shrouded furnishings and said loftily, "Excuse the clutter. We've made arrangements for Todd's belongings to be shipped to New York."

Bethany clenched her hands, a seething sensation rising in her chest. "Todd can't go. He's needed here."

"We both know that's not true," countered Eleanor. "Todd has gone through enough. He needs to get away from this insufferable town and be where he can heal and recover from his wife's death."

"I'll be here for him," said Bethany.

Eleanor's eyes narrowed and her lips formed a mocking smile. "A snippet of a girl like you, taking care of my son?"

"I helped him with Claire."

"Maybe so, but I'm his mother. I've always been the one to comfort him. He knows that."

"Then why didn't you help him with Claire?"

Eleanor ignored the question. "I'm not forcing him to go. It's his own choice."

"I don't believe you."

"Ask him."

Impulsively Bethany strode over and yanked the sheet from the flowered settee. "He can't go. I won't let him." She pulled another sheet off the Queen Anne chair.

Eleanor snatched one end of the sheet, but Beth held the other end tight. "Stop it, Bethany Rose! Don't behave like a spoiled child! Let go!"

"I'll let go when you stop running Todd's life!"

"Hey, what's going on here?"

At the sound of Todd's deep voice, they both dropped the sheet and whirled around to face the door. He stood in the doorway in khaki slacks, brown loafers, and a casual shirt, one hand lightly on Danny's shoulder.

Seeing Bethany, the boy broke away from Todd and ran and hugged her, begging, "Are you going with us? Please come with us! Please!"

Bethany held the boy close. "It's okay, Danny. Nobody's going anywhere, if I have anything to say about it."

Eleanor jabbed a wisp of hair into her silver-gray chignon and looked furiously at her son. "I've told Bethany Rose we have last-minute packing to do, but she insists on seeing you."

"It's all right, Mother. I'm glad she stopped by." Todd walked over and put a reassuring hand on Beth's shoulder and Danny's. "I need to talk to you, Beth, before we leave. I know I've got some explaining to do."

Beth eyed him accusingly. "What's there to explain except that you're running away when you should stay here and fight?"

"If you're talking about the church," he said quietly, "it's not worth fighting when people have already made up their minds against me. Don't you understand, Beth? I'm leaving for the church's sake. They don't have to take a vote that could turn the people against one another."

She searched his eyes. "That's it? You're willing to leave with everything unfinished?"

He wound a strand of her silky hair around his finger. "Dear Beth, I'm only trying to do God's will."

"How do you know it's His will for you to go?"

He shook his head solemnly. "I don't know. I'm ashamed to admit I'm not sure of God's voice anymore. Maybe He's turned His back on me."

Beth's lower lip trembled. "He wouldn't do that."

"Don't you see, Beth? It's become clear to me since Claire died. I've never measured up. Not since I was a boy. I failed my father, my mother, Claire, you, my son, my church. I've wounded every life I've ever touched. How can I expect a congregation to look to me as an example?"

"Stop it, Todd!" Bethany pressed his hand against her cheek, tears welling in her eyes. "I looked to you and you were there. You were there for Claire. You're here now for your son."

Todd smiled grimly. "I know you're trying to make this easier for me, Beth, but God works through circumstances, and we both know how dismal my circumstances have been these days. I'm a weary man."

Eleanor Marshall cleared her throat loudly. "That's why I'm taking my son home, where I can look after him the way a mother should."

"Wait, Todd. Listen." Bethany clasped his hand tightly. "I have news for you. The vote's in."

"What?"

"The church has voted."

"They have?"

"First, let me tell you—Knowl stood up for you. He let the people know what they would be losing. He told them you're a man of principle and honor, a man who accepts his responsibilities, a man who has devoted himself to his family."

"Sounds more like a saint."

"No. He called you a flawed human being like the rest of us, who's wiser and more compassionate because of what he's suffered. Then Knowl admitted he voted against you when you first came to Willowbrook."

"He voted against me?"

"Yes. He considered you—how did he say it?—he said you were too callow and inexperienced, an idealist without the substance, a man who lived by his intellect instead of his heart."

"He hit the nail on the head, didn't he!"

"There's more, Todd. He said seeing your commitment to your wife and son changed his mind about you. He told the people we would be blessed if you remained our pastor."

Todd looked at her intently. "And how do the people feel?" Beth was breathless now, almost light-headed. "Most folks feel the same way Knowl does. Do you hear me, Todd? There were only a few dissenting votes. You've got to stay. You can win over the stragglers and be the minister our church needs. The church can't heal without you."

With a click of her stacked heels Eleanor marched up beside Todd and Bethany, her gloved hands on her wide hips. "Tell her, son. We've made our plans. We're going back to New York where we belong."

Todd seized Eleanor's shoulders and looked her square in the eyes. "Stay out of it, Mother. What I do will be because it's God's will, not yours!"

Eleanor's face blanched. "Why, of course, son. But whatever God wants you to do, *I'm* going home to New York. I couldn't tolerate Willowbrook for another day!"

"I know that, Mother," said Todd, a blend of pity and compassion filling his eyes. "I just want the best for all of us." He beckoned Danny over. "Son, are you hungry?"

The boy broke into a grin. "I'm starved!"

"Mother, take Danny to the kitchen and fix him a peanut butter and jelly sandwich."

"Peanut butter? Really, Todd, I don't—I mean, I won't—"

"Yes, you will, Mother. I need to talk with Bethany alone. Go along, Danny. Your grandmother would love to fix you a sandwich."

Danny reached for Eleanor's hand. "Come on, Grandmother. I'm good at sandwiches. I'll help you."

After the two had left the room hand in hand, Todd led Bethany over to the settee and they sat down, facing each other. He lay his arm along the back of the sofa and ran his fingertips lightly over her shoulder, his eyes somber in his shadowed face. "You probably already suspect, Beth. There's more to my decision to leave than my concern for the church."

She bit back tears. "I know. You don't love me."

"No, that's not it. I'm leaving for your sake, because I do care."

"I don't understand."

He reached up and brushed a tear from her cheek. "My dear girl, for months you've sacrificed your life for me, and for Claire, and for little Danny. You've given up your classes, your dreams, and your own family to see me through the most difficult days of my life. My mother pointed out how unfair I've been. You're a young woman who's just tasting life. You deserve a husband who's free of entanglements. I can't saddle you with a wounded family—a man without a future and a boy without a mother, another woman's child. I can't ask you to take on such an obligation. Don't you understand, Beth? You're free. Go. Find a beautiful life for yourself."

"Todd, I don't want—"

His voice deepened and his eyes grew more intent. "Let me finish while I have the courage to speak. I can't stay here in this house with all the ghosts, the memories, the loneliness, the heartache. Claire's gone. I can't change that. I can't bring her back."

Bethany stifled a sob. "I know. I miss her too."

Todd gently caressed her temple, her hair. "But you're still here, Bethany, so close, so alive, so lovely. Don't you see? To stay in Willowbrook and no longer have you here in my home every day would be harder than I can bear."

For a moment the room was heavy with silence. Bethany slowly removed Todd's hand from her hair and stood up. She walked over to the window and pulled back the velvet drapes. She unlatched the window and opened it, letting in warm, golden sunlight. She yanked the sheets off the sofas and chairs. She opened a cardboard box and emptied out trinkets and curios, dishes and toys.

Todd stood up and stared at her in astonishment. "What on earth are you doing?"

She placed a shade on a jelly jar lamp and arranged Danny's toy train on the mahogany coffee table. "This is the only train Danny will be taking," she announced, her chin raised defiantly.

Todd followed after her as she emptied another carton on the floor. "Have you lost your senses?" he demanded. "Do you have any idea how long it took us to pack those things?"

"Longer than it'll take me to unpack." She hung a painting on the wall, put several framed photographs on a shelf, and returned several hefty volumes of Shakespeare to the sprawling rosewood bookcase.

"Stop, Bethany! Look at me!" Todd clutched her by the arms and held her fast. "Tell me what you're doing!"

She gazed up at him, breathless, her face flushed. "I'm doing what you said. You said I needed to find a life for myself. I have. It's right here. Everything I want is in this house."

"What are you saying?"

"Don't you see, Todd? Everything God called me to be I can be with you. Right here!" She pushed back her tousled curls and brushed a fine sheen of perspiration from her upper lip. Her heart pounded fiercely. She had never felt more alive. "All my life I knew there was something I was supposed to do, something I was meant to be. When I was little, living in our tumbledown farmhouse in Fort Wayne, I dreamed about it, but I never knew what it was, except that it would be grand and wonderful. Now I've found my dream. Please don't take it away. I love you, Todd. I love Danny. I want to stay here with you both."

Todd drew her against him, wrapping her in his arms. "I have no right to you. I'm a man with a past, a man who's failed, but I love you. I'll always love you."

She turned her face up to his. "Todd, are you saying—"

"I'm saying, I'm asking—"

"Todd Marshall, are you proposing marriage to me?"

His blue eyes glistened. "Proposing marriage? Supposing I am? What would you say?"

She pursed her lips just inches from his. "I'd say I do. Would you?"

He smiled. "I do, my beautiful girl. I do!" His mouth sought hers and he kissed her soundly. Between kisses he whispered against her cheek, "Remind me to call the train station about my reservations."

She looked at him with sudden concern. "You're not still going to New York!"

"I'm not going anywhere, darling. I just want to tell them only one person will be traveling to New York tonight."

"One?"

"My mother."

"Alone?" Bethany stifled a smile. "What will you tell her?"

Todd nuzzled her head with his chin. "I'll tell her the truth. I'm not going to New York because the three of us—you, Danny, and I—have a wedding to plan!"

About the Author

Carole Gift Page, considered one of America's best-known and loved Christian fiction writers, writes from the heart about issues facing both adults and teenagers. She has written more than 34 books, including the first two books of the Heartland Memories Series, *The House on Honeysuckle Lane* and *Home to Willowbrook*. She is the recipient of two Pacesetter Awards and the C.S. Lewis Honor Book Award.

Carole is a fiction columnist for *The Christian Communicator* and founder of the Inland Empire Christian Writers Guild. She has published countless articles and poems in Christian periodicals, including *Virtue, Moody, Decision, The Christian Home,* and Focus on the Family's *Brio* and *Breakaway*.

She has taught creative writing at Biola University and served on the advisory board of the Biola Writers Institute. In addition, she is a frequent speaker at conferences, schools, churches, and women's ministries.

Carole and her husband, Bill, have three children and live in Moreno Valley, California.